Now You Have It

by

Zena Livingston

DORRANCE
PUBLISHING CO
EST. 1920
PITTSBURGH, PENNSYLVANIA 15238

Dorrance Publishing Co
585 Alpha Drive
Suite 103
Pittsburgh, PA 15238
Visit our website at *www.dorrancebookstore.com*

ISBN: 978-1-4809-8624-4
eISBN: 978-1-4809-8461-5

DEDICATION

This book is dedicated to the past, present and future. The past is to my mother-in-love, Gertrude, who during her 105 years taught us all how to love and who was the anchor for our family. The present is to my husband, Leon, and our son, Douglas. They are always there, and their love gives me the strength and courage to face life. The future is to Jonathan and Harrison, our grandsons, who are growing up in a world full of challenge. May they find the strength to face whatever is ahead.

CHAPTER 1

It is amazing. All her life, Donna dreamed of the big house, country club, and all the other accoutrements of wealth. These things were the ideals of happiness, and once attained, she thought, happiness was a sure thing. She was willing to compromise everything to get what she wanted, but no matter what, she kept her goals in sight and aimed at her target. Failures along the way did not deter her. She never cared who she hurt or what others thought of her.

Sitting in her newly renovated kitchen, she could not get over the fact that she finally had it all: the big house, which was perfectly decorated by the professional interior design team; the husband with the big bank account; the country club membership where she was still not being accepted because she was a newy but where she was sure she could achieve total acceptance. It amazed her when she thought of how far she had come from being the poor, single mother in the rented apartment in Freeport to this place in Upper Brookville. True, there had been setbacks along the way, but she never lost sight of her goals. To Donna it was as if she had lived several different lives.

June and Alex had done everything they could to give Donna and her brother, Robert, a happy childhood. They tried to always keep their money problems to themselves and not let the children know they could not afford any extras. Alex was an automobile mechanic, but he had a hard time keeping a steady job, mainly because of his drinking and failing to be on time. June worked as a telephone operator for an answering service where she worked part-time at night and earned minimum wage. She believed that when she was at work, Alex would be home watching the children. Little had she known that in reality, Alex would be passed out drunk, leaving Donna and Robert to their own devices. The children, ages twelve and ten, soon became known as the neighborhood trouble makers. Shoplifting and breaking into houses became commonplace for them, and most of the other children were forbidden to play with them.

June first became aware of the behavior of her children when Robert was arrested for breaking into a house in south Freeport. He had taken a television and some jewelry and was trying to steal the television when the police arrested him. As a juvenile, he was released into June's custody and rapidly received the spanking of his life. June then turned her anger on Alex who she, rightfully, blamed for the children's behavior. She knew then and there that she had no recourse but to divorce him and start a new life for herself and the children regardless of how hard that might be. June was a very attractive woman, and she knew that Jim, a local, had always shown an interest in her. She decided that she would cultivate that interest and see where it would lead. Things could not be worse than they were with Alex.

And so a new chapter began for the children. Before long, June was re-married and able to stay home. The children were given strict curfews and expected to conform to the rules of the house. Both Donna and Robert hated having to answer to both June and Jim and often threatened that they wanted to live with their father only to be told that was not a possibility until they reached the age of sixteen when the court would entertain their choice of custodial parent. Until then, they were stuck with June and her rules, like it or not. Little did the children know that Alex had made it completely clear that he wanted nothing to do with any of them once the divorce was final and that he had no intentions of paying child support or anything else. June had accepted his conditions as she knew he was in no financial position to pay anything and she just wanted out of the marriage and to have him out of her life. The children did try to see their father, but he was unavailable and would tell them he had to work or he would be out of town whenever they tried to see him.

Donna was the one most affected by the divorce. She had been her father's little girl. She loved sitting on his lap and listening to his stories and always felt so special when he would take her with him if he went to the store or to see someone. She also loved the way he would touch her and massage her back and her chest. He always made her feel so good. No one else ever touched her like that and she really missed it. She, also, could not understand why June got so angry when she talked about her father and how he would make her feel so special.

Life was not perfect. There was little extra money to spend, especially during the winter months, and this caused tension for both June and Jim. Jim did try to supplement his earnings by taking construction work during the winter, when and where it was available. Often he would be away for weeks at a time. June continued being a stay-at-home mom because she felt that both children needed her supervision. Robert continued being a problem. He was behind at school and was not eligible to play any sports because of his poor grades. No matter how hard June tried to motivate him, he refused to give the needed effort to school work. Donna, on the other hand, was an excellent student. Her grades were good enough for her to skip a grade, but June refused to allow it. June felt that Donna would not be able to handle the social adjustments of being with the older children. Little did she know that those were the very children Donna sought to be with. Donna actually had more friends who were boys than who were girls. By the time she was thirteen, she learned that the boys could touch her in the same ways her father had, and they could make her feel really good, just as he had. She also discovered that the more she allowed them to touch her, the more friends she had. Of course, she never told her mother about the boys and would lie to her about where she was going after school. June would think Donna was at the library when she would actually be at a boy's house or with a group on the hill behind the school. It was easy to lie to her mother because she never claimed to be at a house where June could call and check on her.

By the time Donna was fourteen, her virginity was long gone. She was careful to make sure the guys used condoms because she did not want to risk getting pregnant. She was smart enough to know that would wreck everything. She could not imagine how angry June would be if she turned up pregnant. There was no way she wanted to be saddled with a kid or with one of the boys with whom she was having sex. To her, sex was fun, but she knew she wanted more in life than her poor mother had and she wanted someone who could give her everything she wanted. She had to be older to get what she wanted, and nothing was going to stop her.

Little did Donna know that by the time she was sixteen she had the nickname "The Whore of Freeport." She had the reputation of being easy and that all a guy had to do was touch her gently and he could have whatever he wanted. If he gave her some money to buy something special, he could come back for more anytime he wanted. Donna did not see anything wrong with accepting the money as a gift. Her only problem was sneaking things into the house without her mother seeing she had something new and pretty. Donna knew it would be hell to pay if her mother found out how she was getting the gifts. Donna actually took a job as a cashier at the supermarket. The job served two purposes: it gave her a reason to be able to buy things, and she could also claim she was working if she was questioned about where she was and when she would be home.

She thought she was being so smart until shortly after her eighteenth birthday. She missed her period—something that never happened. She just knew that she and Rob had screwed up, and she even remembered the time they had failed to use protection. Her first thought was to call Rob and arrange to meet with him to discuss the situation. He was shocked, and all he could think about when she told him she was pregnant was that the kid was not his.

"How can you be so sure it's mine?"

"Hell, it is yours. I have not been with anyone else! You know we screwed up that time when you did not use a condom."

"You should be using your own protection. You could get the pill just as easy as I can get the condom."

"That is not the issue now. What are we going to do?"

"Look, I cannot afford an abortion. My parents will have a shit fit if they find out about you and the kid. They expect me to go to college in the fall, and they have already paid the down payment on the tuition."

"You bastard. All you think about is you. What about me? I am not ready to be saddled with a kid."

"You should have thought about that before you started screwing around. I am shocked this is the first time you have been knocked up. After all, any guy who wanted to have a piece of the action had it with you. Your reputation says it all."

"You really are a piece of shit. You know there are tests that can prove you are the father, and then what?"

"You can't afford any tests, so it's your word against mine, and I say I have never been with you."

With that, Rob got up and walked away leaving Donna too stunned to say anything. She sat where she was and just cried her eyes out. Her life had suddenly turned to shit, and the only person who could help her was June, but that help would come at a great cost, if it would come at all. Of course, she could claim it was a one-time thing that she got caught up in. She could also claim that she did not know what she was doing. Then, maybe, June would help her get an abortion. After all, her mother was not a good Catholic; good Catholics did not get divorced. One thing she knew for sure, she did not want this kid.

Donna kept thinking about how she was going to start to talk to her mother. There was no easy way. She knew she would just have to tell her and wait to see how the chips fell. She waited until everyone else in the house had gone to bed before asking June if she could talk to her.

"Of course, baby. In fact I want to talk to you about going to college. You are a smart girl, and your future can be bright. Today, a college diploma is not a luxury; it is a necessity."

"I really want to go to college, but I have a little problem that we have to deal with before I can make any plans."

"What kind of problem?"

"Well, I'm late, and I am never late."

"Are you saying you're pregnant? How is that possible?"

"Mom, I made a mistake. I got carried away with this guy, and I didn't even realize what was happening. Now this!"

"Have you spoken to this guy? What does he say? What about his parents?"

"He is being horrible. He denies he ever did it with me and told me it is my word against his and I could never prove it. I know for sure that I never want to see or speak to him again. I just want to get rid of the kid and go on with my life."

"It is not that simple. That is a human life we are talking about, and you do not have the right to kill it."

"Oh, Mom, don't give me that Catholic dogma. I don't want the kid. I am not ready to be a mother and take care of a kid, and you know it."

"But you were ready to have sex with a stranger."

"I made a mistake. Does that mean I have to pay for it for the rest of my life?"

"Sometimes we have to think before we act. Once we have done something, there is nothing we can do to undo it."

"That's not true. Today, girls have abortions all the time. What I need from you is a loan to have the abortion. That is all I really want."

"That is not happening. I will not help you kill my grandchild."

"What am I supposed to do?"

"Get a job, get an apartment, and when the baby is born, get welfare or give the kid up for adoption. Those are your choices."

"I can't believe you will not help me."

"I did not help you get into trouble! I will give you what extra money I have to help you support yourself. Once the baby is born, I will help you by babysitting so you can work or even go to school. That is the best I can offer."

"You are ruining my life."

"You ruined your life!"

With that, Donna stormed out of the room. She sat in her room crying hysterically and knowing she would never be able to get the money for the abortion before the time limit. Her life was over. She kept wondering how her mother would feel if she killed herself. The only thing that she realized was that she lacked the courage to kill herself; so that too was not an option. She also lacked the courage to stick a hanger up there. That could really hurt, and if she failed, it would all be for nothing.

It was amazing how fast word of Donna's predicament spread. The boys who could not wait to get into her pants avoided her as if she had some kind of sexually transmitted disease. The girls all made believe they were her close friends while they were actually trying to find out who the father was and what Donna planned to do going forward. Donna's only defense was to turn her back on all of them. She devoted herself to work and to making plans to support the baby and herself. She really wanted to prove herself to June and to her boss at the supermarket. June was pleased with the new leaf Donna had turned, and she allowed her to remain in the house rent free. She even promised to babysit so that Donna could work after the baby was born. Unfortunately, Jim would never allow Donna and the baby to live with them. He felt he was well past the years when he wanted to be disturbed by a baby. Donna knew that her mother would never stand up to Jim, so there was no choice but for her to get her own apartment. Things would have been different if Jim were her father.

Where was her father anyway? Donna often tried to get information about him, but June would only say that he abandoned them and she had never heard from him. It seemed strange that a father would just up and leave two small children. Donna had vague memories of him and of them spending time together. She now realized that his touching her was inappropriate, and she wondered if June had known about it and thrown him out. Donna also wondered if her brother had also experienced being fondled by their father. While he never spoke about it, he was certainly strange enough. It seemed really odd that of the two, Donna was the better adjusted. Robert never finished school, and whenever he came to visit, the smell of pot was so strong that Donna thought she could get high from just being near him. June tried tough love with him, but he did not seem to care. He could live anywhere and did odd jobs to get money when he needed it. Jim refused to allow Robert to stay the night in their house. Again June never fought him about that. She seemed afraid to stand up to Jim over any issue involving her children.

What Donna knew about June and Jim's relationship was rather simple. Jim had been her father's friend. They worked together on construction jobs, and Jim often came to dinner. All of a sudden, her father was gone and Jim moved into the house. Whenever Donna questioned her mother about the sudden change of men in her life, June would simply tell her it was none of her business. Now it was obvious to Donna that her mother had been having an affair with Jim long before her father left the family. So it was, and so it would continue to be. For Donna, there were no choices but to accept what she could not change and to try to make the best of a bad situation.

Every penny Donna earned was kept for when she could no longer work. She remained grateful that she was able to live rent free for the present, and she was shocked when she came home one day to find out that June had rented an apartment for her. It was right in Freeport so that she would be near enough for June to babysit.

"It is only eight hundred dollars a month, so you should be able to afford it. I have actually saved some money, so if you are jammed, I will be able to help you," June told Donna that afternoon.

"Wouldn't it be better if we waited until I am closer to my due date? That way I could save more money."

"Rents that cheap do not come along often, and it is a really nice place. The woman who owns the house lives upstairs, and she says she will not mind hearing a baby cry. She actually seems rather like a friendly grandmother."

"Great! Now you are telling me I am going from being watched by you to being watched by a friendly grandmother. That sounds perfect!"

"Stop your sarcasm. The apartment has a separate entrance so you can come and go as you wish. Mrs. Gordon is familiar with having a tenant, and she does not sound like someone who wants to monitor your activities. Of course, I would imagine that if there were to be a steady stream of men coming and going, you could have a problem."

"I am not planning on having a steady stream of men, but I am also not planning on living like a nun once this kid is out of my body."

"I wouldn't expect you to live like a nun, but I do expect you to live like a mother and to protect your child. I would think you'd have learned your lesson."

"Don't you worry! I plan on using birth control so this does not happen to me ever again."

"Let's not put the cart before the horse. Right now you are in no shape to entertain any man. I want you to see the apartment, and then we have to get some furniture and things for it. It is better we do this before you get much more uncomfortable. "

"Why do I have to even see it? You made the arrangements for me."

"Actually, I did not sign the lease. I asked Mrs. Gordon to hold it for us, and I told her I would bring you over there tonight. We need to bring the first month's rent and a security deposit."

"'Like I have sixteen hundred dollars lying around here."

"I have a check for that amount. It is better we give her a check so that when you want to move, you will have proof of paying the security deposit."

With that, June got her purse, and she and Donna left the house. The apartment was in south Freeport in an older house, but it looked well cared for. Mrs. Gordon surprised Donna when they met. She looked like a really nice lady. The apartment itself was clean and consisted of a living room with a small kitchen area and a nicely sized bedroom with an alcove off from it that could serve as the nursery. Being that it was on the smaller size, Donna felt she could use very little in the way of furniture. That was another good thing.

"Can I take my bedroom furniture? It would fit in here nicely, and I could save that money."

"I was planning on you doing that. All we will need to buy is a couch and a table for the living room. I have extra dishes and pots, so you will not have to buy that stuff either."

"There are shades on the windows, so I don't need to buy curtains. I am guessing this is the best I can do."

With that, June took out her checkbook and wrote the check to rent the apartment as of the first of the month, which was two weeks away. Mrs. Gordon told them they could come in and start setting up the place whenever they wanted to as she did not have anyone living there.

"Thank you very much for that offer," Donna said as they were leaving.

On the way home, all Donna could think was that, as usual, June was right to take the apartment now. After all, the baby was due in two months, and this would give her the time to get things in order. In some ways, she was getting excited about having her own place and not having to answer to Jim and June regarding her every movement. It was going to be nice to be able to sleep as late as she wanted on her days off.

Donna was off from work that weekend, so they decided they would start bringing things over and getting the apartment ready. It proved to be fun setting up the kitchen and the bathroom and deciding where to put what. It was like playing house, except this time it was for real. Jim actually helped by bringing over the heavier stuff in his pickup truck. It was when he brought her bed over that Donna knew there was no going back to the house she had always called home.

That night when she got into her bed, she felt a coldness that was penetrating. She had slept alone in her house before, but this felt very different, especially when the baby started moving within her. Her entire life had changed, and its' future direction was unknown territory. She was scared like she never had been scared before. The enormity of her situation finally hit her: she was going to be a single mother, and she was going to have to support herself and her child. Being a cashier at the supermarket was not going to cut it. Staring at the ceiling, she tried to imagine what she would do. In reality, she was prepared for nothing. Her GED might qualify her to be able to go to Nassau Community College, but how would she pay for it? Her mother did not have the money, and Jim certainly would not give it to her even if he had it. A student loan might be a possibility, but then who would watch the kid while she was at school? Trapped by her own stupidity.

Then the thought crossed her mind. Welfare! She would apply for welfare, and the state would help her. Food stamps and a rent stipend could go a long way until she could figure out a better solution.

"I'll go to the welfare office tomorrow. In my condition, they will probably take some pity on me," she said out loud as if hearing it would increase her resolve.

Just then she felt a swift kick. It startled her. "Stop that, you little devil. I am really trying not to hate you before you are even born." So much for maternal instincts, she thought to herself as she began to wonder if she would have them or any real love for the kid. She wondered if every time she would look at him, she would think of Rob and remember the mistakes she had made. June wanted her to learn from her mistakes. That was all well and good, except that her mistakes were going to affect another person.

Then her thoughts turned to Rob's parents. They had money, and this kid was their grandchild. Would they be willing to help her out with things for the kid? She could make it clear that she would not want anything from Rob, but she would let them have a relationship with the kid. They could prove it was his by DNA testing, which she would allow, and she would promise not to make him pay child support if they would help her get on her feet. After all, this kid would be their only grandchild.

"A good thought, but I doubt it will work," she said. "They never liked me and always thought I was beneath them and their precious boy. Oh, well, no one can fault a girl from trying, and try I will."

With that, Donna looked at the clock next to her bed. It was three o'clock. She had been lying there thinking since ten, and soon she would have to get up to go to the supermarket. She knew she was going to be exhausted, but she still could not turn her mind off and go to sleep. Somehow, someplace she was going to find a solution that would work. She knew for sure that she was not going back on the street, because if she did, June would cut her off completely. Another voice in her head kept saying adoption. She kept thinking that was a viable solution, but June was so against it. If she put the kid up for adoption, it would have a better life than she could give it, and she could have a better life than she would if she kept it. Everyone could benefit, and it was not like she was killing the kid. The adoption voice kept getting louder, and Donna knew she would really give that option some serious thought once she saw the kid. There was time for that decision. After all, there were not that many Caucasian children placed for adoption, and there were lots of couples wanting to adopt. There were even ads in the newspaper where couples promised to pay all the expenses for expectant mothers if they promised to sign the papers to give up the child.

Donna put her hands around her stomach and just seemed to hold the kid. With that, her eyes got very heavy, and before she knew it, it was seven in the morning and she had slept for several hours. The sun was streaming into the room as if beckoning her to a new day with new possibilities. All she could think was how much different things looked in the day than they did at night.

When the alarm sounded, Donna could not believe that it was morning. She felt as though every bone in her body was fatigued, and when she went to stand, both legs cramped up so severely that the pain forced her back down on to the bed. Her head kept telling her that she had to get up to go to work, and her body kept telling her to go back to sleep. Listening to her body was not going to pay the rent, so she forced herself to get up and get into the shower. The warm water felt so good as it relaxed her muscles. Almost to the rhythm of the beating water, her brain kept saying, "You can do this, you can do this."

"I can do this," Donna yelled as her resolve returned. She was going to have this kid and then, somehow, she was going to return to school and get her diploma. After that, college and a decent job so she could make a decent life for the kid and herself. Maybe welfare was a temporary answer, but it certainly was a way of putting food on the table. One thing she was certain of; she was not going to use her body to get money. Those days were over, and she hated herself for going down that path. That was dirty money, and she had destroyed her self-respect in the process. Thinking back, she'd started having sex with the guys because she wanted friends, but they had not been her friends at all. None of them even called once she got knocked up. The girls in the group were no better than the guys. It was like they felt it was catching, and they did not want to catch what she had.

"Next time I call someone friend, that person will be a real friend, not a user," Donna said out loud as if by saying it, it would be so.

The shower made her feel better, and after a quick breakfast of cereal, she was ready to go to work. She made sure that she was wearing her sneakers so that she could stand all day at the cash register. No one there cared that it was hard for her to stand all day, and she knew if she complained, she would lose her job. She also decided that during her lunch hour, she would go to the welfare office in Freeport to get the paperwork necessary for her to make an application for aid. Now that she had an apartment and real expenses, she might qualify since she was only earning minimum wage at the supermarket, and they would have to take it into consideration that she would have to stop working. Her New York state disability would also be minimal. Hopefully, she would be able to get by without asking her mother for money, an unlikely thought in reality.

By the time the end of her shift approached, Donna felt really miserable. Her feet were so swollen that the sneakers felt like they were literally cutting into her flesh. Her back was aching, and she felt like she had a basketball attached to her stomach and it was weighing her down. She knew she had to smile at the customers and not let on how she was feeling, but it was getting harder by the minute for her to appear pleasant. Just then, a nicely dressed man came up to the register.

"I've been watching you, and I admire how you respond to the customers."

"Thank you. Everyone here is just so nice. It is easy to be nice back to them."

"I can remember when my wife was as pregnant as you are. She was a wicked witch who tested my patience with every passing minute."

"Being pregnant is hard; there is no doubt about that."

"I would like you to call me after the baby is born as I might have a position for you where you can utilize your people skills in a better way," he said as he handed Donna his card.

"I don't understand what you mean. I would only be interested in a legit job in a legit place."

"I am sorry if I gave you the wrong impression. I operate management services. We manage apartment houses and office buildings. I am thinking you would be perfect on the phones, fielding problems and finding resolutions."

"That sounds great, but I do not have any experience with that type of thing."

"Experience can be learned, and you have the personality that is necessary. I think you can learn the rest of it."

"I will call you once this kid is born. My mother has told me she will watch it while I am at work, and right now, a desk job sounds better than heaven."

"My cell number is on the back of the card. Call that number, and we can talk more when you are ready."

"Thanks, Mr. Sands. You can be sure you will be hearing from me in the near future."

Donna quickly ran her totals and took her cash drawer to the manager. As she walked home, she decided to keep her conversation with Mr. Sands to herself. After all, there was no point in discussing something that was not a reality, and it would be at least two months before she would be able to take any position. She would tell her mother that it looked like she would be eligible for welfare once she stopped working; so that would be a help.

Once in her apartment, Donna felt like she could do no more. All she could think about was putting her feet up and just vegging out. She was not even hungry, something that was surprising even to her. Up to now she felt like she was eating enough to be a construction worker with a pit-less stomach. She did not know how long she was sitting in the chair when the phone woke her.

"You did not call me when you got home from the grocery store," June said.

"Sorry, mom, I was just too tired to think about anything other than sitting down and putting my feet up. I guess I fell asleep. What time is it, anyway?"

"It's eight o'clock. Did you eat dinner?"

"No, I was too tired to eat."

"That's not good for the baby. Do you have anything to eat?"

"There's some food in the refrig. Don't worry, this kid has enough of my fat to nourish him for months. I am afraid to even weigh myself."

"You'll lose the weight before you know it. Now get up and make yourself something for dinner."

"Okay. Just stop being such a worry wart. You wanted me to be on my own. I can do it. I even went to the welfare office, and it looks like I will be eligible for benefits once I stop working. That will be a big help when I am not earning anything. "

"That's good, but go and get some food into you and call me in the morning."

"Yes, mother."

With that, Donna disconnected the call. Instead of going to the kitchen, she went straight to her bed and got under the covers. She did not even get undressed before falling asleep, and that was how she was when the alarm went off in the morning. Besides starving, she was happy to see she had feet and toes instead of the balloons that had been at the end of her legs the previous night. A quick shower and a bagel was all she needed to face the day again. As she locked her apartment door and started walking to the grocery store, all she could think was that this had to end soon and hopefully she would never have to be a cashier again.

At four o'clock, just one hour before the end of her shift, Donna felt a sharp pain that was like someone had taken a knife to her abdomen. Within minutes of the pain, she was overcome by cramps, and she ran to the bathroom. One of the other women saw her and ran after her.

"You're in labor!" Sheila yelled through the locked door. "Open the door."

"I can't be in labor. It's too soon."

"Tell that to the kid. I am going to call your mother, and then we are going to the hospital."

The next thing Donna knew, she heard her mother's voice through the locked door.

"Open the door. You are going to have that kid in the toilet," June yelled.

With that, Donna opened the door. Her face was ghost white, and she was doubled over.

"Can you walk to the car? I have it right outside the front door."

"I have to get my things and close out my drawer."

"Here are your things, and don't worry about your drawer. I closed it out for you, and I will cover the rest of your shift," Sheila told her.

With that, June wrapped Donna's coat around her and helped her to the car. This baby was coming a month too soon, but at this moment, all she could do was to hope for the best. In today's world, babies survive being born too early. Donna, on the other hand, was thinking, "Maybe this will be my way out. Maybe the kid will not make it and I will be free to restart my life. I am too young to be a mother. If this brat survives, I will probably hate it."

It did not take long to get to the medical center, and once there, Donna was rushed to labor and delivery. Tubes and monitors were placed all over her stomach, and doctor after doctor—or should we say resident after resident and intern after intern—all came to examine her. She heard them say the baby was crowning, but nothing else seemed to happen except that the pains were closer and closer together. Finally, she felt them put her legs into the stirrups, and she heard them yelling at her to push.

"Push, my ass!" she yelled back as she felt as though someone was ripping her apart. The next thing she knew, she heard a cry, and she opened her eyes to see the nurse holding this tiny Martian-like thing.

"It's green and horrible looking," she cried out.

"Don't you worry! He will be all pink and nice the next time you lay eyes on him. We have to clean him up, then he will go to the NICU since he made his entrance a little too early. They will monitor him there, and you will be able to go there to nurse him."

"Nurse him! I am not doing that! Give the kid a bottle."

"Are you sure that is what you want? It is much healthier for both of you to nurse him."

"No way in hell! That is too disgusting to even think about. All I want is to have my body back, and I don't want him attached to my tit or anything else."

"You sound like you are giving him up for adoption."

"I wish. My mother would have a shit fit if I did that. I am stuck with the kid, but I don't have to have it attached to my tits. Are we clear about that?"

"I'll let the NICU know your feelings, and they can take it from there. Hopefully, you will develop some maternal instincts and prove to be a good mother to this innocent child. After all, it is not his fault that he has been born."

"Yeah, yeah! I've heard all this before. I am well aware that I will be paying for my mistakes for the rest of my life, but I don't have to like it.

With that, the nurse carried the tiny bundle out of the room and placed him into the bassinette for the short ride to the NICU. All she could think about were all the couples she had seen who were so desperate for a child, and all she could hope for this child was that his mother would treat him well. Life could be so unfair.

CHAPTER 2

DONNA WAS RELEASED FROM THE HOSPITAL the next day. She was told that the baby would have to stay for several days and possibly a week as they would not release him until they were sure that he would suck the bottle and breathe without any problems. June met Donna at her room as Donna could not be released unless someone was able to drive her home.

"Have you registered the baby's name?" she asked.

"I am thinking of naming it Donald after myself. After all, there is no one else. They said I could think about it and finalize its name when I pick it up."

"You have to stop calling the baby 'it.' He is a living person you have to take care of to the best of your ability."

"Yeah, yeah. I know, but right now I have absolutely no connection with that thing. It looks like a monkey minus body hair."

"Give him a little time and all that will change, but your attitude has to change or you should give him up for adoption."

"You were the one against the idea of adoption. What gives now?"

"I am thinking you are an unfit mother, and I am concerned for his safety and well-being."

"I cannot deny that I am hating the thought of taking care of him. I never saw any human that was that small and totally helpless. Right now, I just want to get out of this hell hole and go home. I can decide what I am going to do when I am able to think with a clearer head."

With that, June got up, and together they walked past the NICU where they could see the nurses administering to the little fellow. June watched Donna's face when the nurse held him up for her to see and waved her in to hold him herself. But Donna refused to hold him, so they turned and went back to her room to gather her stuff and leave the hospital.

Walking into the apartment felt really good to Donna, and she was not sorry to have June leave her alone. Once alone, she got into her bed and just laid there hugging herself. It was a strange and empty feeling not to have the baby stirring within her. It had been a long time since she had had her body to herself, and it had been a long time since she was able to really sleep. Sleep was a wonderful thing, and she gladly gave into the need to sleep without being disturbed.

The next two days passed in what seemed like a flash. June came by daily to make sure Donna was eating, but other than that, all Donna did was sleep. The pain in her breasts was intense, and when she called the doctor, all they said was to apply ice and not to express the milk that was coming in as that would help her dry up. All Donna could think was that this whole pregnancy thing was a nightmare. Except for the limited pleasure at conception, everything else about it was marked with pain and discomfort. For her, there was no joy at seeing the creature who came out of her body, and that was exactly what she told the nurse who called her to suggest that she come to the hospital to "bond" with it. June had gone to the hospital to see it and had reported back to Donna that he was gaining weight and breathing on his own. She also told Donna that he would be able to come home soon and she had better decide what she wanted to do. The nurses told June there was a nice couple that they knew about who were anxious to adopt and they could arrange to start the process.

Donna just stared at her mother and did not even acknowledge that she heard what was said. Part of her wanted to be free of that horrible looking thing, but another part just could not say the words. She figured that since she could not make a decision, she would just wait and see what developed. There was no point in asking June for any advice as her opinion did not matter. Had she not followed June's advice in the first place, she would not be in this situation now. She regretted not having an abortion when she still could. But there was no point dwelling on that as it was old history.

A week later, Donna received a call from the hospital that the baby was ready for discharge and that she needed to make plans to pick him up and complete the necessary forms to give him a registered name. It was then that Donna knew she had made the decision to take him home and give him Donald as a name. She had to get things ready for him and make sure the crib was set up and that she had a proper car seat as the hospital would not release him until the car seat was inspected. June was happy to help with all the preparations and readily volunteered to take Donna to the hospital for the homecoming. She seemed genuinely pleased with Donna's decision and even agreed to take her to the welfare office so that she could complete the process to get welfare.

For Donna, it felt good to get up and start doing things. She felt as though she was falling into a hole of depression and knew that was a dangerous place to go. She had heard horrible stories about women who suffered from postpartum depression, and she decided she was not going to be one of them.

When Donna and June walked into the NICU, Donna could not pick her son out. It was not until one of the nurses brought the little pink-looking baby over to her that she knew it was her son.

"He looks so different!" she exclaimed.

"It is amazing what a little weight and caring can do. He is eating like a trooper, and he goes about four hours between feedings. You should be able to take care of him now," the nurse said as she led Donna over to the changing area to give her a lesson in the proper way to handle that necessity. Next was a lesson in giving the baby a bottle. It felt really strange to Donna to be holding the baby, who felt warm and cuddly. Donna began to relax a little and even thought that this whole thing could work out.

Before she knew what was happening, they were placing the sleeping baby in his car seat, the necessary paperwork was done, and Donna was walking out of the hospital carrying the baby. June had hurried to get the car and was waiting at the door as Donna emerged.

"You talk about weird things. This has been really weird. Everyone kept telling me that if I change my mind, all I have to do is bring him back here and they will take care of him. I guess they are afraid I will just abandon him someplace."

"You cannot fault them for that. You never came to see him while he was in the hospital, and they have to think you could do something crazy. It is a big responsibility to raise a child. I think you know that, and I hope you are up to it."

"That is something we will have to see. I do not know what kind of mother I will be, but I am going to try my best. I am really glad you are willing to be there to help and to teach me."

"Lord knows I was not the perfect mother either. Together we will bring this kid up and hope for the best.'

And so Donna's life as a single mom began in earnest. For her, the greatest obstacle was the lack of sleep. The baby was up every three to four hours around the clock, and by the time she finished feeding him, changing him, putting him back down and getting herself relaxed, it always seemed like she was starting all over again. During the day, if June came over to watch him, Donna felt the need to run errands and take care of things, so she did not take advantage of the time to catch up on her sleep. Everyone she spoke with assured her that what she was experiencing was totally normal and would change once the kid started sleeping through the night. Donna often thought she would not make it until then, but she kept on going to her own surprise. There were even times she enjoyed holding him and listening to him coo. He was a good-looking child with the most beautiful skin.

One afternoon, a thought came to her straight out of the blue, and she called Robert's mother.

"I do not want anything from you, nor do I expect anything from Robert. I am just thinking that you might like to see your grandchild."

"I do not know that it is my grandchild, and while your generous offer seems nice, I so do not trust you for a minute. Please do not call here again."

With that the phone was hung up, and Donna could only think, "Like mother, like son." Part of her understood that they wanted nothing to do with her as it could change the course of their precious Robert's life. They had no way of knowing that she would never allow Robert back into her life, but she would have allowed them to be a part of Donald's life. She felt very proud of herself for making the offer but knew she would never make it again.

It was fun staying home and taking care of the baby. Donna was reminded of the days during her childhood when she would play house with her dolls and cardboard dollhouse. The only difference here was it was a twenty-four-hour-a-day enterprise, and while she was enjoying it, money was becoming a real issue. As Donald was growing, his diapers and food were eating up most of the welfare allowance, and though June was still helping her with the rent, she was definitely feeling the crunch. It was just then that she put on her old coat and found the card the man in the supermarket had given her. Her only thought as she stood holding the card was that she really had nothing to lose if she called him and he either did not remember her or did not want to make a real offer for a real job. She definitely was not interested in some make-believe offer that would include sex; those days were done. So she took her phone out of her pocket and called before she could possibly change her mind. To her surprise, he remembered her and asked her to come to his office at nine the next morning to discuss the job possibility. Donna was excited as she placed the next call to June.

"I need you to watch Donald tomorrow as I actually have a job interview at nine in the morning."

"That's wonderful. Do you want me to come to your house, or do you want to drop him off here?"

"It would be better if you come here as I have to dress properly and do my hair and stuff, and you know what a hassle it is to get him ready too."

"I'll be there at eight, and you can take my car to the interview."

"Thanks, Mom, that will be perfect."

With that, Donna disconnected the call and took off her coat. Taking Donald for a walk would have to wait as she wanted to do her nails and put out her clothes for the following morning. She wanted to look business-like for the interview. It was a little hard to decide what to wear as she was still carrying baby weight, and she definitely did not want to look like a stuffed sausage. She finally decided on a black skirt and a silk blouse with a loose-fitting jacket. She tried everything on and was ultimately pleased with her appearance; she looked business-like but not overdressed and certainly not trashy. Next she looked at her hair and was amazed at how long it had gotten. An appointment at the hair salon was out of the question because she just did not have the money for such folly, so she started to play with her hair. Wearing it down and straight just did not seem to go with the outfit . A ponytail was not an option as it was definitely too childish. She finally decided to wear her hair in an up do, and she pulled some loose to soften the look. She was pleased with the look, and with minimal makeup, she knew she would look professional and not trashy.

It was hard for her to believe she had spent three hours on the "get ready project," and she was brought back to the present by Donald crying for his next feeding.

"Okay, little man, Mommy is coming."

June arrived just as Donna finished feeding the baby.

"Here, you take him. I have to finish getting ready to leave. One thing is for sure, I don't want to be late for the interview."

"Go do whatever you have to do. I will take care of the little man."

"Thanks, Mom, you are a gem."

It seemed like only minutes had past, but in reality it was an hour before Donna was actually ready to walk out the door.

"How do I look?"

"You look just fine and very business-like."

"I want to make it very clear that this is all business and nothing personal. After all, I don't know this guy, and I am still wondering why he wants to give me a job."

"Don't judge him ahead of time. Hear him out."

"That is what I intend to do."

It only took ten minutes to get to the office. This time Donna had borrowed June's car, but she knew she could walk there. This was another positive in Donna's mind.

"I am here to see Mr. Sands," Donna told the receptionist.

"He is expecting you. Please have a seat and I will buzz him to let him know you are here."

Donna pretended to be reading a magazine when the office door opened and Mr. Sands asked her to come in.

"Thank you for coming in."

"No, you are wrong; thank you for seeing me. I have been wondering why you gave me your card in the first place."

"You struck me as the type of person I want to work for me. You are kind to people and reliable, and I think you can learn to do the things I need done."

"What are those things?"

"I need a personal assistant. Someone who can handle the calls from the tenants in the various buildings I manage without having to come to me with every single problem. I need someone who can collect the rents and make sure the buildings are operating properly. It takes a strong person to know how to handle the people and to get the job accomplished without seeming too bossy and without alienating the tenants."

"That sounds interesting, but I have no experience in any of the above."

"I watched you at the market. You can handle people whether it is your co-workers or the customers. I think you have a future doing the type of job I am offering, and I think you and I can make a good team."

"What do you mean by team?"

"Don't get the wrong idea. I am a happily married man and I am not interested in any type of relationship outside a business one. I know you were hurt by your former relationships, and I understand you are not trusting of men. My desire is to get someone I can trust and someone who is willing to work hard at a difficult job, and I think you can be that someone."

"No one has ever tried to help me before, so excuse me if I seem confused. I find it difficult to trust anyone, especially someone who seems to want to give me something for nothing."

"I am not giving you something for nothing. I am prepared to teach you the job and to get the effort from you that is necessary to do the job. It will not always be easy and there will be times when you have to work late. My concern is that you will have proper child-care available."

"That is not an issue. My mother is available to take care of Donald. She promised me that when I decided to have the baby in the first place. Now that he is here, she and he have really bonded and she enjoys taking care of him."

"I am prepared to offer you a salary of $40,000. I know that is low for the job I need done, but you have to be trained, and until you can work by yourself, I think it is more than fair."

"I think that is more than fair. I cannot make anything like that at the market, and to be honest, I really need the money. Diapers and formula are really expensive and the welfare check I am getting is barely covering the essentials. I know it is not chic to be honest about my situation, but you seem to know quite a bit about me and I do not think I have much of a bargaining position."

"You are known to speak your mind, and that is something I like about a person. I can tell you that if you do the job well, you will receive raises. What do you think about my proposal?"

"I think I would have to be a fool not to accept the job. My first problem will be getting the clothes I will need. Jeans and sweatshirts will not be the wardrobe I will obviously need. To be perfectly honest, I just do not have the funds to buy the clothes you will expect me to wear."

"Here is a check for five hundred dollars. Use it to buy three suits and some blouses that you can interchange. You should have enough to get your wardrobe started. Now the only question is when can you start?"

"I can call my mother and tell her I am starting right now. Then she and I can go shopping tonight to get the suits."

"You're on! Here is the computer, and this is the program with the rent ledgers. I need you to make sure all the tenants are up to date with their rents. Please call anyone that is more than five days late. You can take the laptop to the desk in the other room. That will be your office, and please feel free to make it as comfortable as possible."

Donna walked into her office and could not believe how lucky she was. The job sounded so interesting and the opportunity so unbelievable that she felt like pinching herself to see if it was all real or a dream. Craig Sands was never going to regret his decision to hire her, of that she was certain.

The next few months proved amazing for both Donna and Craig Sands. They worked very well together, and Craig proved to be an excellent teacher while Donna was like a sponge absorbing the information and putting it all to work. The ledger showed that all accounts were up to date, something Craig had not had the time or energy to effect. She also was able to handle the various problems that came to the office. Donna utilized Angie's List to find contractors who could make the necessary repairs, and she was not shy to bargain with them to get the best price. Tenants were delighted to have their complaints rectified, and Craig was equally delighted with the bottom line.

Best of all, as far as Donna was concerned, Craig remained the perfect gentleman. They became friends as people who work together become friends. There was no sexual innuendo and no inappropriate remarks. Craig would ask about the baby and how he was developing, but he never asked about the father, nor did he question Donna's decision to be a single mother. For her part, Donna kept her word not to allow the baby to be an obstacle for her to do her job. If she had to stay late, she did so without complaint, and if Donald was sick, she still left him with June, who was more than adequate to take care of him. Donna just worried that the babysitting might become too much for her mother, and she planned to get a nanny just as soon as her salary would allow for that expense. Craig was generous and gave her a raise just one month after she started. She was now earning forty-five thousand a year, and to her it seemed like a fortune. She was able to pay her rent and even indulge herself and Donald with some extras. One of the best indulgences was when she had her hair restyled and went to Bloomingdales to have a makeup consultation. She looked good, and knowing that gave her great pleasure.

The only part of her life that was missing was a boyfriend. There just was not enough time in her day for her to meet anyone of quality, and she felt too guilty to ask her mother to watch Donald while she went out to try to meet someone. At work there just were no eligible men coming to the office, and the tenants she met just did not interest her. She felt that she needed to keep all the relationships on a professional level or her job would be compromised.

Before she knew it, a year had passed. Donald was a year old and walking. Donna could not believe that her little premature baby now weighed almost thirty pounds. No year in her life had ever gone by so fast. People had told her that children mark the passage of time, and she was beginning to believe it. It would not be long before Donald would be able to go to a day care so that June could have part of her life back. She knew of one in Freeport where the child could be dropped off as early as seven in the morning and picked up at seven in the evening. Donald would probably benefit from being with other children, and Donna would definitely feel less guilty if she were to impose on June to a lesser degree. June, on the other hand argued that he was too young to be exposed to all the germs at a day care and that she actually was enjoying being with the baby. Donna was sure that a happy medium would be reached where she could do what was best for both Donald and June. Of course, if she could hire a full-time nanny, that would be best, but that had to wait until her salary reached a totally different level. If Craig actually followed through with his plan to start a medical facility, which she would manage, then her salary would allow for a nanny and much more. She had definite ideas about how to bring patients to the facility and how to make big dollars from Medicare and Medicaid. All that she needed to do was to convince Craig and prove that her ideas were actually legal. Donna was sure she could bring homeless people who had proper insurances into the medical facility and have them evaluated by all the different doctors. The doctors would bill for their services, and the facility would be able to take a percentage of the fees as their rent. There were other facilities in Hempstead doing just that, and they were not having any problems with the authorities. Donna looked at it and saw that everyone benefitted: the patients received care they would not otherwise receive, and the facility and doctors made money. Craig worried that it could be considered fee splitting, but Donna insisted it was rent, not fee splitting. She also knew where to go to recruit the patients and knew that if she offered them free shoes or a hot meal, they would come. For her, personally, it would mean a sizeable salary increase with little expenditure of energy. Of course, Craig would make the lion's share of the profits, and he was liking that prospect.

Craig loved to make more and more money. He and his wife were living the good life in the big house on the North Shore. They had the nanny and the country club memberships with all the social accoutrements that went with it. Since Donna started working for him, he had more time to enjoy the things he had and for that he was grateful. The only cloud in his life was his youngest child who was not normal by anyone's standards. She was hyperactive and could not function in a regular classroom, so he had her in a private school that specialized in helping troubled children. His other two children seemed fine, but Michelle and Craig were constantly at each other over Norma, and Donna could not help but notice that Craig was avoiding being with the family more and more. Privatively Donna wondered when Craig would find another woman who would be there to comfort him. After all, he was still a young and very sexy man.

Donna was really excited when she came to work on Monday. Over the weekend she discovered that South Nassau Hospital had vacated a building previously used as an outpatient facility. The building was right on Merrick

Road in Baldwin and would be perfect for their medical center. While she had not seen the inside, she was sure it was already subdivided, so the construction costs would be minimal. Also Baldwin did have a large Medicaid population, so there would be patients who could be attracted to the facility. Then again, it was also close to Freeport where Donna knew she could solicit patients to come, especially if she offered a free pair of shoes or a free meal. Now all that remained was to convince Craig and let him negotiate a deal on the building. She figured it would be best to buy the building and that way they could always sell it at an appreciated value if for any reason the medical facility failed. She also felt that paying rent to someone else was a waste of money. Owning the building and paying yourself rent was the way to go. While she was not an accountant, she knew that there was substantial tax relief for owning the building, and Craig could certainly get a mortgage without a problem.

When Craig came into the office, she started rattling off her ideas, and he could not help but laugh at her excitement.

"Look at you, Miss Businesswoman! I can't believe what I turned you into."

"Don't laugh at me. I am serious about this. I really think it is a wonderful opportunity, and we could make a lot of money with other people doing the work."

"Did I hear 'we?'"

"Yeah, you heard 'we.' If we do this, I want a share of the business. After all, it was my idea in the first place, and I am willing to do the leg work to get it off the ground; but I do not work for nothing."

"And you feel that you are qualified to put this venture together? Where will you get the medical staff, and how would you evaluate them?

"I already looked into the professional journals that advertise positions available. As for their qualifications, I would have to rely on you for that, but I really do not care about their qualifications. All I care about is being able to bill for their services. Once we get the patients to the facility, we can have them see all the disciplines there and bill for consultations. I very much doubt that the people would return for further care, and if they do, so be it."

"You are describing a Medicaid mill. Aren't there laws prohibiting that type of billing?"

"There are laws on the books, but there is no enforcement of them. Also, we will be billing under individual provider numbers not a group number. That way it is harder to trace. It works, and there is a lot of money to be made without negative exposure."

"Let's get in touch with the hospital and find out more about the building itself. There is no point in going any further until we know its availability. Then we can negotiate your share and consult with the attorneys. I would say there is a lot to do before this can become a reality."

"Am I missing something, or aren't you an attorney?"

"Only a fool represents himself, and I am not a fool. There are people who specialize in real estate deals and others who negotiate partnerships. We also need professional advice on whether or not your idea can work. While I am not doubting you, I still need confirmation. I would hate to risk a great deal of money only to find out we cannot do what you are telling me we can do."

"I respect that, but I know I am right, and the sooner we act on it the better. Now is the time to make a killing, and we cannot know how long it will last."

"Go ahead and start your end of things, and I will start mine."

Donna left the inner office with a huge smile on her face. She just knew she was going to make it work and she was finally going to make a financial killing of her own. She could already see herself and Donald living in their own house with a full-time nanny. Life could be perfect! She knew she had come a long way from being a cashier at the supermarket, but she still wanted to go further and to secure financial stability for herself and her son. It was her ultimate goal to never be dependent on someone else.

Things moved along at a very fast pace after that morning's conversation. Craig arranged to purchase the building for what he said was a fair amount, though he refused to tell Donna the exact amount. Donna knew she would be able to find out from the county records, but since it did not impact on her deal, she just let it go. As for Donna, her salary was raised to one hundred and fifty thousand a year plus three per cent of any profit generated by the facility. She had tried to negotiate a ten per cent share of the profits, but Craig refused saying he was putting up all the money, and once the initial output of money was returned, they would look at her percentage. Donna felt she had to accept his offer.

Next, she set about recruiting the doctors for the facility. She immediately had a general practitioner, a cardiologist, a dermatologist, an allergist, a chiropractor, and she was still looking for an orthopedist and a podiatrist. The oncologist refused to be a part of the facility as he knew he would have to see the patients frequently and he was afraid of compliance by the patients recruited to the facility. Unhappy patients could mean lawsuits, and he thought that the people recruited could want the easy dollars from a lawsuit. Donna was having trouble with the podiatrist as he could not see patients under Medicaid in a private office setting and he was afraid of getting involved with Medicare patients. But she still felt she would be able to get one to participate especially since she was filing for the facility to become a Medicaid Center.

The shoes were her next challenge. She had to contact a shoe company and get the out-of-date models for distribution at the center. Nike had a discount store in Oceanside, and she contacted both the store and the parent company as she was willing to take whatever was left over as long as the price was right. After explaining that she was going to give the shoes to the needy and that she was willing to advertise that the company was providing the shoes at no cost, she was able to get a decent supply of shoes in various sizes that she could offer the patients who came to the clinic. A pair of shoes and a hot meal was all she had to promise to get the patients in the door. Once there, the patients were willing to go from doctor to doctor for their free evaluations. Of course, each patient had to have a Medicaid number or a Medicare card or an Obama Care insurance card without a large deductible. Donna had set a policy that all deductibles would be billed to the patient but written off as charity with a notation that the patient was unable to pay the deductible. That way they satisfied the insurance rules for deductible.

Since the building had been used as a medical facility, the rooms were set up, and as part of the deal, Craig got the hospital to leave the examining tables and the cabinets in place. This made it really easy for Donna to get set up. The only thing she did to the building was a fresh coat of paint, which really brightened everything up. So in just six months after first seeing the building, the Freeport Medical Facility was opened with newspaper coverage and the Chamber of Commerce there to celebrate its opening as a facility to service the poor and unfortunate of the Freeport area. Flyers were printed and handed out at the supermarkets, parks, and other areas where the people gathered, and with each flyer given out, the person was told about the free shoes and hot meal. Opening day was marked with a line of people presenting for the free medical care, and Donna and Craig were both extremely excited about the reception the facility was receiving.

Donna personally supervised the billing and the paying of the doctors who each worked as an independent contractor so they were responsible for their own taxes and social security. Craig was really impressed that Donna proved to be such an astute business person. He wondered where she had acquired all the knowledge. When he asked, all she would tell him was that they each had their secrets.

Donna's personal life also changed with the start of the facility. She was no longer dependent on June to watch Donald. She now had a full-time nanny, and she was in negotiation to buy a house in nearby Oceanside. The house was a two-family dwelling, and she knew she would be able to rent the apartment so that her expenses would be covered. What a great idea; she would be able to have the equity and the living space while someone else would be paying most of the mortgage and most of the taxes. Finding a tenant would not be a problem, and she was making the rent high enough to ensure a responsible tenant. She really wanted a married couple as that would mean less partying and less complaints from the neighbors. June, for her part, was happy for Donna and even happier for herself. Taking care of a toddler was no easy matter, and she was finding herself getting much too tired at the end of the day, especially with Donna's hours getting longer with her increased responsibility. Even Jim was starting to complain more and more, and he resented her being away so much.

The only aspect of Donna's life that was not going well was her sex life: there was none. Sure she met lots of men at work, but they were mostly married with children and only interested in a one night stand, so to speak. There was no possible way that Donna was about to risk her reputation and career by getting involved with any of them. The single men she met were just jerks who reminded her of Rob, and there was no way she was about to make the same mistake twice. As for dating web sites, they took too much time and energy, and Donna had too little of both left after working a full day and then trying to give Donald some time and attention. She even thought of going to a matchmaker, but the average fee was five grand, and she just did not have the extra money what with buying the house and getting it furnished. Donna did not even have a circle of friends who could introduce her to someone. That, too, took time to cultivate, and time was her current enemy.

All in all, she was very proud of how far she had come. Here she was, a single mother with an out-of-wedlock child and no college education, making over one hundred and fifty thousand a year and managing a medical center and a real estate company. None of this would have happened without Craig taking an interest in her and giving her an opportunity. It amazed her every day that he asked nothing of her except that she do her job and help him make more and more money. He was a very interesting man, to say the least.

CHAPTER 3

IT DID NOT TAKE LONG for the medical center to start showing a profit. Every morning, Donna went about recruiting the patients, and then she spent time making sure the billing was being done properly. Even Craig was amazed at how simple the whole operation proved to be. While the actual medical care left much to be desired, the doctors did successfully bill for multiple services in each division. There were not many repeat patients, so each service was getting the maximum per patient by billing a new encounter for each person seen. Donna made sure that each doctor was properly rewarded if his or her billing exceeded the expected level, and she personally saw each doc each day. They seemed to enjoy joking with her while she was actually keeping tabs on them.

Donna could not get over the idea that these doctors actually graduated medical school. To her they seemed like total losers who could not make a living without the clinic. It was a shame, in a way, as so many of the people she recruited really needed medical attention and could have benefitted from a proper diagnosis and treatment plan. Being poor really sucked, and being homeless and uneducated sucked even more. Donna felt she could have been one of the hopeless people had June not helped her and had Craig not given her the opportunity.

One day, she came to work to find out that the chiropractor they had hired had not shown up for work. This was a problem because so many of the patients felt relief after seeing him, and their relief was immediate, making the patients eager to recommend the clinic to others. Donna knew she had to replace him immediately as there was no room in her world for people who just did not show up when they were expected to do so. She went right to her resumes and pulled the ones for the chiropractor position. After a few calls that went right to voicemail, Steve Greco answered.

"Are you working?"

"My practice is just getting started, and I have to admit it is a slow go."

"I have a position available at the medical center, and I was wondering if the hours could fit into your schedule. We hire as independent contractors so we can work together to leave time for your private practice."

"There is no doubt that I could use the money, especially until my practice takes off. My only concern is the legal aspect. I know that medical centers like yours work in the gray area."

"There is no gray area. We recruit the patients, and each discipline sees them and bills for their own services. You can bill according to your own moral code, but the more you bill and the more we receive in payments, the more you will make. It is a mutually beneficial arrangement."

"You do the billing and the collections?"

"You only need to see the patients, and we take care of everything else. It is a real win-win.

"Why don't you come over with a list of your provider numbers and a copy of your New York state license and you can work the clinic today to see how you like it."

"How many patients do you expect?"

"Probably thirty or forty—nothing that is not manageable."

"I can be there in an hour, and we both can see how we like each other."

"Great, I will look forward to seeing you."

Steve was a big surprise to Donna when he walked into her office. He was young and very handsome. She could not believe he was having any trouble building a practice of his own. What with his looks, women would love to have him put his hands on them. It goes to show you that one never knows what is happening in someone else's life.

"Thank you so much for coming down to help us out today."

"Thank you for the opportunity."

"Come on, and I will show you your office space and introduce you to the support staff. I think you will really like them."

"I am not used to having a support staff. Right now I am doing it all myself. Hell, I even answer my own phones and make appointments for the patients."

"I have been told it is really hard to get a practice going."

With that, Donna took Steve down the hall and introduced him to everyone and then left him to start seeing the patients who were there. Later that morning, she popped her head into his office to see how he was doing, and all seemed to be going well. He had a nice way about him as he spoke to patients and made them feel comfortable being treated by him, and he was relatively fast, so he could see all the people on the schedule. Donna told Craig that she felt she had a real find with Steve, and Craig seemed pleased as well.

At the end of the day, Steve came into Donna's office and asked when she wanted him to return.

"I take it you enjoyed your day."

"It was more than interesting, and it gave me the chance to try new things that I am hesitant to try on my private patients."

"These people are more interested in the hot meal and the free shoes than the medical care being offered, so I guess trying new things in this arena is probably just fine. Since the clinic is currently open three days a week, I would appreciate it if you can be here all three days."

"I can do that as I am finishing up early enough to still see patients at my office in the afternoon and evening. That is when I am busier anyway."

"Good, so I will see you on Wednesday at ten. I try to have the first group of patients here by then."

"See you then."

As he left her office, all Donna could think was how cute he was. She could see herself becoming interested in him, if he proved to be single.

Donna began paying more attention to her appearance when she knew Steve would be coming to the center. In the beginning, he seemed not to notice her as anything more than the director of the center and, in essence, his boss. Then gradually as he became more comfortable in his surroundings, he started joking with Donna, and the two of them could be heard laughing when they were together. Donna's interest in him piqued when she found out he was not married and did not have a steady relationship. It seemed odd to her that someone so personable and good looking would not be involved, and she began to hope that he would pay attention to her on a personal level. When he failed to make the first move, she decided to try to bring their relationship to a more personal level.

"How about getting a drink after we're finished here tonight?"

"Never thought you'd ask," was Steve's reply.

"Hey, isn't it usually the guy who asks a girl to go for a drink?"

"Not if the girl is the guy's boss. I've been wanting to ask you out for dinner, but I've hesitated. Most people don't like to mix business with pleasure."

"We're both just employees here. I really don't feel that I am your boss."

"That's where you are wrong. Everyone here knows you run this place. You're the boss lady! I am about to start brown-nosing the boss lady as I think she is one sexy lady."

"Let's not get ahead of ourselves here. We are going to get a drink and nothing more."

"A guy can hope. Seriously, when I leave here, I keep thinking about you and have been doing so since the first day."

"Flattery will get you anywhere."

Once out of the office, the two of them really began to hit it off. They discovered that they both loved being near the ocean and walking on the beach. They liked the same type of television shows, and their taste in food was almost identical. Gradually, they started spending more and more time together. Steve was great with Donald and would even take the kid to the park and play on the floor with him. While he never asked any questions about Donald's father, Donna felt compelled to tell him everything, including her previous reputation.

"What was, was. I really don't care about the past. It is quite obvious that you have totally turned your life around and that you have done your best to provide for this little guy. I respect that. All too many women would have made different decisions if they were in your shoes. You chose the harder road, and that says a lot about your character."

"I got lucky in that I met Craig, who gave me the opportunity to turn my life around. I never would have dreamed of being able to earn this much money and to be able to own my own house. I really owe that man, and I will never forget what he has done for me."

"I am hearing that you have proven to be a giant help to him, and everyone at the center says you really earn your salary."

"I am glad to hear that because I really try. That is my only way to thank him for what he has given me."

"Are you and he involved?"

"As in a sexy relationship?"

"Yeah!"

"Craig has never been anything short of the perfect gentleman. The only relationship we have is a business one. To be extra blunt—I have not had any sex since I became pregnant with Donald. I promised myself not to make the same mistake twice and not to get involved with any man whose only desire would be a roll in the hay. At work, all the men who could possibly interest me are married with kids, and I really don't have the time or the energy for the bar scene or the internet dating gig."

"Believe me, I know that route. I have been there and done it but have never met anyone I would want to have a relationship with. Most of the women lie when they write their resume, and most of the pictures are from another generation. It can actually be scary when you meet for the first time. I would only meet at a Starbucks so it could be a fast cup of coffee and out of there."

"That's hysterical. I never thought about it being hard for a guy to meet someone."

"Quality is hard to find."

And so Donna's life as a single mom began to change. She, Steve, and Donald would do things together on the weekends. Most of the time, it would be simple things like going to the beach or the park or a barbeque in the backyard. Often, June and Jim would join them for dinner. June really liked Steve, and she often told Donna what a great guy he was and how she should treat him nicely and not scare him away.

"Don't worry, Mom, I am treating him nicely, and I have to say he does reciprocate. He treats me like a lady, and I am beginning to feel there is a future in the relationship. I am actually going to meet his parents next weekend, and we are going to bring Donald with us. Steve is excited to have his folks meet us, and while I am nervous, I guess I am a little excited too. I just hope they can accept Donald and that they can like me for who I am and not think of me as who I was. I guess I am a little burned by how Rob's parents treated me and Donald. That can never happen again."

"Don't judge Steve's parents by Rob's. Rob's parents had big plans for their wonder boy, and you could have stood in the way of them seeing their plans manifested. I have heard that wonder boy has been a failure at everything. He actually failed out of college and has been supporting himself by selling drugs on the street."

"That is unbelievable. How did you hear that?'

"Freeport is a little town, and not much goes down around here without everyone knowing. People know how he and his parents treated you, and they take great pride in telling me about his failures and comparing them to your success."

"I hope he eats his heart out if he knows how far I have come. Now there is no way he can ever be a part of Donald's life, and neither can Mr. and Mrs. Know-It-All. But they are the past, and Steve is the future, and I promise not to compare his parents to anyone in the past."

"Someone once told me to see how a man treats his mother, because a man who treats his mother well, treats his wife even better."

"How did Jim treat his mother?"

"I never knew his parents; they were gone before I met Jim. From what he has told me about them, I think I would have liked them very much. Remember, Jim and I were quite a bit older when we met."

"I have never asked you why you left my father."

"Your father was an abuser who terrified me, and I always feared he would hurt you. Jim used to work with him, and he would come to our house. One thing led to another, and he offered me a better life. Case closed."

"You do know that my father used to touch me in my private places. That was probably the real reason I started to act the way I did."

"It is probably a good thing that I never knew about it. I would have killed the bastard had I known. "

"I always thought you knew but you just did not want to acknowledge it."

"I did not know. Please believe me."

"I guess I am glad to know that, and I do believe you. You were always a good mother to me. I love you."

"I love you, too."

CHAPTER 4

TENSIONS AROSE when Steve came into her office at the end of his shift to discuss some billing concerns he was having.

"I just received an explanation of benefits from Medicare for a patient seen here. There were numerous services that were not in my note, nor do I recall performing them," he said with some concern in his voice.

"Maybe we should just check the note and make sure it shows what was done."

"You are not getting the point. I know I did not do them. That is of concern. The last thing I want is to get into any trouble with the government."

"Steve, it must have been a billing mistake. The easiest way to rectify it is to correct your note. If we do anything else, we can raise red flags, and no one needs that."

"I just would appreciate it if you could tell the billers to just bill what is in my note and nothing more. I understand they are aggressive, and I do not care what they do with the doctors. I just want my billing to be the same as my note."

"I promise to do that first thing in the morning, and you can check your billings, if you want to do that."

"I can try to do so, if time allows. This place is getting so busy. Please don't misunderstand, I like it here and the money is really good, but I know it can be a nightmare to be on the wrong side of Medicare."

"I got It! Now, how about we go for a drink to calm you down some?"

"That's a great idea.

"Well, let's do it, and let's not make a bigger deal out of this. We can keep it to ourselves, if you get my point?"

"Got it and will make sure to do it!"

With that, Donna took her bag and prepared to leave the office while Steve did whatever he had to do to leave. They decided to go to the City Cellar in Westbury as that was far enough away from Freeport to possibly ensure that no one from the center would see them together. Donna knew Craig disliked the place, so it would be unlikely that he would be there. He was the only one that she did not want to know she was seeing one of the docs after work as he would not approve. But Donna said to herself, "A girl has to do what a girl has to do."

Donna was almost giddy when she saw Steve walk into the restaurant. He looked so handsome. She felt so proud when he sat down beside her. She almost could feel the eyes of the other women at the bar staring at her. Her only hope was that he was going to be able to put their previous conversation behind him, and she wondered how she would handle the billing of his cases going forward. It was in the best interests of the center to bill for as many services as possible, and he was not one to perform all the possible manipulations that could be billed. Hopefully she could get him to understand that he had to note and perform more if he was going to be one of the docs at the center. She was sure she could get him on board once he realized the more services he billed and recorded, the greater his salary.

The drink turned into dinner. Steve seemed to relax, and Donna decided not to pursue any conversations about the center and billing. That would have to happen at another time, and she was sure she would get him on board. Money talks and bullshit walks, after all is said and done. Time seemed to fly by, and before long Steve was actually the one who became concerned about Donald's babysitting arrangement.

"Babysitting is not a problem. I actually have a live-in nanny who can put Donald to bed and have the rest of the evening at home to do her own thing. She understands I have to work late, and I am good to her by giving her time off. It's a mutually convenient arrangement, and she has room and board, so she actually sleeps at my house even on her nights off. She gave up her own apartment to save the money. The whole thing works out well for both of us, and if for any reason she cannot be there, my mother is always available."

"Does her being there preclude my sleeping over?"

"Cindy is one to mind her own business. She has a separate living arrangement, and once I am home, she goes to her own area and closes the door. We both respect each other's privacy, and I am sure she has her own guests come when I do not need her services."

"Sounds perfect."

"It works, but if you do stay the night, it will be a first. I wonder how Donald will react."

"He will love waking up to me being there, and we will have all kinds of fun making breakfast together. Remember, I am a kids guy."

"Let's give it a try."

With that, they both went to their cars and left. Donna could feel her whole body tingle in anticipation of the rest of the evening. Now she could only hope for good sex as everything else seemed so perfect.

CHAPTER 5

THEIR RELATIONSHIP BLOSSOMED. Both Steve and Donna found that they could easily talk to each other and yet could also enjoy periods of silence. Donna was especially pleased by the way Steve related to Donald. He seemed to truly enjoy playing with the baby and never complained about spending time with him. Donna could tell that he was genuine about his feelings, and even June seemed pleased about having him around. Things seemed to move quickly, and before she knew it, Steve was spending nights at her house and they were behaving like a normal family. The time after Donald was asleep was the best as Steve knew just how to reach her sweet spots and make her tingle all over. Of course, she responded in kind, and he really enjoyed the sexual parts of their relationship but never questioned her about how she knew to do the things she did. She had told him in the beginning that what went before stayed in the past and that she had no interest in knowing about his past and expected him to understand that her past was just that: the past. Donna never wanted to deny her past or to glorify it. She confessed that she had taken the wrong road as a teenager but had changed paths.

One day Steve came to her house and declared that it was stupid for him to continue paying rent on an apartment he seemed to never use.

"I am here most nights, and if we combine the costs, it will be easier to maintain this place and still have money left over for fun things. Even more importantly, we will be able to spend more time together, and Donald will have a real family."

"I really am able to maintain this house on my own. Money would not be the reason for me to change my lifestyle."

"I guess what I am really thinking is that I want to be a permanent part of your life. I want us to have a home together and to be a real family. I want to marry you and adopt Donald. That's what I want."

"This is moving along too fast for me to digest everything. I can see all types of problems with us living together and working together. Up to now we have been able to keep it quiet at the center, but if we really live together, everyone will know and will think you are getting special privileges."

"The hell with what other people think. This is about us, and I love you and want to be with you. I can stop working at the center if that would make you feel better."

"I am concerned about what Craig will feel about us. I owe him so much, and I never would want to do anything that would make him angry or would disappoint him."

"That seems easy enough. We could speak to him and ask his blessing. I know how fond he is of you and how much he appreciates your work. I doubt he will run any interference in you being happy."

"I guess that is a good suggestion, but what if he does not approve?"

"We can both get new jobs and start a new life together. Neither you nor I are married to that center, and what with all you have learned and your reputation, you could get a job anywhere. As for me, my private practice is doing better and I could just give up the center in a minute."

"Let me think about this, and we can talk more over the weekend."

And so a new chapter of her life began. Donna went to Craig the following Monday and told him all about Steve and how she felt about him. While Craig said he was not elated about an intra-office relationship, he did not want to stand in the way of Donna's happiness. His main concern was if they were to breakup. He wanted them to consider a plan in that event so that the work place would not be affected. He also wanted Donna to be sure that she could still be Steve's superior at work.

"Look, I understand how hard it is to find someone you love, especially when you work the hours you do and then have to go home to take care of your son."

"I really have never been able to meet anyone who cares about me the way Steve does. He really likes Donald, and we can be a real family. I love him, and he loves me, but neither of us want to leave the center."

"So make it work; that's all I ask of you. You have always made it work. Your work ethic is impeccable. I really depend on you to run the center and to manage the properties. If this relationship is what you want, make it work for both of us. That is all I ask of you."

"You have been more than good to me, and I owe you big time. I promise my work will not be affected by my private life. I just want a life away from work, and I love Steve."

"Good luck. You have my blessing."

With that, Donna knew she was about to start a whole new life, one she'd never expected to have. She was happy beyond words.

CHAPTER 6

THINGS WERE REALLY BUSY FOR DONNA AND STEVE. He moved all of his stuff into her house and, just like their relationship, everything seemed to fit right in. Donald was so excited to have him there that he started calling him "Daddy" without anyone ever asking him to do so. It became obvious to Donna that he had missed having a father figure, and having Steve fill that role was perfect. Then there were the nights after Donald went to bed. Sex had never been that good for Donna. Never before had a man cared about her satisfaction. It had always been she that tried to satisfy the guy, and now Steve always tried to reciprocate and find her sweet spot. She was so grateful that she knew she would always do whatever he wanted, and his sexual appetite was insatiable. Their love making took hours, and at the end, they both would fall into a coma-like sleep only to awaken and think about doing it all over again.

Just as she had promised Craig, Donna made sure her work did not suffer because of her new life. She was just as attentive to the details of the real estate responsibilities. Rents were collected on time, and all the problems were solved in a timely manner. Craig was happy, and so were the tenants. The only place she was a little less effective was the medical center. Everyone there knew of her relationship with Steve, and they were quick to accuse her of favoritism.

This diminished her ability to manage the other doctors and the general staff. More and more, she began to rely on Steve to take over the day-to-day management. The staff really responded to him in a positive way, and they tended to do what he asked of them more quickly then when Donna asked the same of them. Craig, again, did not seem to mind the new relationship at the center as the bottom line kept increasing. Services were up, and so was the billing. Steven had even managed to recruit new doctors in different specialties. Now the center had a dermatologist, a neurologist and a vascular specialist, a podiatrist, and even a dentist. The dentist could even make sure the patients got dental insurance on the spot so they did not have to worry about being paid by the patients. The center was now advertising head-to-toe care in one facility and was attracting more and more people, many of whom could go elsewhere but liked the fact that the center offered a complete "head-to-toe" examination in one building at one visit.

As Steve took over more and more of the administrative responsibilities, Donna felt compelled to split her percentage with him. He really enjoyed making the extra money and often expressed his delight at being able to afford to have a family. Steve's private practice was also doing better even though he had limited time there. The patients really seemed to like his laid-back attitude and the fact that he took the time to listen to them as well as adjusting them. When patients really needed to see him and he was not available to do so at his office, he would arrange to see them at the center if they had acceptable insurance. Of course, there were patients who refused to go through the center's litany of doctors but the center still made enough from Steve's referrals to make Craig happy. Donna was delighted that all parties were benefitting and getting along. The other doctors resented Steve's arrangements, but when Donna suggested that they bring some of their private patients to the center, they quickly quieted down and politely refused. The best part of the entire situation was that Donna was able to get home at a reasonable time each day so she could spend an hour or two with Donald. He really seemed to enjoy the time he spent with her, and the two of them were getting closer and closer with each passing day. It was even better when Steve got home early enough to join them, whether it be for dinner or a walk at the park or a trip to the playground. This was what life was supposed to be like in Donna's imagination, and she was delighted to have it for real.

Donna was also loving having money to spend on beautiful things. She loved buying things for the house to make it look more beautiful than any place she had ever lived before this. She made sure all the furniture matched exactly and everything was new. Even Donald's room looked like a decorator had created it, and it was beautiful enough to be featured in a magazine. The master bedroom was totally something else. The headboard was tufted to match the fabric of the drapes, and even the side chair matched exactly. She had special lighting installed to create an exceptionally sexy atmosphere. She wanted the time she and Steve spent there to be extra special in every way possible. He often said that he never could imagine sex being so great and so exciting. This was something that Donna took great pleasure in because she was sure she would keep him with her and not wanting outside adventures. As for her, sex was becoming more and more just okay. Steve did try to satisfy her, but her best organisms were still when she was alone and touching herself. For her, sex became the same old, same old thing. She had been there and done that before, and it seemed like there was just nothing new to try. She also knew that there was no way she would ever let Steve know her true feelings. She was a very good actress and could fake an organism better than Sally in the movie *When Harry Met Sally*.

One day Steve came home and really shook Donna's world. "Let's get married," he said.

"Married? Why would we want to do that? Things are good, and we certainly don't need a piece of paper to make things any better."

"I want to have children so Donald can have a sibling, and I want us to be a stable family going forward. I am a little old fashioned, and for me, it is essential that we be married before we bring any children into this world. I love you to pieces, and I want you to be my wife, not my significant other."

"I've never thought about marriage. You really are taking me by surprise. I almost think that being married could change our relationship, and I really don't want that to happen."

"I don't see how it could do that. If anything, being married can cement our relationship. We could share everything and stop the nonsense of your accounts and my accounts. Most importantly, we would share the same last name. I would adopt Donald so he too would have the same last name, and then we would be a real family."

"That all sounds nice. It's just that I've never thought about marriage. I need some time to digest the idea."

"Take whatever time you want. I just see it as the necessary step in our relationship, so I hope you will come to agree."

"Do I detect an ultimatum in this conversation?"

"I would not say that. It is just what I would want and I hope you will agree to be my wife and the mother of my children."

"Give me a little time to get used to the idea."

"You got it!"

With that, Steve took her hand and lead her into the bedroom where he proceeded to make love to her like it was the first time for both of them. Donna felt his passion and let her mind shut down so she could just focus on his love making, but a little voice could still be heard within her telling her it was time to make a decision, and she hoped she would be able to make the right one. The biggest obstacle for her would be combining her accounts with his. She had worked so hard to accumulate the savings she had, and it represented her independence, something she had vowed she would never relinquish. She could not help but wonder why he even mentioned combining accounts with getting married. That would be something she would have to discuss before any decision could be made. She also needed to determine if she really loved him enough to spend the rest of her life with him. Up to now, she could always have walked away from the relationship if she wanted to do so. Steve was a good man, a man who helped her, a man who cared about her son, but he was not the most exciting man in the world. She needed to decide if his good qualities were enough for her. The other question that kept popping into her mind was the thought of having more children. More children would mean more responsibilities and would further tie her to Steve. She loved her life as a professional woman, and even with a nanny, more children would encroach on the time she could spend working. She had vowed that she would never allow herself to be dependent on any man, and now Steve was setting the stage to create that type of dependence, something she was really afraid of.

"Man, life can get so complicated so quickly," she said to herself just before she drifted off into a troubled sleep.

Donna was grateful that the morning did not start with a continuation of the marriage conversation. She decided she was definitely not going to bring up the subject and would wait for Steve to initiate it, which she was certain he would do. She knew that she would not be able to give in on joining all their resources, even if it would mean the termination of their relationship. She decided that she would be willing to have a joint account going forward, but the house and her savings would have to remain hers and hers alone. She also felt that any savings Steve might have accumulated would remain his and his alone. The idea of children and all that stuff would have to be worked out, but there was no point in thinking about that until the financials were settled.

Donna felt good about her decision, and she also felt that she could be happy with Steve. After all, he treated her with respect—something other men never did—and he did have the potential to be a good provider. It was kind of exciting to think of herself as a doctor's wife. Who would think of her as being a doctor's wife after most people just thought of her as a whore? She could see how much she would enjoy rubbing everything in the noses of Rob's parents and the rest of the crowd she used to hang out with. She actually laughed to herself when she thought about having a newspaper article announcing her marriage and introducing her and Steve as Doctor and Mrs.

"What a kick that would be," Donna said out loud.

Of course, June would be happy to have her married. June had often said that was what was missing from her life. In June's mind, a woman had to be married, especially if there was a child involved. Marriage was a social status which gave a woman credibility as well as respect. No matter how much money a woman could make, if she was single, she lacked the social status. Donna could see the validity in the argument, but she really did not want to marry just to marry. She wanted a special relationship, one that would keep her from looking elsewhere and one in which she would respect her husband. Ironically, Donna was sure that Steve would give her the social status and the validity, but she could not help but wonder if he could provide the excitement she so wanted. Life is a series of compromises, and she needed to decide what compromises she would be willing to make.

Life continued just as it was for quite a while. Steve said nothing more about marriage, and Donna certainly did not bring the topic up. They were both busy with the medical center and Donna was even helping him with his private practice. She did follow up calls and the bookkeeping so that he was free of those things and could just concentrate on seeing patients, something that was getting busier and busier. She loved seeing how much people seemed to like and respect him, and she was proud to be introduced as his fiancé.

On a Sunday several months after the initial conversation about marriage, the topic again emerged. This time Donna was ready with all of her requirements, and Steven listened patiently as she gave him the details of what she wanted to keep and how they would manage their finances going forward.

"While I can understand your position, I do think you are being a little selfish. After all, during this whole time, I have been contributing to the finances and you are able to save more money than you would be able to do if we were not living together," Steve said after listening to all that Donna had to say.

"There is no doubt that I have been able to save extra money during these eight months, but that does not equal what I had saved prior to our relationship. The house is something I paid for, and I have been paying the mortgage out of my salary. My savings account had one hundred thousand dollars in it before we met, so that is totally mine. If you cannot see that, I cannot marry you. I need to know that if, for any reason, things go south between us, I have my nest egg. I have been burned before, and I never want to be in that position again."

"Believe me, I get it. I also know that without you, I would never be in the position I am in today. You helped me when I was failing, and I am grateful to you for that. I also can tell you that I never expect our relationship to go south for any reason."

"That's all well and good. I really do not expect it either, but I have to have the protection. The house must remain in my name and my name alone. My savings must do the same. Once we are married, we can have a joint account for the money we save while we're together. Your practice must remain yours alone since that is something you started before we even knew each other."

"But you have been helping me build that up. You are entitled to something for your time and efforts."

"I help you because I want to do so. I am not looking for money, and as your wife I would realize that your practice is a benefit to both of us. The more money you can make, the more money we can save in our joint account. Who knows, maybe one day we can even buy a bigger house together."

"What would you do with this one?"

"I cannot imagine ever selling this house. My first thought is that if we were to buy something together, this would be an income-generating rental. But that is the future, not the present."

"You drive a hard bargain, but I can see where you are coming from, and I understand your need for underlying security. If I agree to your terms, will you marry me?"

"I will as long as we agree to a prenup. Craig can draw it up for us, and we can both sign it."

"Have you discussed this with Craig."

"Not exactly, but I did ask him if he would be willing to do a prenup for us, and he agreed to do it, but as of now, he does not know the terms."

"Draw it up, and I will sign it. It is interesting to think of a marriage that has yours, mine, and ours, not just ours."

"Today that is the way marriages are. No one can guarantee the success of any marriage, and when the couple has assets, they need to be accounted for before the marriage."

"I get it, and while I really do not like it, I agree to your terms."

"Great! Now that we have that hurdle settled, let's go to dinner and celebrate. June can watch Donald because the nanny is off today."

"Sounds good, but there is one more issue that we have to settle before we celebrate."

"What is that?"

"I want to have children with you and for you to be the mother of my kids. Are you willing to have a couple more children?"

"I can do that as long as Donald is never left out. He will always be our son."

"That is not an issue. I love that child as though he is my own flesh and blood, and I will always treat him as such. I am sure he would love to have a brother and a sister if that is how it works out."

"Sounds good to me, and you can include that stipulation in the prenup if you so desire. Now let's drop Donald off and go to a romantic dinner at a restaurant of your choice."

As Donna prepared to go to dinner, she was pleased with the way the conversation had gone. If Steve had not agreed to her terms, he would have had to move out immediately as she was not about to back down. Now they could go about planning the wedding and starting their life as a married couple. It was exciting to think about being married and Donald having a mother and a father, especially a father who loved him. How perfect would that be? Donna knew there was still one issue that remained to be discussed. It was important to her that she remain the administrator at the center. She was happy to allow

Steve to handle much of the day-to-day issues, especially since he got along with the rest of the staff even better than she did. Some of the doctors resented that they had to take orders from her. After all, she was not a doctor, and they felt they knew better than she did. He did not have that issue even though he was just a chiropractor. But Donna still wanted the ultimate control, and she knew this was something that had to be discussed, but tonight was not the right time.

That night they went to a quiet French restaurant where they had a table in the back. For dessert, Steve ordered Jell-O, something that really surprised Donna as she had never seen him eat Jell-O. When the Jell-O came to the table, all Donna could do was smile as in the middle of it was the most beautiful ring she had ever seen.

"I was afraid to put the ring into ice cream because I was afraid you would not see it."

"How hysterical! It is absolutely beautiful, and I will wear it proudly."

"I want it to be a symbol of our love. I want our love to be as enduring as this diamond."

"I can't believe this is happening to me."

"Let's just enjoy all the preparations for our wedding. Whatever your life was like before, is over and done with. I want no explanations. We have spoken about this before, and you know my feelings. You are a beautiful person and a wonderful mother. Donald and I are lucky to have you in our lives, and we both love you dearly. Is that clear?"

"I am too excited to speak. I can only say thank you for all your support."

CHAPTER 7

JUNE WAS SHOCKED when she learned that Donna wanted a church wedding with all the trimmings. The guest list included the staff from the center and many of Donna's friends from high school as well as all the relatives.

"This is going to cost a fortune," June exclaimed as she looked over the list.

"I plan on only getting married once, and I want it to be perfect. I also want everyone to see how successful I am and how happy I am."

"I get that, but can't we do this on a smaller scale?"

"I am planning on having the reception at The Coral House, which is not that expensive. I've priced it out, and the whole thing will cost about twenty thousand dollars. We have that saved, so it is not going to put us in any debt."

"I am sure you could use that money for something more substantial than a four hour party."

"It is my wedding, my money, and what I want. Stop being such a dishrag, and let's enjoy it. You are always too practical."

With that, June just shut up and decided to let Donna do her own thing. After all, she did have a point. She was not asking for money; she was only asking for someone to enjoy the experience with her. In her heart, June could understand that Donna was making a point and that she wanted to show off her new, successful husband and new lifestyle. Everyone had been so sure that Donna was always going to be a street person and never make anything of herself. Now, here she was about to marry a doctor and earning a six-figure salary on her own.

"When are we going for the dress?"

"That's what I wanted to hear! Let's go and look for one this Saturday. I need to know how long it will take to get the dress before I actually book the reception. I want one that will make me look beautiful and successful so everyone will notice."

"Everyone always notices the bride as she walks down the aisle or into the reception. That is not something you have to be concerned about."

"The dress cannot be trashy; it has to be classy."

"I get it, and I agree. Nothing off the rack for my girl. Saturday it is," June replied, smiling at her change of tone and enjoying the ideas behind it. She was going to enjoy Donna's statement.

Planning the wedding was simple. Donna realized she had made all her plans as a little girl, and she knew exactly what she wanted, who she wanted there, and how everything was to look. Now it was a matter of just implementing her plans, and she did so with complete ease. Before anyone knew it, the invitations were printed, and the flowers were ordered with explicit details as to how they were to be arranged. The photographer was given a list of the mandatory photos he was to take, and most important to Donna, the band was engaged and given a list of the songs that were to be played. She even instructed the band as to when they could play loudly and when they were to play soft music as she hated going to weddings where everyone was constantly yelling to be heard. Donna was leaving nothing to chance.

Steve was not really consulted since he told Donna this was her gig and that all he wanted was to invite a few friends from his childhood as well as some of his closer relatives. Donna arranged to have his guests sit at a table right near the center table so that Steven could interact with them easily. On the other side of the center table would be June and Donna's closest relatives.

At the center table, there was going to be Steve, Donna, and Donald, who would also have a seat at June's table so he would never be left all alone.

Once all the plans were in place, Donna just sat back and waited for the day to come. She was giddy at times thinking about the wedding and how perfect it was going to be. She was also excited to know that everyone in Freeport was going to know about her perfect wedding and how successful she was personally and how she was marrying a doctor. The satisfaction was almost more than she could take, especially since she knew that Rob was a total failure and a major disappointment to his "wonderful parents." How perfect could life possibly be? It was going to be she who had it all!

The wedding went off just as planned. Donna was elated as she walked down the aisle at the church and heard the gasps from those in attendance. She knew she looked beautiful in the form-fitting gown, which flowed over her body as she moved. Steven's smile was the best assurance that she did indeed look beautiful. The reception that followed was a dream come true. There was no doubt that the dance lessons had paid off, and Donna could only hope that the rest of their life together would be as perfect as that moment. Even Donald cooperated and seemed to enjoy all the attention showered on him. He definitely was an amazing little boy who was mature far past his years.

CHAPTER 8

THE HONEYMOON CAME TO AN ABRUPT END when Donna and Steve returned. There were problems with the staff at the center, and the general census was markedly down. Craig was getting nervous and requested that Donna make her presence known. He made it clear that only she could get the census back up and resolve the staff discord.

"The doctors are crying that Steve is getting preferential treatment now that he is your husband, and they are threatening to leave *en masse*," Craig told Donna during a meeting at his off-site office.

"That is absurd. Steve was the assistant manager before we got married, and that is exactly what he is now."

"They feel they do not have to take orders from a chiropractor when they have medical degrees."

"I get it. Do you have any idea of who the ring leader is?"

"No, they came to me as a unified group with no one doc showing any leadership."

"It probably all boils down to dollars and cents. If I get the census up and we can pay more, they will probably quiet down again. I will set up some re-cruitments at the local supermarkets and banks, and I will get more patients into the center. In addition, I will start looking for fresh staff. Once we fire one of the docs, the others will shut up."

"We don't want to cut off our noses to spite our faces. It is not easy to get these docs trained."

"That is why I am going to appease them now, but I will not tolerate their insurgence and I will get new docs in place. The center is our golden egg, and we do not know how long it will last, but while it does, we need to maximize our profits."

"I totally agree with that. After all, we are dealing with the government to pay for the services, and that could end at any time."

"I am back at the center, and it will have one hundred per cent of my attention. I got these docs for us, and I will take care of the problems. Have no fear."

"That is the tough Donna I have grown to respect and love. Go to it, girl!"

Donna went directly to the center after leaving the meeting with Craig. She could feel the tension in the building as she walked down the corridor to her office. She immediately notified the front desk that she wanted food ordered for the next day when they were going to bring a busload of patients into the center for lunch and medical services. She had made the center profitable the first time, and she was going to do it again. Except this time, she was going to surpass anything that had happened before.

The next thing Donna did was to call Steve into her office. She promptly told him about the meeting with Craig.

"What's going on here? Have you had any negative discussions with the other docs?"

"I thought everyone was getting along well. I have never had anyone say anything differently to me. My only guess is that some of those guys are jealous now that we're married."

"I want you to back off completely. Just act like one of the docs, and I will take over the management of the center for now. I need to get everyone back in line and to get the census up. Once that happens, we can do whatever is necessary for you to retake over the management."

"I get what you are saying, but I am not liking it. You are demoting me and diminishing me in front of all the other doctors."

"You may not like it, and I get that. But that is what we need to do at this moment. Once the census is up and the center returns to great profitability, I will weed out the troublemakers and replace them with docs who will understand that you are the manager. These docs were hired by me and think of me as the manager. They were willing to take orders from me, but not from anyone else. They think they know what's best, but they don't. They are all failures and will continue to fail without leadership. I am going to whip their asses into line, and once I fire some of them, they will all fall into a more manageable place for you to take over once again. You are different from these bozos. You can be successful on your own, and I totally get it if you want to devote more time to your private practice and use that as an excuse for relinquishing the management here. I will make sure that you are paid the same as always."

"That is a thought for now. It would allow me to save face with these docs as I do not want it to look like my wife is punishing me."

"Fear not. I will never allow it to look like that. I respect you and know the man you are. I just need to get this place back on track, and I know I can do it. Tomorrow I will be bringing in a busload of new patients, and I will want all staff here and ready to process them. After that we can figure out how we will arrange your time between here and your private practice."

And so it went with Steve. Donna was certain he got it and would cooperate with her. She next sent a memo to all the staff regarding the activities for the next day. Some of the docs quickly came to her office to tell her they had other plans for the time she wanted them to be in the building. Donna just laughed and told them it was not an option and that all other plans had to be cancelled or their employment would be cancelled immediately. She made it completely clear that it was a matter of "get with the program" or leave the cash cow. Everyone, in the end, said they would be at the center, and the meeting ended with a feeling of renewed dedication. Donna felt like she was a cheerleader and was elated and encouraged by the reception she was getting. She was once again the old Donna, pushing the buttons to make things work.

That night Steve did not come home for dinner. When Donna tried to call him on his cell, there was no answer. When he finally came home, she could smell the alcohol on his breath.

"You've been drinking."

"I did not enjoy being called to the principal's office."

"That center is my baby. I started it; I made it grow; I hired you. Neither you nor anyone else is going to get between it and me. If I need to make changes to keep it successful, I will do whatever I have to do to achieve my end result. Am I making myself clear?"

"Clear."

"There is no way I want our work relationship to come between our private relationship. You are my husband, and here we are totally equal, but I am still your boss at the center. I can differentiate between the two. Can you?"

"Honestly, I do not know if I can. "

"Then you will have to leave the center. There are no choices. I have to answer to Craig, and he is not happy with the current losses and the discontent among the staff. He feels that they resent you because you are my husband, and they feel you get special privileges. That cannot be the perception. I need your cooperation. But most of all, I need our work not to interfere with our marriage, and that is what is happening now. I love you and want us to be happy and successful. I know we can work this out and come out ahead in every way. Your private practice will benefit, and eventually you will resume your responsibilities as the manager. Just let me get things going again."

"I'll try. I do love you, and I also want things to be good for us at home."

"It is even more important than ever before. I wanted to tell you over a great romantic dinner, but I think you need to know right now. I am pregnant with your child. So you can see why time is important to me."

"Donna, that is great news. I can't believe it happened so easily. Everyone I know has had a horrible time getting pregnant."

"Everyone is not me. I know how much you wanted this. Let's enjoy the moment and let our work be our work and our home be our home. We can do that; I know it. But coming home drunk is not the answer."

"I am so sorry for the way I acted. I get it loud and clear."

CHAPTER 9

DONNA WAS AMAZED at how easily her pregnancy proceeded. It was so much easier on her body this time than it had been with Donald. It was also nice having someone to stand by her and help with the daily chores. Steve was being good to his word about coming home directly after work and being supportive. He was actually thrilled when they learned that the baby was a girl, and they were having fun picking names for their baby.

Work at the center was going well. Donna was showing that she was the practice administrator, and all the doctors accepted her in that role. Steve was relegated to being another doctor and not someone in charge of the implementation of policies at the center. For his part, Steve seemed happy in his new role as it definitely gave him more time to devote to his private practice, which was showing a steady improvement in revenue. Patients seemed to really relate to him, and his return rates were excellent. Donna could only hope that the trend would continue after the baby was born and that she could even spend more time with the baby than she had with Donald. She felt that she could monitor the center from home more, especially now that she actually had a computer at home and that she had staff who could bring patients to the center to keep the census positive.

All was good until she reached thirty weeks and started having premature labor. The doctors insisted that she have bed rest to allow the baby to continue to develop and that she not have any stress.

"You have to be kidding me," Donna exclaimed. "If you put me to bed, the stress will be intense. After all, I have a three year old, a demanding job, and a household to manage."

"If you want a normal and healthy baby, you have no choice. If that baby is born now, she might not survive or might have permanent brain damage along with other disabilities. The decision is ultimately yours, but we have to inform you of the consequences."

"I get it, but I do not like it one bit. Everything was going so well. I do not understand how this could be happening."

"Pregnancy can change course in a moment. It is nothing you have done, but we have to address what is happening. Bed rest is the easy answer. If we can get four to five more weeks, we can be out of the danger zone. You will be allowed to go to the bathroom and to shower, but otherwise you are to stay off your feet and be lying down. Am I making myself clear?"

"Clear as day. I guess my mother will have to take care of Donald while Steve is at work, and any problems at the center can be handled on the telephone. That's the best I can do."

When Steve heard about the doctor's advice, he was devastated. There was no way he wanted to jeopardize his baby's well-being, and he quickly declared that he would take over whatever responsibilities Donna had so that she could remain on bed rest, even if that meant resuming the duties of the manager at the center.

"Let's take this one step at a time. If I can continue to manage the center by telephone, I will do it. If I need you to do something specific, we will talk about it. I just do not want to upset the applecart again with the other docs."

"They have to understand that this is an unusual set of circumstances and that you have to do what is best for yourself and our baby."

"I spoke to Craig, and he is going to tell them exactly that. So let's just see how it all plays out. For now, I need you to take over the household and the shopping. June is willing to watch Donald when you are working and he is not in daycare or with the nanny. So that will work out. I know you or Cynthia can cook a dinner and that you are good with takeout, so I think we can survive the next five to six weeks if she can," Donna said, pointing to her stomach.

"We will all make it!"

And so life continued for Donna and Steve. Each day was like a lifetime for Donna, who hated staying in bed. She actually wished that she had some girl-friends who could stop by and gossip with her. That was something she had never had the time to cultivate and, she thought, going forward she would try to make friends with some of the women she met at the preschool program where Donald was going. She was resolved to change her life once again. She was going to have a family life, and everything was not going to revolve around work and more work. Obviously, the center could function without her constant attention.

It was a big deal to Donna when she had to go to the doctor for her weekly checkup. Just getting dressed was a major ordeal. Usually it was June who would accompany her as Steve would be working, and it was ridiculous for him to lose the income, especially now that his income was their primary one with Donna only receiving the small amounts from disability. After each doctor's visit, Donna found she had to come home and take a long nap before she could think of anything else.

Four weeks into the bed rest routine, Donna felt the first sharp pain that she knew was the beginning of her labor. It was close to four in the afternoon, so she immediately called Steve, only to have the call go directly to voicemail.

"I don't care what you are doing, and you had better have a good reason for putting your phone on voicemail. I am calling my mother to take me to the hospital, and I strongly suggest you get there really quickly, or you will never see your daughter or me. "

After leaving the message, Donna called her mother to come and pick her up, and then she called the doctor who told her to come directly to the hospital, which is what she expected to hear. June had already gotten Donald from day care, so she told Donna she would be right over and help her get her things together. June diplomatically did not ask about Steven as she knew he was unreachable, or Donna would have just told her to keep Donald and not ask her to bring her to the hospital.

As they were leaving for the hospital, they both noticed that no return call had come from Steve.

"I am sure there is a good reason why his phone is off. After all, it is obvious that you could have to go to the hospital at any time now," June said, trying to calm Donna down.

"Yeah, I am sure the good reason is that he is shacked up with some broad and does not want to be interrupted."

"Just maybe, you are wrong and there is a legitimate answer. You should hear his side of this before you allow yourself to get so upset and destroy everything. This baby deserves a real family life and you know how much Steve means to Donald."

"Talking about Donald, where is he? It is too bad that today is Cynthia's day off.

"I left him with Jim. They have dinner, and Jim is perfectly willing to watch him under these circumstances. Don't worry, he will be fine, and I can stay with you for as long as you want me to."

"Thanks, Mom, you are the greatest!"

"Not really. I am a mom, just as you are, and we both will always do what is best for our children. Remember that."

They drove the rest of the way in silence. Donna did try Steve's phone again only to go to voicemail yet a second time.

Upon arriving at the hospital, the triage unit took Donna's blood pressure and immediately called her doctor because the pressure was so high. June tried to explain that she had been very upset on the way over, but they refused to accept that explanation. Donna was rushed to the emergency unit of the labor floor where her doctor was waiting for her. He quickly explained that a c-section might be needed if her blood pressure did not stabilize. This news only served to further elevate her blood pressure as Donna was becoming more and more agitated.

June excused herself and went into the hall to try Steve once again. This time he answered and tried to explain that he was in a meeting with Craig and could not answer his phone. "I am on my way to the hospital as we speak."

"I really don't care why you could not answer your phone. In my book, there are no excuses, and I am sure Craig would have understood given the circumstances. Donna is so upset that her blood pressure is dangerously high and the doctors are considering a c-section. How long will you be before you get here?"

"I should be there within ten minutes. Please let Donna know that I am on my way and why I did not answer the phone. It might calm her down some."

"I'll do that, but I doubt it will be of any help now. We are in the emergency unit on the delivery floor, so get here as fast as you can. I will try to have them wait for you, but I make no promises."

"Thanks, June."

June went back into the room, and quietly spoke to Donna, telling her that Steve was on his way and should be there within minutes. She also tried to explain that he was in a conference with Craig and that was why he had not answered the phone.

"Yeah, sure! We'll see about that later. I know Craig would never have stopped him from taking a call from me."

"Donna, stop working yourself up. You are hurting yourself and the baby, and there is no point to this. He'll be here soon, and after the baby is born, you and he can talk this over in a calm way and work things out together. Now is not the right time or place."

"You are always so level-headed."

"And you are always so hot-headed."

With that, the doctor reappeared and told them he wanted to proceed with the c-section as it was in the best interests of Donna and the baby. He voiced his fear that Donna would stroke out if they did not act quickly.

"Her husband will be here momentarily. Can we wait for him?"

"As long as it is really soon. I am going to make the necessary arrangements, and I'll be back."

Just as the doctor left the room, Steve came rushing in. As soon as Donna saw him, her pressure again spiked.

"I am so sorry, baby. I did not think you would be going into labor this soon, so when Craig asked me to turn off my phone, I did so. You can talk to him, and you will find out I am telling you the truth. "

"They want to do a c-section, and I am scared out of my mind right now. This is all I can think about."

"We need to do whatever is best for you and the baby. You have confidence in Dr. Brown, so let's listen to him. I cannot think about the consequences."

With that, he sat beside Donna and started to stroke her face. June was amazed to see the blood pressure decrease for the first time since they had arrived, but it still seemed too high and went right back up with the first labor pain. It was obvious where this was going, and all she could hope for was that the end result would be good.

Dr. Brown came back into the room. "Ready to rock and roll."

Steve asked the question Donna was going to ask, "Can we wait and see if her pressure stabilizes?"

"It is not in her or the baby's best interest. There is entirely too much stress being placed on her body, and it will affect your daughter. We have to do what is in the best interest of the patient, and waiting is not."

"Can I stay with Donna?"

"Of course. Dads are allowed in the delivery room. Just don't pass out on us as we don't need another patient."

"Worry not; I'll be fine."

"Grandma, have a seat in the waiting room, and I'll be out as soon as possible to let you know all is well."

"Don't rush."

The c-section went well, and both Donna and Steve were thrilled when the nurses placed the little, dark-haired girl on her chest. Her skin was a beautiful pink color, and she seemed to just snuggle into Donna as though she was waiting to do just that for a very long time.

"I have never seen anything more beautiful than our little girl," Steve exclaimed loudly enough for everyone in the delivery area to hear him.

"I know, she is just perfect. Now we have our boy and our girl. What more could we ever want?" Donna responded, looking into Steve's eyes and hoping to find the answers she really wanted there.

She could not get it out of her mind that she was sure he was having an affair, but she was hoping against all odds that he would stop it now that the baby was here and they could again have a real life together with their little family. She was well aware of the fact that the past few months would have been hard on any relationship, but that was all over now. She knew in her heart of hearts she could forgive him and forget all that had happened, but that would be predicated on him being devoted to the family and stopping seeing whoever he was fucking. She also knew that words were cheap and actions were what really mattered, so it was pointless to listen to him declare his love; she would wait to see how he showed it. She also knew that she would throw him out just like the garbage if he did not change. If things were to come to that, she also knew, she would do everything possible to destroy him professionally. But now was not the time or the place to discuss any of this; now was the time to appreciate their beautiful daughter and to revel in the magnificence of their creation.

When the nurses removed the baby from her chest, there was an emptiness that Donna had never experienced before. It had been a long time since her body was hers alone. It was at that moment that she became aware of the pain where the incision was. Up until then, she had felt no pain.

"I guess the damn anesthesia is already wearing off and this incision really hurts."

"I was expecting that," replied one of the nurses. "I have some pain meds ready for you. They will take the edge off things, but you will not be sleepy, so you will be able to hold your daughter when they bring her back to you."

"Where did they take her?"

"She is in the nursery. They have to do the vitals and complete all the necessary paperwork. Once that is done, they will bring her back to you. No worries."

Donna eagerly accepted the meds and then turned her attention to Steve to ask about June.

"She knows all went well and saw the baby before they took her to the nursery. She is waiting outside as she felt it was best for you and me to have some time alone together."

"That's my mother. Always the romantic! Please let her come in as I know she will feel better when she sees I am really okay."

From that point on things moved quickly. Donna was transferred to her private room, and the baby was brought back to them and they could actually hold her. It was Steve who seemed the most excited, and he kept looking at her and admiring each body part as though it was a unique creation. Donna tried to stay awake but found herself drifting off into never-never land as a result of the pain meds, something she was definitely not accustomed to taking. Because of this, the nurses gave Steve a bottle for the baby as they felt Donna was too groggy to attempt to nurse her.

It was shortly after his giving the baby the bottle of glucose that Donna woke up and commented that the baby did not look as pink as she did initially. Steve tried to dissuade Donna from being alarmed, but she insisted that the nurse be called.

"The baby is getting a grayish hue, and I am really concerned," Donna said as the nurse walked into the room.

It did not take her long to rush the baby out of the room and down to the NICU. Steve ran after her, demanding explanations, but none were forthcoming. Once at the NICU, the doctors took over and placed an airway into the baby's nose. They then explained that the baby had a form of apnea and was stopping breathing. They were going to keep her on the respirator and monitor her breathing. She would be staying in the NICU until she was stabilized, but they did stress this was not an uncommon occurrence and that he should not be overly concerned.

"My baby is stopping breathing, and you do not want me to be overly concerned. Come on now!"

"We have seen this many times before, and I can assure you we will handle this. She will be fine."

"Good luck explaining that to my wife. She is going to be hysterical."

"Go back to your wife. She needs you more than the baby does right now."

Donna was inconsolable when Steve came back to her room. All she kept saying was that this was the result of them having to give her anesthesia to perform the c-section. The drugs must have affected the baby's ability to breathe.

"I did everything right. I gave up my life for weeks so she could have a life, and now look, it has all been for- nothing."

"You are being melodramatic, and you know it. It is nothing that you did or the doctors did. This happens to babies all the time, especially if they are a little early like our little girl. She just needs a little help, and before you know it she will be home and doing just fine. Now let me get a wheelchair and take you down to the NICU. I think it will be helpful for her to hear your voice and feel your touch."

"I really don't want to go. I don't want to get too attached to her and then lose her."

"That is absurd. You are already attached to her, and you know it. You love that little person and always will. Besides, I repeat, I think it is in her best interests to know you are there for her."

"She does not even have a name."

"What do you want to name her? It is funny, but we never discussed this during all the time you were doing nothing but staying in bed."

"Since she is really your first child, what do you want to name her?"

"You are Donna, and then there is Donald, so why don't we stay with the D's and name her Debbie?"

"I like that. Let's see if we feel it fits her."

"I'll get the wheelchair. Thanks for taking my advice."

As they entered the NICU, Donna could not help but yell, "Look, she is pink!" The nurse came over to reassure the couple that their baby was doing just fine. In fact, she told them there had not been another episode of her stopping breathing or any indication that she was having any problems.

"We'll certainly keep her here for a couple of days just to monitor her, but my experience says, she will be going home a normal and happy baby. This type of thing happens, and once she does go home, we would recommend a monitor be attached to her crib just to give you additional peace of mind. Now would you like to nurse your baby?"

"I am afraid to touch her what with the wires and all."

"Have no fears, I am here to help you, and it is good for the two of you to bond."

Donna was delighted to be holding her daughter. It so reminded her of holding Donald when he was this size. She knew now something that she did not know the first time: time would go by faster than anyone could realize, and she had to enjoy this time with her baby before the time passed her by. With Donald, she had been eager for him to reach each step, and she remembered showing him how to stand and walk long before it was time to do so. This time she was going to enjoy the baby stage and not rush it as she was convinced this would be her last pregnancy.

Steve, too, was delighted to stand and watch Donna nurse their baby. He viewed this child as a true extension of himself and was excited to think about the things he would be doing with his daughter. While he had fun with Donald, it was always in the back of his mind that he was not really Donald 's father, and he would never really see himself in the child. This was going to be different. This baby and he shared DNA, and he was always going to be there for her to share the good and bad and to make her life as perfect as he could. At that moment, he knew he would never cheat on Donna again if for no other reason than the fear that Donna would shut him out of the baby's life just as she had with Donald's father and his family. Steve made a silent promise to his daughter that he would forever be a part of her life and would forever take care of her no matter what sacrifices he would have to make to do so.

CHAPTER 10

LIFE RESUMED as it always did for the little family. Donna went back to working at the center, and June resumed her role as grandmother and babysitter whenever Cynthia was unavailable. The only one who seemed somewhat unhappy was Steve, who was now reduced to being just another doctor at the center and not the administrator. He hated taking orders from his wife and often showed his displeasure at inopportune moments.

Donna tried to ignore him but finally decided to call him out on his behavior.

"I think you should stop working at the center. I can get another chiropractor to take your place, and that way you can concentrate on your private practice and we can have separate professional lives. I know you have an issue with working under my supervision, and I have an issue with you showing your discontent."

"You know I still need the income from the center, so I cannot give up my position. I just need you to back off and not show everyone you are the boss. You do not realize it, but you tend to single me out and ridicule me in front of the others."

"I need you to be extra special and set an example for the others to follow. I also need to show that you do not receive special treatment because you are my husband."

"But I do receive special treatment—negative special treatment—and that has to stop."

"Stop or what?"

"This is not a threat. It is a discussion. I love you as a wife, but I hate you as a boss."

"There are things in life over which we have no choices, and this is one of them. If you are going to stay on at the center, you have to work under my supervision and accept the way I do things, or you can leave. Have I made myself clear?"

"You are like two different women: the one at home and the one here at the center. I like one and hate the other."

"I thought you loved one!"

"Let it go. This is not the time or the place for that discussion."

"Just know that if you do not love me, leave me. I will survive, and my children will survive. We can do it with you or without you; it is your choice."

"Now who is threatening who?"

"Not threatening, just making a statement. This entire conversation has deteriorated to a very bad place, and if you want to continue it, we have to do so at home. This is neither the time nor the place."

"Don't expect me home for dinner tonight. I need some time and space."

"Take all the time and space you need, and maybe we will still be there when you come crawling back. No promises made."

"Whoa, you can be one solid bitch."

"Don't think for one moment that I was unaware of your affair while I was lying in bed to save your daughter. I never challenged you about it because I really wanted us to be a family. You are the one making it hard for me to forgive and forget. You are the one creating issues and making out relationship harder than it needs to be. We started out with me being your superior, and that has not changed nor will it. If it comes down to one of us leaving, it will be you. Get that through your head. If you want to leave both relationships, that too is your decision. But don't take too long deciding or I will make the decisions for both of us."

Steve just stood there, unable to think of anything to say. Shaking his head, he turned and walked out of Donna's office, wondering if indeed he was also walking out of her life. He felt totally emasculated by her and knew this was going to be just the beginning of a negative spiral that could easily spin totally out of control.

Donna just sat down at her desk and put her head into her hands. All she could think was that Steve had been acting strangely ever since she was put on bed rest. Then when she came back to work, the strangeness had just become magnified. He just made it obvious to everyone that he resented having his role as the administrator diminished, but there was nothing Donna could do about it. When push came down to shove, Steve had to be able to take instructions from her, like it or not. As to their personal relationship, that too was up in the air and Steve just had to accept who she was and what she was or he could leave. She had worked too hard to get to where she was, and she was not about to change for anyone or anything. Before Steve, she had managed well, and she could do it again. Of that she was sure!

She was shocked when she looked up and saw Craig standing in front of her desk. He rarely came to the center, and his expression was one of stress not friendship.

"We have a problem, and it seems as though your lover boy is at the center of it."

"Can we start at the beginning so I can understand what you are talking about?"

"I received a love letter from Medicaid today stating that they are investigating Steve for submitting claims for patients he did not see."

"I do not understand. Are there notes about the treatments in question, and did the patients sign an encounter form?"

"There are detailed notes, but suspiciously, the encounter forms are nowhere to be found. It looks very suspicious, especially since all the visits were during your absence from the center. I understand he was filling in as the administrator and was the one responsible for checking the claims submitted. It would have been very easy for him to produce the claims so that his census would be improved. Before coming to you, I did check, and his census was definitely up during that time."

"I find it hard to believe he could be that stupid. What proof do they have that the patients were not actually seen?"

"I understand that they actually called several patients and asked. The patients vehemently denied having any chiropractic care. They do say the patients were here but that they were here just for follow-up care by one of the other doctors. I did check with some of the docs who were seeing the patients for follow-up, and they too say there was no reason for the patient to have seen Steve. This could be a real problem for us, and it could actually close down the center. I really think you have to have a heart-to-heart with lover boy."

"That could be a problem since he and I are having problems. He stormed out of here just before you appeared, and I am not sure he will even come home tonight. He resents taking orders from me and feels I am overstepping my position here. He made it quite clear that he does not respect me as the administrator. Personally, I do not think he respects me as his wife either."

"I am sorry to add to your burden, but this is something that we have to deal with immediately. I would like to give him the respect of hearing his side of things before this goes any further. But, if he is guilty, he could face charges and could even lose his license. This center will not protect him as that would put everyone in jeopardy. "

"I get it. I really do, and I agree with you on all counts. I am just sorry that my medical problems could have negative ramifications for the center. I really thought I could trust Steve to do the right thing. I can only say that I guess I really do not know the man on any level."

"Let me know what's up after you speak with him."

"Of course. I just cannot help but wonder how accurate the patients who are involved really are. Is it at all possible that they were really seen? I know for a fact that some of our docs resent Steve and would love to hurt him."

"Good try, but I doubt that will float the boat. Medicaid is saying that they are suspicious of the increase in his census as it is out of range with the number of patients being seen and with the comps from last year. It is looking bad, and I am worried that there is no defense."

"Whoa; this sounds like you have known about it for a while. Why didn't you come to me sooner?"

"I wanted to have some concrete proof before coming to you. After all, he is your husband, and I was sure you would want to defend him at all costs."

"Wrong. My first allegiance is to you and the center, and if he has done anything to hurt you or the center, I could never forgive him. That is especially the case since I put him in the position and he misused it."

"I appreciate your loyalty. Let's hear his side before we do anything else."

"Please give me a list of the claims in question. I would like to look into the matter myself before we even speak to Steve."

With that, Craig handed her a folder and walked out of Donna's office. All she could do was to put her hands over her eyes and put her head down on the desk. She had to squelch her desire to call Steve immediately and demand a meeting with him. Instead, she decided that she needed more proof that he was billing for times he was not physically in the building. That would be the easiest to prove as all the entry-exit records were kept for a year, but no one other than Craig and herself knew about their hiding place, so they could not be altered. Now she needed the dates involved and the exact patients for whom the claims were submitted. She did not want to think about the personal ramifications, but she knew if she proved he was not at the center, she would have to believe he was with someone else because he certainly was not with her. All the time she had spent in bed, he kept telling her how busy he was at the center, especially since he was doing much of her work. She had really wanted to believe him, but all along there were the little voices in her head telling her he was lying. She just did not know how she could possibly be that bad a judge of men.

It took several days for her to accumulate all the data for the claims in question and to compare the entry and exit records. Steve was not in the building during the times of the visits in question, and the claims for his services were processed days later and processed directly by him. All of this was not according to the normal procedures. Billing normally processed all the claims for the doctors, and the only contact Steve should have had was to check the claims after they were done and prior to their submission. In addition, Donna was able to confirm that Steve had reported seeing over fifty percent more patients than he had during the same time period in the prior year. This also did not make any sense since Donna had been out and not recruiting patients the way she had done during the same period last year.

"Oh my God," Donna exclaimed when she called Craig. "I cannot believe he could be so stupid to think he could get away with all of this."

"Obviously, we have to get him in and talk to him as soon as possible. I would like to hear his side of the story before taking any legal action against him."

"Good luck with that. I have not heard from him since he stormed out of my office days ago. He is probably shacked up with someone as he has not even been to his private office in two days. I called there, and the receptionist had not heard from him and he had not answered his cell even when she calls him."

"You are married to one sick puppy. I suggest you call him, and if he does not answer, leave a message that he is in serious trouble and needs to call immediately. Also text that to him so if he does not pick up his messages, he will see the text. In the meantime, I will contact our legal staff and get their advice as to how to proceed so that we protect the center. I really hate to do this as it will affect you personally, but I do not see how we have any alternative."

"Don't worry about it affecting me. I am done with him and better off without his nonsense. I told you my allegiance is to you and the center. I have taken steps to protect my house from him and have spoken with a divorce attorney who told me that what was mine before the marriage stays mine and he would have no rights to it. I never put the house or anything into his name even though we had talked about doing so after we were married. I just never got around to it, and now I am so glad I didn't. Besides, I do have a prenup that simply states what was mine is mine and what was his is his. The only good thing that comes from my marriage is Debbie, and she is really adorable."

"You do realize that Steve can demand visitation with his daughter and that you will have continued contact with him."

"I get it, and I did discuss spousal support with the attorney. He said that since Steve's W2 is higher than mine for last year, he should have to pay child support but that maintenance will be at question, especially if I go on to earn more than he does. That, of course, will be a possibility if he were to lose his license. He really does not have any other means to support himself."

"He should have thought about that before he allowed the wrong head to influence his actions. He had a good thing being married to you and working here. He really screwed up his life, and she had better be worth it."

"How did you know there was a she involved?"

"I am a man, and to me it was obvious that he was fooling around even before this thing with Medicaid erupted. He just looked too happy for a man whose wife was bedridden."

"Why didn't you say something to me?"

"The point would have been what? You had all you could deal with, and there was no point of adding to your stress."

"I get it. I just don't understand how I could be such a poor judge of character. I really thought he loved me and he would be a good husband and father."

"We all make mistakes. Look at me. I am still in a loveless marriage because I cannot afford to get out of it. Believe me, if I did not have a special needs child and a long-term marriage, I would leave Michelle in a heartbeat. But there is no point to this discussion. Please do your best to get him here as soon as possible, and I will take care of the legal department."

With that, Craig walked out of the office and left Donna to make her call, a call that was going to change her life as she currently knew it to be, but one that was totally necessary. Her second call was to her mother, who also confirmed that she'd had suspicions that Steve was fooling around and that she was not surprised that Donna was going to initiate divorce proceedings.

"You will be better off without that freeloader in your life," June said. "You did it before, and you can do it alone again. Just remember I am here to help."

It took two days for Steve to respond to Donna's call and text. When he agreed to come to the center, he walked into her office to find Craig and a group of attorneys there, each with a very serious face on.

"What is this—a kangaroo court?"

"No, we just know what was going on here with your billing, and we want to hear your side of it," Donna said without allowing her voice to shake.

"You bitch. You take their word for things without even thinking that they are wrong. You should be married to Craig, not to me. Do you forget that I am your husband? Where is your loyalty anyway?"

"Loyalty is a funny word for you to use. Where was your loyalty when I was bedridden to save your daughter and I trusted you to do the right things here at the center? I really do not care who you were shacked up with as we will deal with that at another time and another place. I only care about your fraudulent billing and am waiting for you to explain how you thought you could get away with billing patients you did not see. We have conclusive proof that you were not even in the building when you claimed to have treated patients."

At that point, Craig took over the conversation. He patiently explained that the center was going to acknowledge that there were billing errors and that Steve, himself, would be expected to return the money billed to Medicaid. He also explained that, should the government want to prosecute, the center would do nothing to protect him, and should he lose his license, then so be it.

"Look, I don't have that kind of funds to pay back the claims. There is no way anyone can get blood from a stone," Steve exclaimed.

"You signed the claims. They are your responsibility, and we cannot protect you."

"So, in essence you are sending me down the river in a boat with no paddle."

"Every action has a consequence, and you should have thought about that before you did what you did. You put every doctor here at risk, and the credibility of the center is damaged."

"If you continue to refuse to help me, I will expose the fraudulent billing that goes on here all the time. I know how you bring patients in and have them see everyone on staff even if they really do not have a medical problem. You realize that the two of us can play the same game. I, too, have kept proof of your billing tactics, and I am sure Medicaid and Medicare would be delighted to know about them."

"You are really one solid piece of work. I expected this response, and now the attorneys will take over this conversation. After they are finished with you, I expect you to remove all personal belongings from this building and to never set foot in it again. Your office has been gone through, and all paperwork has been removed from it.

"I, too, expect you to remove all personal belongings from my house. All of your paperwork has been destroyed, so don't even bother looking for it," Donna said with a look of disgust on her face. "You will be notified as to when you can come to get your things."

"So now I am being kicked out of the center and out of my home! Nice, real nice."

"You made your own choices; now you can live with them," Donna said as she turned her back on him and walked out of the office.

Once out in the hallway, Donna started to shake, and Craig actually had to grab her to keep her from falling. It was obvious to him that what had transpired had taken a toll on her, but he also knew she would survive.

Somehow Donna made it home. All the way home, all she could think about was packing up all of Steve's belongs and throwing him out of the house and out of her life. All that changed when she entered the house and Donald asked for Daddy and wanted to know when Daddy was coming home. Her children loved Steve, and having him in their lives was a positive. It was also clear that supporting the house and the lifestyle they had developed was going to be a challenge on her salary alone. Steve's private practice was definitely doing well enough for him to be able to contribute to the household expenses. She also began to question if their relationship could actually improve now that he was no longer her underling and no longer obligated to taking orders from her. The big question that remained was if Steve would even come home and would want to resume their relationship after what had gone down at the center. There could be no doubt that he had been totally emasculated in front of everyone present. On the other hand, he deserved it as his actions were going to affect everyone at the center.

So, considering everything, Donna decided not to do anything. She would not call Steve as the only way it could possibly work out would be if he came back on his own. She was not going to beg him or show any other signs of weakness. She still wanted to have the upper hand in their relationship and make him feel grateful that she was taking him back into the family. After all, the wrong doing at the center was only secondary to his having an affair, and he had to know that both would never be tolerated again. If he did not accept her terms, she would just pack up his things and throw him out lock, stock, and baggage. The only thing she knew for sure was that she would survive and so would her children.

A week passed without Donna hearing from Steve. The days were packed with activity as everyone at the center was trying to right the wrongs and save the center. Medicaid was informed of the fact that a billing mistake had taken place and reimbursement was going to be made for the erroneous claims. For the time being, Medicaid seemed satisfied, but everyone was on notice that they could expect closer scrutiny going forward. They even put in place a patient signing requirement for each claim being submitted. In addition, patients were no longer going to see all the providers on their initial visit and would only see the necessary doctors to treat their complaint. This was going to have a negative impact on the center's bottom line, but under the circumstances, it was necessary, at least until things cooled down. Donna was also busy interviewing for a chiropractic replacement. She was surprised at how quickly they had resumes for chiropractors wanting the position.

Each night, Donna would get home just in time to see the children before they went to bed. Each night the nanny would tell her that Donald kept asking for Steve, and each night Donna had to strengthen her resolve not to call him but to continue to wait him out. Finally, on the seventh night, the doorbell rang at nine o'clock.

"I thought my stuff would be all boxed and waiting for me," Steve said as Donna opened the door.

"I thought we might talk first."

"You did your talking at the center. What is there left to talk about?"

"Us, our marriage, the children…"

"You have to be kidding me. Now you want to talk. You threw me out as though I was garbage, and now you want to talk."

"Our work relationship is definitely over; but it is up to you what you want in regards to our personal relationship. You have placed too many obstacles in my path, but I am willing to try to make the marriage work and keep the family together, if you are willing to change. I mean no more affairs, no more disappearing acts, and no more lies."

"Holy shit, Donna, you want to treat me like a puppy dog. You want to hold the bone over my head, and as long as I do what you want, I get the possibility of getting the bone."

"I never thought of it that way. I know you love the children and you want to be a part of their lives. I want them to have a stable home with two loving parents, and if you want the same thing, I am willing to try to make it work. I won't live in the same house with a man who cheats on me and lies to me, and you cannot deny that you have done both. If you cannot change, then we will all be better off without you. It is your decision, and if you want to think about it, go ahead. It is my terms or no terms."

Steve just stood there with his mouth open. It was obvious that he did not know how to respond. Donna, on the other hand, just turned her back on him and started to walk away. The moment was broken when Donald came running up to Steve. Donna had thought the boy was sound asleep, but he must have heard them, and there he was in Steve's arms. She could see the tears running down Steve's cheek as he cuddled the boy in his arms.

"Good to see you, little man."

"Daddy home?"

"Daddy's home; don't you worry. Now go back to bed, and I will see you in the morning."

With that, Donna came over and took Donald in her arms and carried him back to his room. When she came back to Steve, he was still standing near the door.

"Sometimes little people make the decisions for us," Steve said. "If that scene had been in a movie, it would have been unbelievable."

"Now you know why I am willing to try to make this work. That little guy really loves you, and Deb deserves to know her father and to love you as much as Donald does."

"Where do you want me to sleep?"

"The guest room works for now," Donna said as she again turned her back and walked to her bedroom and closed the door. She was prepared to allow Steve back in the house but not in her bed; that would have to take some time, if it were ever to be again.

CHAPTER 11

It PROVED INTERESTING to be living with a man in a purely platonic relationship. They continued to do things with the children and even ate dinner as a family whenever they were all together at dinner time. Donna really liked it that way as it seemed very uncomplicated, and yet the children seemed happy to have Steve with them, especially Donald, who looked at Steve as his real father and who was old enough to appreciate being with him. Debbie was still too young to appreciate anything, but Donna took great pleasure in hearing her laugh whenever Steve played with her. She was going to be a daddy's girl, of that Donna was sure.

Everything changed for Donna in a flash. A friend of hers introduced her to Mark, who was involved in a pyramid vitamin business. Jack thought that Donna was a natural at convincing people to do things they never thought of doing and that she could make a lot of money selling vitamins and selling positions in the pyramid. Mark was also a wheeler-dealer, and he immediately thought that he and Donna would be a perfect business fit. However, Donna did not see Mark as a purely business associate, nor did it disturb her that he was married with his third child on the way. To Donna, he was sexy, rich, and easy pickings. She also liked the fact that he had a big house on the water with a boat, a big car, and all the other accoutrements of wealth. She even liked the idea that he was a doctor who earned big money from his practice and did the vitamin gig on the side. There was no doubt in her mind that he represented a major improvement over Steve, who continued to struggle in his private practice and remained resentful about being fired from the center. In Donna's mind, it would be better to be with a rich man than with a man struggling to maintain himself and who could still be facing charges for Medicaid fraud.

It did not take Donna long to lure Mark into her bed. They each found it easy to have time together in one of the nearby motel rooms, and they both found the sex exciting and satisfying. It had been a long time since Donna felt satisfied, and she was really enjoying her new found sexual experiences. Mark had also been feeling deprived. His wife believed it was good for the children to sleep in their parents' bed. As a result, their sex life was extremely limited and unsatisfying. Now that she was pregnant again, sex was even less frequent and much less exciting. Mark had never found a pregnant woman to be sexy, and he was even more resentful and more turned off because he did not want to have a third child. He had always told Sara that two children would be his limit, and he really had no idea as to how it happened that she was again pregnant. He even went so far as to accuse her of having an affair that had resulted in her pregnancy. Mark's resentment made it even easier for Donna to lure him into a relationship.

Mark and Donna decided to go on vacation together using their business association as an excuse. They each told their spouses that they were going to a vitamin convention in Florida for four days. For Donna, this was an opportunity to evaluate their relationship. She wanted to be sure that she could get along with Mark on a twenty-four-hour basis, and that was something they could never do while at home. It was going to be wonderful not to have time limits and not to have to be sneaking around and making up stories as to where she was going and what she was doing.

The trip proved to be everything Donna had hoped for it to be. They swam with the dolphins, spent time at the beach, and enjoyed hours of exploring each other's body. There was something special about having sex without having to watch the time. Of course, there were cell calls from home that they each had to field. While the calls were intrusions, they were kept short using the excuse that there was a meeting that had to be attended. Sara seemed more skeptical than Steve did about their excuses and even questioned Mark about the reality of the convention since there was nothing on the website about it. Mark just told her over and over again that this was a private meeting for the top people in the organization and that they did not want to put it on the website because they did not want to open it to all the people in the pyramid. She then questioned him about the hotel not having a booking for the organization. At that point, Mark got angry with her and accused her of checking on him. He disconnected the call, cursing out loud.

"She is one solid bitch and always has been. I should never have married her in the first place. It is my mother's fault that I married her."

"How is it your mother's fault?"

"She told me to either marry her or let her go. She felt it was wrong to keep her on the hook, so to speak, if I did not want to marry her."

"So you married her, why?"

"Because there was no one else and I thought she was as good as I could get. It was also a matter that she had been a virgin and I felt I owed her. It was not so bad in the beginning, but once the children were here, it all changed. She is a good mother, but mothering took all her time."

"That is not something that can ever be said about me. I have a nanny who gives the children uninterrupted attention. It's great that I can still have a life even though I have two kids."

"I like that idea."

It was during the trip that the two of them came up with the idea to have dinner with their spouses. For Mark and Donna, it was a kick to think about being together in front of Sara and Steve. They set the Saturday night when they were returning to Long Island as the time.

Saturday night came, and both couples met at the Nautilus Café in Freeport. Mark told Sara that they were going there since it was centrally located for both couples and explained that he really wanted her to meet Donna who, he explained, was going to be his business partner.

"I thought I was going to be your business partner in the vitamin business?" Sara exclaimed.

"We both know that you are too busy with the children, and especially now. Soon there will be three of them, and I doubt you will have time for anything else. Let's be honest, you don't even have the time to straighten up the house."

"I've told you many times that I need a housekeeper. We don't need anyone sleeping in, but a day worker would be nice. She could do the housecleaning and such."

"And what will you be doing?"

"I take care of the children, and if you do not think that is work, try it for a day or two. They might even benefit from having some attention from you."

"Now you want me to be Mr. Mom as well as tending to my practice and doing the extra work that the vitamin business requires. You like the lifestyle I provide for you."

"The children will only be children once, and you really do not have a relationship with them. You should make some time for them, and no one is saying you should be Mr. Mom. Robert is a great little boy who needs his father to be a role model for him."

"Nag, nag, and more nag is all I get from you. You are never happy."

What Sara wanted to reply was, "Cheat , cheat, and more cheat is all I get from you," but she decided to hold her tongue as she was sure a big argument would ensue and more things would be said that she might regret later. She simply turned her back on him and proceeded to dress for dinner. She really wanted to look good, but everything she tried on just seemed boring. It was hard to look good with the big belly, swollen feet, and all. Some people actually said that pregnant women looked special, but this was not Sara's opinion. She just saw herself as fat and ugly and totally not sexy.

The Nautilus was its usual busy place on Saturday night. The noise level actually made conversation hard. Sara sat between Steve and Mark, and all through dinner, she found herself annoyed by Donna and her display of familiarity toward Mark. Mark even seemed to enjoy her little remarks, and his smile only confirmed what Sara thought. To her it was totally obvious that they were having an affair and that they considered the evening a joke on both Sara and Steve. By the time dinner was over, Sara could hardly contain her anger, and on the way home she totally refused to even speak to Mark, who was so self-absorbed that he failed to even notice her silence.

Once home, Sara erupted, and all her anger came pouring out.

"You may think I am stupid and that you and your little mistress can flaunt your affair in front of me, but you are so wrong. I saw the way the two of you look at each other, and I caught the innuendos. You had better clean up your act or be ready to face the most horrible bitch you will ever encounter in the divorce court. I will not be made a fool of by you or anyone and you will pay big time, of that I can promise you."

"I'll sleep in the guest room tonight as I can barely stand the sight of you."

"That's fine with me. Go to your man cave and lick your wounds like the dog you are. Just think about what that bitch will cost you."

Mark went directly to the guest room and texted Donna wondering if Steve had had a similar reaction to the dinner. Her only answer was that he was too stupid to even notice anything and that she was surprised that Sara had picked up on the true situation. She was sorry that they'd had their little joke as it definitely was complicating Mark's life.

CHAPTER 12

MARK CONTINUED TO USE THE GUEST ROOM whenever he was at the house, which was not that often. He started staying later and later at the office or meeting Donna for dinner and company. Sara chose to totally ignore him when he was there, but she did go through his things and check his computer when he was out of the house. She made copies of his e-mails and continued to collect proof of his affair and the fact that he was hiding his assets. She knew she would need the proof once they went to court for the divorce she was sure was coming. She knew he was staying in the marriage until the baby was born because he would look like a heel if he left her what with her being eight months pregnant. Sara also did what she could to prove her involvement with the vitamin company, and she kept withdrawing money from their joint account and putting it in another bank under her maiden name. As part of her preparing for the obvious, she bought things she might need if she was the one having to move. She knew there was no way she could ever support the big house, and she really did not want to live there any extra time. The house was just too full of bad memories for her. She could not help but wonder if, had they lived in a more economical fashion, Mark would have been different. As their lifestyle became more and more expensive, he seemed to feel the pressure to make more and more money. That was why he became involved in the vitamin business. Without that, he might never have met Donna. He was definitely a different man from the man she had married, and she had no use for the person he had become. Regardless, Sara felt he owed her for the ten years they had been married, and she was going to get every last dime owed to her when they ended the marriage.

It was really strange the day the baby was born. Mark felt compelled to be in the delivery room as the c-section was performed and the little baby girl was born. When he came out to the waiting room, he smiled as he saw Donna sitting there—apart from the grandparents but there never the less. Her greeting to him made all four grandparents just look with disbelief on their faces. Of course they were all aware of what was going on, but the fact that she and he had the nerve to be together at the time of the birth of his daughter was too much for them to take. Sara's parents just left the room while his parents just shook their heads. They wanted to say something but thought better of it as there was no purpose in having a scene at the hospital. Instead, they just left the waiting room and went up to the nursery where they could see the new baby before leaving the hospital.

For Donna, this marked the beginning of the end of Mark's marriage and the start of their life together. Up until the birth, she had maintained some appearance of still being married to Steve. It was easy as he was still sleeping in the guest room, so other than having dinners together with the children or going on an outing with them, there was no personal contact between them. She was fine with the arrangement, and she was trying to protect herself once the divorce proceedings started. Like Sara, she too removed money from their joint account and, in addition, she had Craig review her prenup and the deed to the house to make sure Steve would have no claims on her income or the house, which she had purchased solely. Since she did not want or require child support, Craig had advised her that the divorce would be a fairly simple exercise and they would only have to settle on things that had been acquired since the marriage.

Steve, on the other hand, seemed edgy and uptight. It was clear that he wanted to change their living arrangement and resume being a husband with all of the rights associated with being a husband. He kept dropping hints that it would be nice to be in the master bedroom again, but Donna continued to not take the bait.

It all came to a head one night when, in the middle of the night, Donna awoke to see Steve looming over her. He came into her bed and proceeded to rape her with a vengeance that Donna had never before experienced in any sexual encounter. When he was finally finished, Donna just laid there sore and totally upset, too upset and shaken to even talk to him.

The next morning, after Donald left for preschool, Donna knew she had to take Steve on over what had happened.

"That was real manly what you did last night."

"I am your husband, and as your husband I am entitled to have certain rights. I have been faithful to you, and you just continue to treat me like a piece of dirt that you can boss around. I have had it. Living with a bitch is not what I want to do. And just so you know, Sara called me and told me about you and Mark. I did not believe her at first, but after thinking about it, I know it is true. I just wanted to have my piece of the action."

"Then you can just pack your things and get the hell out. I don't want to live with a rapist, and after last night, I can never have any respect for you or trust in you. You cannot control yourself."

"What about my share in this house and all the stuff in it?"

"I bought this house, and it is in my name and my name alone. So you can just fuck yourself on that idea. You can take whatever you bought as far as the furniture and stuff is concerned because I don't give a damn about any of it. I just want you out of my life."

"It's not that easy, bitch. We have a child together, and I don't intend to allow you to have custody of her. In my opinion, you are an unfit mother who puts her career ahead of her children and never gives them the time or attention they deserve."

"And you are a fit father? Let me remind you that you committed Medicaid fraud and cheated on your pregnant wife."

"Anyone will testify that I am a dedicated father and have been one to your son as well as my daughter. If I were you, I would think about what you are threatening to do. Once I leave, I promise your life will be hell and I will fight you in every court until I get custody of Debbie. I will also go to the government and let them know how you recruit patients and make them see all the doctors in your precious center, even if they are just complaining of a hangnail. You forget I know how you operate. If you want trouble, you are looking at it right now."

"You really are a bastard."

With that, Donna again turned her back on him, leaving him alone in the kitchen. She went directly to her bedroom and locked the door. She knew that from this point forward, her door would be locked and the children would be in her bedroom with her. She did not want to give him an opportunity to take Debbie out of the house, and she did not put such a thing past him. Her first thing to do was to call Craig and to get his advice as to how to handle Steve's threats. The center had to be protected, no matter what, and Donna's first loyalty was and always would be to Craig. In her heart, she was greatly relieved that she no longer had to live a lie and pretend she was happy in a marriage that was dead and buried.

CHAPTER 13

SARA KNEW HER TIME IN THE HOUSE was growing shorter, and she decided that she had to get the things she really wanted out before she lost the opportunity to do so. Joanie, her sister-in-law, was good in that she gave Sara an area in her garage where she could store the boxes of things she wanted until she had a place of her own. Sara was careful to take things that Mark would not immediately miss. She chose the wedding gifts from her family, the holiday china and silverware along with the extra linens and towels that they had accumulated. Pots, pans, and kitchen utensils also found their way into the boxes that Sara carefully took out of the house during Mark's office hours. She was careful not to let the children know what was happening because she did not want them to tell Mark, so most of the boxes were moved while they were in school. Sara was rather proud of herself for acquiring her nest egg.

It all became a reality when, one day, as she returned from her brother's house, Mark told her that a patient of his who was a real estate agent had a house for her to see in the next town.

"To facilitate this, I am willing to put up the down payment on the house. Between the maintenance and child support you will get, you should be able to carry the house with no problems. I think I am being very generous, and if you do not immediately accept my offer, I will withdraw it and you can go fuck yourself. Remember, I am more than willing to be the custodial parent and have the children live with me," Mark said with a smug smile on his face as he knew Sara would never consent to him being the custodial parent and there was little chance than any court would award him that request.

"I guess there is nothing to lose to see the house. To be very frank, I want out of this sham of a marriage as much as you do. I hate seeing you and I hate knowing you are in the same house as I am."

"I can fix that immediately."

"Why don't you do that. I am sure your whore would love to have you on a full time basis."

"You cannot keep even the most civil conversation going without resorting to name calling."

"If it fits, wear it." With, that Sara turned her back and walked out of the room. She knew she had to accept his offer regarding the house because she had no choices but she did not have to like talking to him or be civil when it came to referring to Donna. Her only hope was that that bitch would make his life a living hell in the long run. Sara knew she would enjoy seeing him suffer, and she also knew who the bully would be in that relationship. Donna was destroying Steve's life both personally and professionally, and Sara actually felt sorry for the guy. He would be lucky if he even got to see his daughter. That was not her problem, and lord knew she had enough problems of her own with which she had to deal, and deal she would. Her children had to be a priority now and always. No matter how she hated Mark, he was still their father, and a bad father was better than no father. She knew she would never talk badly about him in front of the children, but she doubted he would do the same when referring to her in front of them. However, she was sure she would be able to make the children understand that she was not a bad person, that she was and always would be dedicated to them.

Mark stopped coming home after Sara saw the house and accepted his offer. Sara knew he was staying at Donna's house, and that was just fine with her. It gave her more time to move things out of the house. She was no longer afraid of the children saying something about her boxes as they rarely saw Mark. She would not allow him to take them to Donna's house, so they only saw him when he came to pick up some of his personal belongings. Robert, the oldest, was showing signs of really missing his father. Sara found it hard to reassure him that he would be seeing his father soon. However, Becky did not seem to even notice that Mark was not home and, of course, the baby was too young to know anything. Sara had even asked her brother to help out with Robert and give him some fatherly attention, which seemed to really help as Robert loved his uncle and really enjoyed playing with him and his sons.

Time seemed to fly by, and before she knew it, it was time to close on the house in Oyster Bay, a community adjacent to Mark's but where the prices for houses were lower and yet the schools were good. They closed on a Friday, and it was decided that Sara would move in over the weekend and have all her personal belongings out of Mark's house by Monday. Donna was planning on moving into the house by the following weekend as she and Mark were anxious to begin their new life together even though neither divorce was final. To Sara, this just showed what a horrible person Donna really was and how selfish Mark was. It was like she was being cast aside and the old being thrown out and the new taking over. No one could believe how callous they were.

Sara worried about how the children would feel when they went to Mark's house for visitation and had to deal with Donna and her children being there. The attorneys had negotiated a joint custody agreement that gave Mark every other weekend and dinner with the children on Thursday nights. Sara had wanted it to be with Mark alone, but the judge ruled that was not possible since he had the right to have anyone there he wanted during his time with the children and could not dictate to him or limit his access to the two older children. As for Marcie, since she was a baby and was being breastfed, Sara did not have to allow Mark to take her until she was on regular bottles, something Sara planned to delay as long as possible.

After the first weekend at Mark's house, Robert was really quiet. He did not want to talk about what went on there and just refused to answer any questions that Sara presented. Becky, on the other hand, was a chatterbox. She told Sara how she felt that Donald and Debbie got all the attention and she was left to be with the nanny and that Mark was really too busy to give her any time.

"Daddy just keeps kissing Donna and hugging her, and he just ignores me as though I am not there at all. He even told me that I am just like you; a nag. What is a nag anyway?"

"To your father, that is someone that thinks for herself and does not just do what he says or wants."

"Then Donna is a nag too. She keeps telling him what to do and when to do it, and he just does whatever."

"My guess is that will not last too long. He is not a man who likes to be told what to do; he is one who likes to do the telling. Time will tell, but for now, just ignore her and make the best of your time with your father."

"He likes being with Robert more than with me."

"I am sure that too will change. You are a very special girl."

"They keep telling me that Debbie will be prettier than me."

"Always remember that you are pretty both inside and outside, and more importantly, you are smart."

"I love you, Mommy, and I wish I didn't have to go to that house ever again."

"We do not have choices until you are of legal age, and then you can make your own choices. Just remember that no matter what is said, I love you and I am here for you always. If you ever feel you are being mistreated, just call me, and I will come and get you."

With that, Becky ran over to Sara and gave her the biggest hug ever. Sara knew that the bond she had with her daughter was stronger than anything Donna could ever undo. She could only wish that the same was true for Robert, who seemed to really want a relationship with his father and who seemed to be willing to do anything to attain that.

Sara also found some comfort in knowing that Mark's parents would be visiting when the children were there. They were excellent grandparents who really loved the children, and Sara knew they would do whatever they could to protect them. She just hoped they were strong enough to stand up to Mark's bullying and Donna's demands.

CHAPTER 14

LIFE CONTINUED ALONG ITS MERRY COURSE. The weeks seemed to fly by, and the children seemed to adapt to their new situation. As for Sara, money was a problem. She knew she would have to get a job to help sustain them and that there was no point in asking Mark for anything. In fact, she was not able to speak to Mark directly. Only Donna would return her calls, and Donna made it perfectly clear that she was going to be the one deciding how any money would come to Sara and what the children really needed. Sara felt her stomach turn every time she spoke to Donna and soon decided it was not worth the effort. Instead of calling, Sara resorted to texting, and that way she did not have to hear Donna's voice and listen to her refuse to pay a doctor's bill or give the children extra money for school clothes. Sometimes Sara even had to resort to asking her brother, George, for money, something she hated to do because she knew it was not a loan but charity at this point.

Jobs in hospital administration were few and far between. Since her degree was in that field and since the only jobs available were in the city, Sara knew she had to look for other employment. She did take a job as a receptionist at a local gym. The hours were good, and George and Joanie were willing to have the children stay with them while she was at work, so she did not have the expense of child care, which would have consumed her entire salary. On the weekends that the older children were with Mark, it was really easy as Marcie was a very good baby and Joanie loved taking care of her. Sara wondered how single moms did it without the help of their family.

The gym also proved to be a meeting place where Sara made friends with other women in the community. Soon there was a network of moms with whom she shared childcare and car pools. As she became less and less dependent on Joanie, she felt herself grow as a person. She had never had to live on her own before as she went from her parents' house to marriage to Mark, and she began to like being able to make her own decisions and to be able to do what she wanted when she wanted to do it. She often wondered what her marriage would have been like if she had asserted herself and demanded more respect. She was Mark's dishcloth, and he had used her and discarded her. No one was ever going to do that to her again.

Once Marcie was a year old, Sara could no longer keep her from Mark's scheduled visitation. Marcie cried whenever he would pick her up, but though it broke Sara's heart to hear her cries, there was nothing she could do about it. The divorce was just about final, and the court ordered that Marcie be included. The first time the baby was gone, the house seemed to echo as Sara walked from room to room. She was truly alone, probably for the first time in her life, and she wondered how it would be to have a holiday alone as Mark would be getting the children on alternate years for the holidays. As hard as that would be, Sara knew she would be able to accept it. There were other moms in her circle of friends who had similar arrangements, and she knew she would be with them if she was not with her family during the holidays. She also knew that the weekends the children were all gone would be excellent opportunities for her to take courses and do home studies. She was determined to make a life for herself, and she decided to study nursing.

Sara enrolled in Alephi University as it was close to her home and she could take as little as two courses a semester. The courses were offered in the evenings, and she arranged a babysitting agreement with one of her friends who watched the children, and in return Sara watched her children while she was at school. Going back to school was hard after so many years away from academics, but the times the house was quiet proved to be an asset as she could really concentrate on her studies. It was also a good example for Robert and Becky, who saw their mother doing homework while they were doing theirs.

Between her hours at the gym and her time at school, Sara had little or no time for a social life. Men at the gym continually asked her out for drinks and dinner, but she felt she could not accept the invitations. All the free time she had, she wanted to spend with the children if they were with her, and if they weren't, she needed the time to study and catch up on the housework. For now, she was content not to have any man in her life, but she knew someday that could change.

CHAPTER 15

Donna was having severe doubts about her situation. All was good when it was she and Mark and his children were not there. But when Robert and Becky came, it was a whole different story. They were not used to having a nanny, and so they kept coming to Mark for everything. Closed doors meant nothing to them, so privacy was a total thing of the past. Donna repeatedly spoke to Mark about the situation, but he turned a deaf ear to her complaints, telling her they were his children and he needed to spend time with them. To make matters even worse, Mark's parents felt they had to come over every weekend when the children were there so they could spend time with them. Donna kept thinking they were not there to spend time with the children but rather to spy on her and to report back to Sara as to how the children were being treated. This was definitely more than Donna had bargained for. She had thought she was going to be queen of the hill, so to speak, and that Mark was going to do everything for her, especially on the weekends when she was off. Donald and Debbie had their nanny and were only with Donna and Mark when they wanted them to be there. Donna knew she was going to have to effect changes or the entire situation was not going to work for her. The question was, how was she going to get what she really wanted, which was for Mark to be totally devoted to her at the exclusion of all else, including his children and his parents? She knew it was going to take time to get what she really wanted, but she also knew that if she didn't, she would bag the whole thing. There were other fish in the pond, and she felt certain she could catch an even bigger one if she set her mind to doing so.

On the immediate agenda for Donna was changing the house. There was no way she was going to live in little-miss-housewife's home. What little furniture Steve did not take, Donna brought with her when she moved in. Luckily Sara took many of the things that were in the living room and dining room, so it was easy to convince Mark to buy new furniture for those areas. As for the bedroom, all she could think was how unsexy it was, and Mark made it even worse by putting his desk in the room, so the computer's monitor would light up the room at night because he never wanted to shut it down.

"We have to do something with the bedroom. I feel like I am sleeping in an office, and I hate it," she complained to Mark.

"What do you want me to do? You closed down the man cave and changed it into your daughter's bedroom. I need a place to do my work, and I need it secure so that the kids don't touch the computer and wipe everything out. We need to be a little realistic here."

"Realistic is not sexy. We had something special going on, and now it's like we are old, married people with no interest in sex or each other."

"Aren't you being overly dramatic? Things change when we are living with four children and a nanny. It is different from our lunch breaks, I agree. This is real life with real responsibilities."

"Well, you had better start thinking of me and my needs. Remember, you tired of Little Miss Mother. You wanted someone exciting and sexy in your life. Now it almost seems like you want me to become Miss Mother, and you are not going to get that-ever. I hate it that your children think nothing of barging into our bedroom without even knocking. I feel like I have to hide in the closet just to get dressed."

"That was always the way it was here. Our door was always open to the kids."

"Well, maybe if it were locked, your marriage would have survived and you would not have gone looking for someone more exciting. Now that you have that someone, your door has to be locked or I'm out of here; it's that simple."

"Are you threatening me after everything I've done for you?"

"What have you done for me? I am under the impression that you wanted me to move in here so we could start our life together. Right now, that life stinks, and I feel like you are trying to mold me into the same image as Sara. Let me tell you something, buddy, that is not going to happen. I am not now or will I ever be like Sara. I have no interest in housekeeping or cooking or taking care of the children. That is what a nanny is for. I want to have fun, to have sex, to feel good, and to have excitement in my life. If that is not something you can provide, let's end this now. I am sure Sara will take you back in a minute, and the two of you can just resume your life together as though it was never interrupted."

"Don't you try to bully me. It will not work. I am not Steve who needed you for his livelihood and who you could boss around like a puppy dog. If you don't want to stay, leave and take your kids and your nanny with you. I am not saying that everything you have said is ridiculous. I agree it is inhibiting to have the children be able to just come into our room unannounced. That is easily corrected; we can have a lock installed on the door so you will be able to parade around nude if that is your desire."

"That is a start. Now, what about the computer? You know, you can shut the monitor without shutting down the computer and you could straighten up the desk so we don't have to feel like we are fucking in an office."

"I'll do that if it will make you happy. We can even get a screen to hide the desk if you want to do so. I really don't care, but I need to have the computer safe and away from all the little fingers."

"How about rearranging the furniture in the bedroom? The mirror is wasted with the headboard up against it. We could position the bed so we can actually see the mirror while we fuck."

"Sounds good to me. Do whatever you want with the furniture. Just remember, don't try to bully me or threaten me. That cannot work. You cannot tell me you are leaving if you don't get your way with me because under that type of arrangement, I will do nothing for you that you may want. I don't like to be bullied."

"I get it. You like to be the bully."

"Don't call me names either."

"Oh, so it is all right for you to call me names but not for me to follow suit?"

With that, Mark stormed out of the room. He felt there was no point in continuing the conversation, and he also knew that Donna would be back on his lap making nice-nice in just a few minutes. She had the unique ability to change from a tiger to a pussycat within minutes. She knew she would get whatever she wanted; all she had to do was touch him, and he would give into her, especially if there was credible grounds for her complaints. She was definitely right about the children barging into the bedroom, and he would make sure that was put to an end. He did agree, even though he did not want to admit it, that the children were affecting his sexual performance.

Donna felt as though she had won the battle this time and that she had learned a great deal about how to handle Mark. He definitely did not respond well to being threatened, and she decided that the next time she wanted something, she was going to leave the threats out unless she was really ready to carry them out. She knew she could use sex to get whatever she wanted, and she was not above doing just that. She was going to be the head of the household whether or not Mark knew it.

That night at dinner, Donna called a family meeting. She told the children that from now and going forward, if a door was closed, they were not to enter until told to do so. She also told them that for routine things such as being hungry or thirsty or needing someone to settle a dispute, they were to go to the nanny before coming to her or Mark.

"Everyone needs some privacy," she said.

"Does that mean that if our door is closed, you will not enter without knocking and waiting for a response?" Becky asked.

"It means just that unless we have reason to believe that you are doing something against the rules of this house. We do not want you using your cell phones in your bedrooms or using the computer behind closed doors. Believe it or not, this is to protect you as there are bad people out there who prey on youngsters like you."

"What if I want to talk to a friend in private?'

"Do it in the den."

"Daddy, I object to this rule. There are times when I want to talk to my mother and do not want to do it in front of Donna. Why does she have to know everything I say or do?" Becky asked.

"You can talk to your mother as much as you want when you are with her. When you are here, you have to follow the rules of this house. I think I am making myself perfectly clear. There is nothing to be said that either Donna or I cannot hear, and let's be clear, we are not interested in overhearing every word you have to say. No one here will ever mistreat you or your brother or sister."

"I just think we have to have the same respect you guys are demanding. If my door is closed, I expect you and Donna and Donald and Debbie to respect my privacy."

"We will do just that. Now can we all go for ice cream?" Mark answered.

With that, the meeting was over, and Donna and Mark went directly to their bedroom, and Donna closed the door.

"Let me tell you something. That Becky is one tough kid. She is the only one who had anything to say about the new rules," Donna exclaimed.

"She will always be a thorn in my side. She is unwilling to just accept any-thing, and she has my personality. I wish Robert had some of her spunk, but he is just a real pushover. He takes after his mother."

"I'll take him any time over her. Now I can hardly wait to see how the baby will fit into this mix."

"I really do not know Marcie at all. I even wonder if she is really my kid."

"That is a whole other story and one we cannot solve right now. The children want ice cream, so let's get it for them, and later I will reward you for standing up for me."

Donna knew she had just won a battle but not the war. The children were always going to be a thorn in her side, and she knew that if she did anything to anger them, they would go directly to their mother. She wanted to avoid that scenario at all costs as it could easily end up in a court battle. Since she was not married to Mark and could not be until the divorces were finalized, she knew she had to be careful. There were still judges who would frown on her living with Mark and the children without being married, and any judgement to that effect would severely hamper her plans. Especially now that the center was having serious problems maintaining the bottom line. Craig had actually told her to expect it to close as he was getting tired of fighting the rules and regulations of Medicare and Medicaid and the personalities of the losers they employed. What Donna really wanted was to take control of Mark's practice, but she knew she would have to get rid of his parents and brother to accomplish that. Right now the word was no wives or girlfriends in the practice.

Thinking about his parents made her shudder. They had a special bond with the children, and when they were at the house, the children completely ignored Donna and Mark. Donna could feel her blood boil, especially since Donald and Debbie seemed to be caught up in their web. Even June and Alex were no match for Mark's parents when it came to playing with the children and bonding with them. Donna knew she was going to have to limit their exposure to the children, but she also knew that would take some time to accomplish. Mark seemed to need them to be at the house when the children were there, and he was not open to discussion of the matter. Donna knew she would have to work on him and she would have to take her time doing so. She also knew in her heart of hearts she would eventually win, but she would have to have the wedding band on her finger first. Right now, she had to enjoy her victory to have the door closed, and she was definitely going to have a lock installed to ensure her privacy. Children were like sponges; they could absorb things that were not their business, and they poured out the information without reservation. The last thing Donna wanted was for Sara to know her business.

CHAPTER 16

BECKY COULD NOT WAIT for the weekend to end. As soon as she returned to Sara's house she started telling her mother all about how horrible Donna was and how much she hated being there.

"All that bitch wants to do is fuck Daddy," Becky yelled at her mother.

"Becky, that is no way to speak. Where have you learned such horrible language?"

"Where else but from her?"

"Well, we don't speak that way here, and I expect you to adhere to my rules when you are home. Am I making myself clear?"

"I am sorry, but she is one horrible person who is manipulating Daddy to do things. We are not even allowed to go to him if we need something. We have to go to the nanny, who only cares about Donald and Debbie. I really hate going there."

"Sometimes we just do not have choices. You and Robert have to take care of each other."

"Robert is a real wuss, and you know it. He just does whatever so that Daddy does not get mad at him. I think if he were told to jump off the roof, he would do it."

"Maybe you could learn something from him. It is often easier to join forces than to continue to fight."

"That is why you are getting a divorce. You never learned to fight."

"I have learned to pick my fights, and that is something you should learn. You have to go to your visitations, and you have to learn to make the best of it. I would love to keep you here with me, but a judge's order has to be adhered to whether we like it or not. However, if she is ever abusive towards you or Robert, let me know. I will not tolerate that."

"Is it abusive for her not to allow us to use our phones?"

"No, it's her house, and she can set the rules as long as you are not being physically harmed. I am talking about physical abuse where you are in danger of being hurt. Did she say why you cannot use the phones?"

"She does not want us to call you if she cannot hear what we are saying. When you call, the phone has to be on speaker and there is a recorder going."

"Nice. I will have to take this up with my attorney, and I will find out if she can continue doing that. For now, we have to think of emergency codes that will let me know if there is a serious problem while you are at your Dad's. I am thinking the easiest would be for you to say "Mommy, Mommy," and by you repeating, "Mommy," I will know there is a problem."

"Mommy, Mommy—I get it. I only hope I don't screw up with that."

"Think about it. It can work since you usually call me mom."

"It makes me feel better. I think I can remember the code, and I promise I will only use it if I need to."

"Remember the boy who cried wolf. If you misuse it, I would not be able to respond even if it were to be a real emergency. It will be even more important once Marcie has to go with you. She cannot defend herself, so you have to protect her."

"I get it. She will be sharing my room with me."

"That is good, and it makes sense that the two sisters share a room."

"Of course, Debbie has to have a room of her own."

"So be it. It is really better that Marcie be with you, so I am happy that you are together, and I really do not care what Debbie has or doesn't have. It is not our concern."

"Don't worry about Marcie. I will take care or her."

After that conversation, Sara was sure that Donna was up to something. It was obvious that she was manipulating Mark to get whatever she wanted, and she probably did not want to have the children there as they were cramping her style. Sara doubted that Mark would ever cave and not have the children, but anything could be possible, and if that were to happen, she would be very happy. She really hated it when they were with him.

That night Sara decided to call Jan, Mark's mother. She knew that Jan and Fred were at Mark's on Sunday, and she hoped she could gain some insight from her.

"I am sorry to bother you. Do you have a few minutes to talk?" Sara asked when Jan answered her call.

"I always have time to speak to you."

Sara went on to explain what Becky had said and asked Jan for her impressions about how Donna was treating the children.

"When we are there, it is as if she is a candidate for 'Mother of the Year.' I cannot help but feel it is all phony and that she is putting on a show for our benefit, but I cannot prove that. There is no talking to Mark about her, and if anything is said that is in any way disparaging, he flies off the handle."

"How does he treat the children?"

"Mark is Mark. He is the same as when you were with him if we all agree there are no issue, but if anyone disagrees, it is hell to pay . If Becky puts up an argument, the bully comes out. You know this all too well. Fred and I are doing our best to blend into the woodwork so that we can be with the children."

"Becky also says he says horrible things about me."

"Don't you know it was totally your fault that the divorce is happening? Are you surprised at that? Mark always has to be the victim. I can't help but wonder what we did wrong to make him that way. My only guess is that we always tried to make life easy for him, especially since he was such a sickly child."

"You and Fred were great parents, and you continue to be not only great parents but great grandparents. You should not blame yourselves for what he is doing. I am just grateful that you are there for the children as they really need some stability."

"We are trying, and rest assured, we always tell them that you love them very much and that they are lucky to have two parents who love them. Fred and I will not participate in any discussion that includes bashing you."

"Thank you for your support. It really makes me feel better knowing you are there when the children are with Mark. Hopefully, once the divorce is settled, he will calm down. Who knows?"

"Who knows is right. My guess is that things might get better, but every time he has to write a support check, his mood will be foul. You know how important money is to him, and it is even more important to her."

"That is too damn bad. I need the support to carry this house and take care of the children. There is no way I can have a full time job what with Marcie being a baby and all. "

"Good luck with it all. If you need anything, please remember we are here for you."

"Thanks."

With that, Sara hung up the phone feeling she knew nothing more after the conversation. Obviously, Donna was putting on an impressive act in front of Mark's parents but felt she could do and say whatever she wanted to when they were not within earshot. Becky was too dramatic to have her word taken seriously by any judge, who would feel that the child just did not want to accept the divorce. Now if Robert complained, it would be a tale of a different story since he was the oldest and tended not to be as dramatic. But Robert was being Robert. He was just accepting whatever Mark did in hopes of having a relationship with Mark. He'd even told Sara that a bad father was better than no father. All she could do at this point was hope for the best and give the children all the love she could give.

Jan was despondent when she hung up the phone. It was obvious to her that the path ahead was going to be rocky at best. Mark was so busy trying to please Donna that his judgement was totally marred. Jan felt that Donna wanted to be the boss and wanted to control Mark in every aspect of his life. Jan could not help but feel that it would be only a matter of time before Donna succeeded in turning Mark away from both Fred and her. It was obvious to her that Donna resented her being the office manager and having an influence on Mark. Jan saw how angry Donna was when Fred said that no wife was welcome to work in the office in any capacity and that the only exception was ever going to be that Jan was to continue there as long as she wanted to be there. If steam could have come out of Donna's ears, it would have done so. It was obvious that she was planning to be the office manager so her control would be complete. When Jan voiced her concerns to Fred, all he would say is, "Too bad. That is the way it is going to be." Fred felt strongly that for the good of the practice, Donna had to remain out of it no matter what Mark wanted.

"What will happen if he decides to leave the practice? You know that is a possibility," Jan asked.

"If he leaves, we will most likely be better off than we are now. His attitude is negative, and patients are complaining about him. He talks about his divorce all the time. Patients want to be listened to and to have their problems addressed. They do not want to hear the doctor's problems."

"My guess is that a breakup of the practice will be ugly."

"I am sure you are right. He is just so accustomed to having his way, and he is so selfish that no matter what we do to appease him, it will never be enough."

"Are you going to try to keep it together?"

"I will try, but you can be sure I will not do anything that will jeopardize Howard's position. After all, he is also our son, and he just joined the practice. He has to be protected from Mark's avarice. In my opinion, Howard is a far better doctor and surgeon than Mark will ever be. He cares about the patients and really wants to help them. Mark just wants the bottom line to be the best it can be. This is why I feel so strongly that Donna cannot be in the office. She would do everything possible to hurt Howard and even make sure he is out of the practice so that she and Mark can have it all to themselves one day."

"My guess is that they would throw you and me out of the practice as well."

"You are probably right. Loyalty is not a virtue of Mark's. The only loyalty I see that Donna has is to that guy, Craig, and who knows what their real relationship is?"

"The story I heard is that he gave her her first real break and helped her make something of herself."

"That's all good and well, but it is unusual and does not change anything as far as our practice and we are concerned. Don't fool yourself for one moment, she has no good feelings towards us and is only tolerating our being there for the time being."

"I fear for the children."

"You are right to fear for them, but children have a way of surviving, and while I would love to protect them, we will have to see where this all goes and how it all works out. I cannot compromise everything I have worked for and Howard's future."

"Believe me, I get it loud and clear."

"I do not want to talk about this anymore. There is nothing we can do at this point. I will tell you this. I am going to the bank on Monday and changing all the accounts so that he cannot sign any checks without my being the cosigner. I do not want to find out that our accounts have been wiped out. "

"Do you really think he is capable of that?"

"I think he is capable of doing anything that benefits himself. Now no more talk."

With that, Jan grabbed her coat. She needed to get out in the fresh air to clear her head. The entire situation was getting worse by the minute, and she could feel the family being broken apart. Family had always been the most important thing to her, and she knew that she had made many concessions to try to always keep the peace within the family. Now she feared that she was going to have to make painful choices. She knew she would always stand with Fred. He was a unique man who always treated people with respect and kindness. Anyone, whether it be a stranger or a son, who could hurt him, was someone she could cut out of her life in a heartbeat. She knew she loved him when they married, but after forty five years, that love had grown, and so had the respect she had for him as a person. Life was full of choices, and Jan knew she would always choose Fred before anyone else, even her own son.

CHAPTER 17

When Jan walked into the office on Monday, she could not believe the reception she received from Mark.

"I am not talking to nor will I ever speak to you again," he declared.

"What is with you? I do not get it."

"How dare you speak to Sara! You are a traitor to me and my children. I will not tolerate you telling her things about the goings on in my house. Nor will I accept you speaking about Donna. I am done with you."

"I am shocked. Sara called me to ask about how the children were dealing with being with you and Donna. I said nothing but positive things about Donna and how she is treating the children. You are just totally out of control, and you cannot tell me to whom I can speak or when I can do so. You can bully other people but not me."

With that, Mark started yelling at the top of his voice and accusing Jan of stealing from the business and being totally disloyal. The anger his face showed made her worry about her safety, what with her being alone in the upstairs business office. When he stood over her pointing his finger at her face, Jan did the only thing she could think to do. She called down on the pager and asked Fred to come upstairs immediately. She knew he would leave whatever he was doing as she never placed such a demand. When Fred came into the business office, he too was astonished by the tone of Mark's voice and his outrageous behavior.

"You are no better than her. You two always stick together and conspire against me. I am the big money earner of this practice, and if you think you can continue to be successful without me, you are crazy. Don't for one minute think that Howard can take my place here. He is not as good as I am and will never be able to do the surgeries I can do and will never be accepted by the other doctors. I am done with both of you, and as far as I am concerned you should both leave this practice and my life. I guarantee you will not be part of my children's lives either. You do not deserve that honor."

"Get something straight and get it straight right now. I started this practice. I am still the majority owner of this practice, and I will not tolerate you speaking to your mother or me in this manner. The one who should leave is you. Your brother does not deserve you speaking about him in this manner either. He has done nothing to you, nor has your mother. Her only mistake is being too good to you and accepting you no matter what you do or who you hurt. You have become an animal since you have been involved with that woman, and you do not care who you hurt. I am well aware that she wants it all, but she will never have that as far as this practice is concerned. She will never work here or make any decisions about the management of this office. You are totally out of control, and you should be ashamed of yourself."

"I am out of control?! You will regret ever saying that to me, you old man. You are an antique, and you should retire before you hurt someone."

"The one who can hurt a patient is not me but you. You are a mental case, and your lack of control is detrimental to this office, any hospital at which you work, and your life in general. You need professional help."

With that, Mark stormed out of the room, slamming the door behind him. Fred could only take Jan into his arms and allow her to cry herself out. It was obvious that the family was shattered and probably would never be the same. As for the practice, he really believed what he had said; the practice would be better off without Mark. Other doctors had complained about his behavior in the OR. Many of the doctors who had always referred patients were no longer sending patients to them and were open about their concerns about Mark's behavior. Fred had often been told that Howard was the only one to operate on their patients.

"Do you want to go home?"

"No way! He will not chase me out of this office. I put my entire life into helping you build this practice, and I will not give him the satisfaction of seeing me run away from him. I promise I will get myself together and get my work done."

"That's my girl. No matter what happens, you and I are a team. Never forget that. I have to go back down. I actually left a patient in the room. I knew you really needed me. In all the years, I've never heard such a page."

"Now you know why. I really thought he was going to hit me."

"He is a horrible bully, and he cannot control his rage. Of course, he sees it that he is the victim, just as he sees himself as the victim in his divorce. That is all a part of his sickness."

All Jan could do when Fred left the room was sit at her desk and shake. Family always had been the most important aspect of her life, and she could see that it was shattered, and she knew it would never be the same. She had to wonder where Howard would stand in all of this. Her instincts were that he would be with her and his father. He had always resented the way Mark treated him and the way Mark always fought about paying him. Jan knew the brothers had had words in the past, but she had always tried to patch things up between them to help keep the peace and to keep the family together. It was always important to make Mark happy, even at the expense of everyone else. That was the mistake she and Fred had committed. No one could ever really make Mark happy. His ego, selfishness, and avarice were too great.

Throughout the day, Mark was true to his word. He completely refused to talk to Jan even when she came to him for him to help a patient who was in pain. Jan tried to act as though nothing was wrong, but it did not take long for the entire staff to be talking about the argument. Jan knew there were staff members who would be loyal to Mark, but there were many more who were loyal to her and Fred and Howard. She felt that those who would side with Mark were not people she would want to be around, and if they were to leave, so be it. The practice would survive, and those who would stay would benefit from the pay scale and the pension benefits the practice offered. She was sure that Mark would never be as generous as Fred had always been with the staff.

That night, Howard met Fred and Jan at their house. He had heard about the argument even though it was his day off. Right away, Howard assured his parents that he would do everything possible to make the practice whole and successful and that he would always support them and have a place for them in the practice for as long as they wanted to work.

"It is to my benefit to have Dad in the practice. People see it as his practice, and we will stress that everywhere we go. Dad's reputation is impeccable. Doctors at the hospital always refer to him as the ultimate gentleman, and they cannot believe that Mark is his son. I am sure that we will be able to recapture the referral base and re-staff the office once those who want to go with Mark leave."

"It is going to take a major effort on all of our parts. Who knows what demands he will make in regards to his shares of the practice."

"In the morning, we will contact a lawyer I know who is one tough guy. He will help us. Just do not make any statements to Mark about anything. We will let Steve do our talking."

"Smart suggestion! I agree completely."

"I just feel sorry for Mom. She really wanted to keep this family together."

"Don't worry about me. I am strong, and my loyalty will always be with you and Dad."

"With that, we cannot help but prevail. I love you both more than words can say, and I appreciate all you have always done for me. I know the sacrifices you made for us. Not every parent makes sure that the kids graduate without student loans. No matter what I ever needed, you were there to make sure I had it. That is the difference between me and Mark. He always feels he is entitled to everything. I know you guys gave him the down payment on his first house. But to hear him talk about it, you would think you never gave him anything in the way of financial support or moral support."

"We always tried to make Mark happy," Jan said sadly.

"That was part of the problem. He can never be happy. I am sure that he and Donna will have a rocky road to travel. They are two peas in a pod. Both of them are grasping and selfish, and neither will be willing to give in."

"It is just that Donna has a power over him. I am sure she has him thinking with the wrong head, if you know what I mean," Jan said.

"Yeah, the power of sex. I am sure she is good at that. Let's be frank, she has had a lot of practice. Give her some time, though, and she will ruin him just as she ruined her last husband. That poor schmuck is taking all the heat from the center, and I heard he could even lose his license to practice."

The next day, Sara called Jan. She was very upset.

"I am so sorry about what happened. It is all my fault."

"No, don't think that for a minute. What happened would have happened over anything. He was just looking for an excuse. I am sure that Donna put him up to it in her desire to get total control, especially now that she is losing her job at the center, which I hear has to close. She has it in her head that she will work with Mark and together they will build a practice bigger and better than ours. I am only sorry that, under these circumstances, I will not be seeing the children."

"I'll make sure you can see them."

"That cannot happen. I do not want to put them in the middle of things. He will make their lives hell if he knows they are seeing us. It is wrong to make the children be sneaky or lie. Just please let them know we love them and always will. Our door will never be closed to them, but we do realize a bad father is better than no father, and there is no way we would want them put into a position where they would not have a relationship with Mark."

"That is very big of you. I know of many people who would not do what you are doing for the good of the children."

"Love is love. Please remember that if you need anything or if they need anything, we are here for you."

"Thank you for taking the time to talk to me. You have made me feel better. I was so ridden with guilt. I am sure the children heard me speaking with you, and one of them probably said something to Mark or Donna. I am sure it was an innocent thing on the part of the kids."

"Children hear and understand more than we give them credit for."

With that, Jan said her goodbyes and hung up the phone. She was shaking, but she knew she had done the right thing. Who knew what he could do to them if he were to find out they were seeing Fred and herself. Maybe someday when they are liberated from his control, they might want to establish a relationship with their grandparents. She could only hope that day would not be too late, but for now she had other things to attend to, and those were more important.

CHAPTER 18

DONNA COULD NOT HAVE BEEN HAPPIER than she was when Mark told her what happened. Finally she was going to be free of his parents and especially Jan. She did not understand why Mark, a grown man, had always sought his mother's advice. He had even asked her about rearranging their bedroom before he would allow Donna to make the changes she wanted. Now Donna was free to do whatever she wanted whenever she wanted to do it. It was not only Jan that she resented. She also resented Fred for not allowing her to be part of the office. After all, she was a good administrator, and she could have helped the practice immensely. Now she would be the force behind the new practice, and she was convinced she would really show them all what she could do. She decided that they were going to rent a building where Mark could have his practice and where Donna could set up a multidisciplinary facility which could generate referrals to Mark right from within the building. She had several doctors from the center who were looking for space and with whom she knew she could work. Of course, she now knew she wanted nothing to do with Medicaid and as little to do with Medicare as possible. That had proven to be a costly lesson for her. She also knew she would not have patients see all the doctors when they presented to the building. Instead, each doctor would have an independent practice administrated by her, and each would pay her a salary. There was no way she would ever be dependent on Mark for her money.

As for Sara and those awful children, Donna knew she was about to make life miserable for them. She was about to take over all dealing with Sara, and she knew she would make her crawl for her support checks and would make sure there were no extras. The children would have to learn to live by her rules when they were in her house, and she was going to make sure that Mark put the needs of Donald and Debbie ahead of those of the other kids. It was going to be easy to do this now that Jan was out of the picture. She was always the good grandmother making sure that everyone was treated equally.

Donna felt she would prove to Mark how smart she really was. Right after the showdown at the office, Donna met Mark there after others had left. Together they copied all the computer data and made a complete list of the referring practitioners. She knew the others would be too upset to think about Mark being in the office without them being there, and they never would think it possible for anyone to copy their data. It is just not how they thought, but it was how Donna thought. Their plan was that as soon as a suitable location was secured and set up, Mark would send out notices that they had moved. He would make it appear that the entire practice had moved, not just himself. Of course, if someone were to call requesting Fred or Howard, the person would be told that doctor was on vacation or simply out of the office but that Mark was there and would be happy to help. She felt relatively safe legally because it was true that Mark moved. If challenged about saying the others were out of the office, that too was true. In the end, any legal action would take years and be extremely expensive. So it was unlikely that would happen. Donna had discussed the legal ramifications with Craig, and he, too, felt that legally they would be all right, though he did say that morally the plan was questionable.

"I am not interested in morals. I only want success, and Mark only wants to crush them. In fact, we want you to handle any buyout agreement," she told Craig.

"You can be sure I will do everything possible to cost them money in legal fees and to annoy the hell out of them, if that is what you want. I just do not understand why you personally hate them."

"They are controlling people, and I want Mark to be his own man."

"Donna, let's be honest here. You want to control Mark. I've known you a long time, and I know how you operate. You really think that you can get more money with your plan than you ever could if Mark stayed in the family practice?"

"They refused to allow me to be a part of that practice."

"I get it, and if I were them, I would feel the same way. If you were the administrator, Howard would have to leave."

"He is useless, as is Fred. Fred is old and going senile. That is why Mark is better off leaving than to be associated with those failures."

"I imagine that, had the center not failed, you would probably not feel this way."

"Had the center not failed, I would still be earning my own money. Now, Mark feels as though he is giving me everything, and I do not like being in that position, and you know it."

"You could still work for me. I still need someone to manage the real estate properties."

"Thanks for the offer. You cannot afford to pay me what I need, and you have done enough to help me through the years. It is time for me to move on and to not be dependent on you. I see this as my opportunity."

"Let me get this straight. You are not doing any of this to help Mark. You are really doing it to help yourself, and you are using Mark in the process."

"I have never lied to you, and I cannot start now. I am doing what I have to do, and Mark will benefit as well."

"Donna, you are one solid bitch, and I have always been glad to have you on my side."

"We did well together while it lasted. It probably could've continued if it weren't for the stupidity of Steve."

"Let's be honest here. You threw Steve under the bus. Medicaid would have come down on the operation whether he was the manager or you were. We both know that to be the reality."

"It was more convenient for him to take the fall. He deserved it."

"Because he had an affair?"

"I ascribe to the theory that it is my way or the highway. He did me wrong, and I can never forgive that. My God, he was screwing some broad when I went into labor with his kid."

"Revenge is sweet, and I would say you have gotten yours. It looks like he is going to lose his license to practice."

"It doesn't effect me. I don't need his child support, and our divorce agreement states that I owe him nothing, as you know."

"You had a good lawyer."

"The best. Now are you on board with this new project?

"Just for the record—I will do whatever you need, but I am not liking everything here. It is not like you to try to destroy good people."

"I do whatever is necessary to achieve my goals."

"What will happen to our relationship if I disappoint you in any way?"

"Craig, let's not be stupid. I owe you and will always owe you. It is just too bad that you could not leave that bitch you are married to. We could have done beautiful things together."

"I think it is safer this way. You are a real ballbuster, and I, for one, do not want my balls busted."

"Very funny. Now get to work preparing the necessary papers, and let's get the ball rolling."

When Craig got in his car, his head was spinning. He could not believe what he had heard. How was it possible that the pathetic girl in the supermarket could evolve into such a cunning bitch? It was shocking that she had not stood behind Steve when the problems hit the fan at the center, but Craig could almost understand that since Steve had been unfaithful. However, to completely ruin him seemed excessive. Then to go after a married man whose wife was pregnant was immoral. He had to wonder if she really loved Mark or was just using him as a stepping stone to greater wealth. Now she was after his family, who had done nothing to hurt her except exist. Was she jealous of the influence Jan, Fred, and Howard had on Mark? Did she want to eliminate them so she could completely control him? Obviously that was what she wanted, and Mark seemed to have nothing to say on the matter. Craig was astonished since he too had a family practice and knew the dynamics of working with family. It could be wonderful, and it could be challenging, but it was always there, and no matter what, someone was there to watch your back.

Then there was the remark about Michelle's and his marriage. Thank God he had never succumbed to Donna's advances. Donna had always appeared to be interested in having a different relationship with him, but he had always insisted on keeping it a business one. He was grateful, at this moment, that he had not mixed business with pleasure. No matter what Michelle's faults were, she had proved to be a loyal wife, and they were happier now than ever before in their marriage. Maybe it was simply that the children were getting older and less needy. No matter what, he was content.

Craig knew one thing for certain. After this was over and Mark set up his practice, he was going to separate himself from Donna. No more business deals and no more legal representation for free. If she ruined another man, he was not going to be a part of it. He was actually feeling guilty that he was about to be part of her plan to ruin the family. In his heart, he knew he would do whatever he could to attenuate her demands.

"Call it manly pride," he said out loud to himself as he drove away from Mark's house.

CHAPTER 19

AFTER CRAIG LEFT, Donna poured a glass of wine to celebrate the start of her plan. She was going to ruin Jan, Fred, and Howard and enjoy seeing their practice diminished while Mark's would grow and be the ultimate success. She was also going to enjoy her new role in his life. She was going to be not only his wife, but his confidant, manager, practice administrator, and the only person who controlled him and made his decisions. It amazed her how easy this was all proving to be. In her heart, she'd known she could control him when their relationship first started, but she never really had expected it would be to the extent it was now. His weakness could prove to be a breaking point in the future, but she would make sure she secured her financial status first.

Mark was insisting on a prenup agreement. Donna decided she would sign it to prove good faith but knew she would make him void the agreement in the future. Mark made a big deal out of having the house in his name only, and she had countered with keeping the money from the sale of the Oceanside house in her name only. There was no doubt that the Brookville house was more valuable, and it was definitely in her best interest to be on the deed. Tincture of time would allow that to happen, of that she was certain. The other stumbling block was his pension. That money would be transferred to a new plan once he left the practice. She probably would manage the plan as part of her responsibilities, and she knew she would be able to figure out a way to gain complete control of it so she could liquidate it if needed. That power would give her even more control over Mark.

The children were another thorn in her side. Once Jan was removed from the scene, Donna knew she would be able to do whatever she wanted to do in regards to the children. Jan was always saying how important it was to treat all the children equally. Donna knew she would always protect Donald and Debbie's interest above those of Mark's three brats. She had already told Mark that Debbie was to have her own room and his two daughters were to share a room. Robert and Donald could share a room, but the nonsense of not allow-ing Donald to play with Robert's things was going to end. She knew she would be buying Debbie new clothes, and the other girls would be getting her hand-me-downs since Debbie was the biggest of the girls. It was going to be that way with singing lessons and whatever they needed. Debbie would come first, and she would make sure of that. Let their mother provide the nice things for them. After all, Mark was paying her enough money, and that bitch could cer-tainly go to work. Donna knew she would make sure that Sara did not get one extra penny. That resolution was going to be the easiest to effect since Mark resented having to pay the child support and maintenance that the courts de-termined he had to pay. It was proving interesting that he really felt that Sara was to blame for their divorce, and it was all her fault that their marriage failed. Donna could not believe how easy it was to manipulate him and his thought process.

Donna was grateful that the children were only there on alternate week-ends. She had stopped the weekday dinners and the sleepovers during the week. That, she had convinced Mark, was a burden and hindered their ability to set up the new office. She also had convinced him that they could not be involved in any of the planning or any of the discussions regarding the new office. She was convinced that whatever they heard was going right back to Sara, and she was sure that Sara would tell Jan everything she heard. Whenever the children were in the house, she insisted that all conversations between her and Mark were conducted behind locked doors, even though she knew this irritated the children. They hated being excluded, but it was just too bad. Becky was the biggest problem. She looked like Jan and was as strong willed as her grandmother. That girl thought nothing about telling her father off if she was displeased with anything he did, and she would go directly to him if she felt that Donna treated her or Marcie improperly. It was as if Becky thought she was in control and everyone needed to do what she thought was best. Donna knew she was going to be a constant problem and that she would have to convince Mark to put that child in her place or there was going to be hell to pay. None of this really came as a surprise to Donna. She knew she would have challenges from the children when she met Mark, but she also knew she would overcome them. Becky, she felt, would be more manageable once she realized that Donna was there to stay and that it was in her best interests to be more compliant. Donna was going to show her that she would get nothing she wanted unless she did what Donna wanted and that her father would not fight for her.

Donna felt good that she had a plan. She knew the first thing she needed to do was to neutralize Jan. For whatever reason, Mark had an unusual relationship with his mother. He actually looked to her for advice whenever there was a pending decision. That was going to end and quickly. Donna decided it would be in her best interest to completely eliminate Jan from their lives and to make it such that she was no longer a part of the children's lives. Donna knew she could do this by challenging Mark's self image and by making him feel that Jan was manipulating him. Donna wanted Jan banned from seeing the children whether it be at their house or Sara's. She would then take Jan's place of advising Mark, and there would be no one to monitor her behavior with the children. To do this, she decided to convince Mark to make it clear to the children that they would have to choose between him and their grandmother. This proved easy to accomplish, and during their visitation, she actually heard Mark saying, "Remember, a bad father is better than no father. If you do not stop calling and seeing your grandparents, you will not be allowed to use the bathroom in the house and you will have to go outside like a dog. I promise, I will cut you off completely and you will get nothing from me. I swear if you lie to me, I will find out the truth and make your lives miserable. Am I making myself clear?"

Robert was the first to accept his father's demands. He did not want to be deprived of the fishing trips and ball playing he had come to love doing. Becky, on the other hand, continued to argue, hoping to attenuate Mark's demands. When she realized she had hit a stone wall, she too agreed to the demands, but not without telling him it was a shame what he was doing.

"I know Donna put you up to this. I will never forgive her for what she is doing to our family," Becky yelled.

"Donna has nothing to do with this. It is my desire. Get that straight, young lady."

Marcie was just too young to be involved in the drama. Mark knew she had no real relationship with her grandparents and would just accept this as the way things were.

As for Sara, she too would have to accept his wishes or face financial repercussions. She would not be happy to have late checks and not to be able to pay her bills on time. Late charges could be a bitch. What was going to be interesting was Jan's reaction. Mark wondered if she would take legal action to demand visitation with the children. It would be expensive to fight it out in court, more expensive for her than him, as he had Craig. But in his moments of clarity, he knew Jan would not want to put the children in the middle of the fight. He truly believed she loved them too much for that. Donna felt the same way, and she guaranteed him there would be no court fight on this issue, especially since Jan was totally consumed by the challenges facing the practice.

Next on Donna's agenda was to get married to Mark. There was no way she was going to work and help him build a practice without some guarantee that her future would be secure. After all, he had left his wife for her. There was no saying he would not do that again if some younger woman set a target on him. She decided she would sign the prenup and then she would work to have the house put in her name as well as his. That would afford her extra security as she was sure Mark would do anything to keep the house. The money from the sale of her house was already securely invested in her name alone, and that would have to remain that way. As for the actual wedding; it would have to be a simple ceremony with just her parents and the children present. She wanted a Justice of the Peace to officiate at the ceremony as that way neither religion would be represented. She knew for sure there would be no conversion on her part, and she planned on making sure her children were being brought up in the Catholic faith. Mark probably would not force her to celebrate the Jewish holidays now that his parents were out of the picture.

Everything was falling into place nicely. One problem remained, and that was Steve. He was insisting on having the children at his house. He was willing to include Donald, saying he felt as though Donald was his son and he was sure that Donald viewed him as his father. Donna felt that she was losing some control with the children staying at his house for the weekend, but she did not want to go to court as she was sure she would lose and then he would really be empowered. So she set up a schedule that coincided with Mark's visitation, giving them every other weekend alone. She hoped that she and Mark could have some fun on their weekends alone, but so far, he was too taken up with setting up the practice to even think about anything else. The weekends when the children were away proved to be lonely times for her, and her resentment was growing with each time. The result was it was getting harder and harder to be the sexy wife, and she even sensed that Mark was beginning to lose interest in her. They were beginning to argue about insignificant things.

On the weekends when the children were all at the house, things were chaotic. There was no end to the things that had to be done even with the nanny being there. Each child had activities, and some overlapped. Donna soon demanded that Sara not make plans for the children without Mark's approval, and if they had an activity that he did not want to go to, they had to miss it. Becky resented this the most. She had signed up to play soccer and had to miss most of the games because they were on Mark's weekends. Her resentment was increased by the fact that Donna's children did not have to miss any of their activities because Donna was willing to take them.

"Why can't my mom take me to the games?" she asked.

"She can take you on her weekends, but not on our times. You have to abide by your father's wishes when you are at his house."

"They are not my father's wishes. They are yours. You are ruining my life, and I hate you for it."

"That is no way to talk, young lady. I am not ruining anything for you, and if you have any complaints, take them up with your father."

"He has no balls! You control him and everything in this horrible house."

With that, Becky turned her back on Donna and ran into her room, locking the door behind her. She knew she had gone too far and that her father would be there backing Donna up in short order. It was clear to Becky that she was rapidly becoming an unwelcome person in the house, and she truly wished she did not have to come. Unfortunately, her mother wanted her to go because she wanted her to protect Marcie. While she understood this, Becky just felt it was all unfair to her, and she had no one to stand up for her. Robert also had no balls when it came to standing up to Donna. He so wanted attention from Mark that he was willing to do anything necessary to get that attention. He actually had it better than Becky because Mark loved playing baseball and basketball and he was willing to go with Robert to his games. Mark just did not think it was important for a girl to play soccer or any other sport.

It was not long before the knocking on her door started.

"Go away. I don't want to talk to anyone."

"Open this door now, young lady," Mark yelled.

"No. I know you are mad, and I know what you want to say. I hate you almost as much as I hate her because you brought her into our house and ruined our family."

"You cannot speak this way to me or to Donna. Do you understand?"

"I understand. Do you understand I do not want to come here anymore?"

"You do not have a choice. I am your father, and I am entitled to have proper visitation with my children."

"You can visit me through the locked door. I am not coming out."

"You are a very stubborn girl. You will have to open the door eventually, and we will have a conversation face to face at that time."

"I am calling my mother to come and get me. I am afraid of you and that horrible woman, and I will call the police if you threaten me or prevent me from leaving with my mother."

"Your mother will not come here."

With that, Mark walked away from the door wondering if Becky would actually call her mother. He was somewhat surprised she had a phone in her room as Donna had a rule that all cell phones were to be given to her once the children came into the house.

"Did you take Becky's phone when she came here?" he asked Donna.

"I guess I forgot to collect the cell phones this time. Why, is she threatening to call her mother?"

"She is threatening to not only call her mother but to call the police as well. This is the last thing I need right now. You and I both know that the police will take any complaint seriously, especially under these circumstances. We'll have child services all over the place, and if the newspapers get word of it, it will be all over town in a heartbeat. You really need to be more understanding and gentler in your dealings with that girl."

"Oh, now it is my fault alone."

"This time I think it is your fault. You are the adult, and you need to understand she is unhappy with the entire situation."

"She is right, you do not have any balls when it comes to dealing with your children. You are willing to give in any time there is a crisis, and you side with them over me."

"You do the same when your children are involved, and you know it."

From her room, Becky could hear their voices rising. She smiled to herself as they continued to yell at each other. Maybe he would come to realize what a bitch he had married and he would leave her. Then she started to feel guilty. Had she gone too far, and was she ruining everything for her father? She really knew there was no going back in time. Her mother had said repeatedly that even if Mark wanted to return to them, she would never allow him back in her life. As these thoughts came to her, Becky started to cry and to wonder what would happen next.

"Becky, open the door, I want to talk to you."

"Talk through the door. I am afraid to let you into my room."

"Let's not be overly dramatic. I am your father, and you know I love you. Open the door. I promise we will just talk."

With that, Becky unlocked the door but quickly returned to her bed and buried her face in her pillow.

"Look at me. I want you to know you are very important to me. I want you and Donna to get along, and I want you to know you can always come to me if you are unhappy."

"You do nothing if I come to you. You just let her decide, and she is unwilling to consider how I feel. It is important to me to be a part of my soccer team, but I cannot be if I am only there every other week. I told Donna that my mother was more than willing to pick me up and take me to soccer if you guys can't do it, but she refuses to allow mom to come and get me. I just don't understand why I am being punished because you guys don't get along."

"You are not being punished. It is just that if we have plans as a family, we want you to be a part of that and not off doing something else."

"Plans to just hang out and do nothing. That really makes sense. Believe me, I get it. If Debbie has to go to singing lessons or whatever, Donna is Johnny on the spot. All of us have to live our lives by her children's schedules. I just want to be able to go to my games. That is not asking too much, especially since I can get rides back and forth."

"Then you will be spending more time with you mother than you spend with me."

"Be honest; you do not really spend time with me when I am here. You are busy with office stuff, Donna, and Robert. All of that doesn't matter to me, but I hate having to spend the entire day in my room when I could be with my friends doing something I really like. I would be happier, and Donna would be happier too since I would be out of her hair for a part of the day."

"Do you promise to come right back here after the games?"

"Sure, that is not an issue. I would even miss a game if we were doing something special as a family."

"That sounds very mature. If your mother agrees to bring you back here, I think we can work this out. I do need you to be nicer to Donna. She feels you hate her and that you are trying to destroy our marriage."

"That is ridiculous. I am just a kid, and I have nothing to say about your marriage. I am well aware that you and my mother are done, and for that I am sorry. I am also aware that Donna destroyed our family and now she wants to control everything just as she made sure our grandparents are no longer here with us. Do I resent her? You bet I do, but that is not something that is up to me. Mom tells me to stay out of it, and I think she is right. Mom says that if I ever want to have a relationship with you, I have to put-up with Donna. I am willing to do that so I can see you, but she has to be fair in the way she treats me and Marcie. I hate being a second-rate citizen in my own father's house, the house where I have always lived."

"You are not a second-rate citizen in my eyes."

"Then open your ears and listen. I am not as pretty or as smart as Debbie. She is talented, I am not. She deserves all of Donna's time, and I deserve none. Isn't that being a second-rate citizen? I really want to spend time with you without Donna being there. I want to do some of the things we used to do before the divorce, such as going shopping together or just going for a long walk at the beach and talking to each other."

"I hear you, and we will try to do some of that going forward. Just try to be a little more respectful toward Donna. You have to understand she feels your resentment and that makes her very unhappy."

"I can only try, but she has to try too. After all, she is the adult in this mess, and I am still a kid. She doesn't have to resent my mother, who only wants to help me and doesn't have any other interest in this mess . Hell, Donna even makes it difficult for mom to get her checks. Do you know she sends them certified mail so mom has to go to the post office to pick the check up? Really, Dad!"

"I think she does that to have proof that the check was sent on time."

"You have proof it was cashed, and I know you can see the date it was cashed. Donna does it just to annoy my mother and to make her life more difficult. Get a clue, Dad."

"I really do not want to deal with your mother any more. I have asked Donna to take over all the dealings so we do not have constant disagreements. Divorce changes the way people see each other, and I know your mother resents me and blames me for everything. Divorce is never one-sided. You are old enough to understand that I was unhappy being married to your mother, and I believe I can be happier being married to Donna. What caused our unhappiness is none of your business, and I really do not want to speak badly about your mother."

"Funny, she says the same things about you. When I complain to her, she is the first to defend you and tell me you are my father and you have always been a good father. I stopped complaining to her, but I am sure she would be upset if I were to tell her how Donna treats me."

"Let's work together to make things better. Your mother can pick you up and take you to your soccer games, but you have to promise to come right back here after the game. No visiting with your friends or going back to you mother's house. If I am available to take you, then you will let your mother know, and we can use that as our time."

"What will happen if my mother comes to the same game as you do?

"Nothing. We will not sit together or talk."

"I am willing to try this out if you are."

"Good, problem solved. Now I would like you to apologize to Donna for being so nasty to her."

"One more thing; I want to keep my phone while I am here. Debbie is allowed to use her phone in her room, and I want to be able to speak to my friends or my mother if I want to without having to ask permission."

"Okay, but no more threatening to call the police. That was really not called for, and you were wrong to do that."

"I will apologize for that."

With that, Mark took his daughter into his arms and hugged her. It was totally clear that Becky was having a really hard time and that Donna was not helping. He wondered who was more insecure.

When Mark returned to their bedroom, Donna was sitting in a chair looking out the window. He went over to her, but the look he got was frightening. It was quite obvious that she was furious with him, and he knew it was because he had taken Becky's side in the argument.

"You can't expect me to keep order in this house if you don't back me up."

"I don't expect you to keep order. I only expect you to treat my children nicely and not to make them miserable. If they do something you do not like, let me know, and I will address it. The way things are now, you have a collision course on your hands and no one will come out ahead. We do not need nor do we want to give Sara any grounds to take us to court and to complain that the children are being mistreated."

"You know the girl does not like me, and she will do and say anything to put you against me."

"I am well aware that she blames you for me leaving Sara, but if you continue to show your resentment, it will only make matters worse for all of us. Becky is a very smart girl, and she has heard and remembers things. She knows all too well that if she builds a case, the authorities will listen. You are the adult in this, and you have to be smarter than she is. After all, the children are here only two weekends a month. Be nice and win her over to your side. It will be easier than fighting her. Do some things with her that she likes to do, and help her to bond with Debbie so that they can do things together. It would be helpful if the girls all got along and were able to entertain each other."

"It is hard, especially since Debbie has so many activities on the weekends."

"Encourage Becky to do the same activities. That way the two of them can be together and you will have only one place to go."

"You make that sound so easy, but what if Becky still wants to play soccer and Debbie wants to take singing lessons?"

"I will try to take Becky to her soccer or we can allow her to call her mother to take her. She tells me Sara is okay with that, and as much as I hate having her spend extra time with Sara, it will solve the problem. I can do the running around on Sunday but not Saturday when I have to be at the office."

"Now you are taking time away from us."

"We have all week together and every other weekend. I think we can manage to be apart for a few hours here and there, especially if it helps keep the peace around here."

"I hate it when we are apart."

"I do too, but sometimes we just have to do what we have to do. Please try to understand that the way things have been going here, you are losing the battle and I do not want to see you lose the war. Becky resents you. In her mind, she has good cause to do so. It is not lost to her that now, not only have her parents divorced, but she has also lost her grandparents to whom she was very attached. She does not understand that I am the one who severed that relationship, and in her mind, you are the one responsible. She is too young for me to explain that they were sucking me dry and taking all the profits from the practice while I was the major earner."

"Maybe you should explain that to little miss know-it-all."

"When the time is right, I will, but right now she is not ready to hear it. I am sure that Sara has given her a totally different view of the situation, and I do not want to fight that fight with her right now."

"By 'with her' do you mean Sara or Becky?"

"Since I have no intention of speaking to Sara now or in the future, I mean Becky. I am expecting you to handle Sara for us, and I really don't care how you do it. Just make sure she does not have any grounds to go to court, and you can enjoy yourself making her life as miserable as possible."

"I get it. You are the good cop, and I am the bad cop."

"If that is the role you want to play, play it. I just think it is easier to give Sara exactly what she is entitled to get and no more. There is no reason for us to be friendly or have detailed conversations with her. You can pass along any necessary information via e-mail. It is really a good idea to do things that way as you have a permanent record of what is said and what is done."

"Good idea. I will start using e-mails to communicate with her, and I will continue sending her her checks via certified mail so she has to sign a receipt and cannot claim she did not get the check on time."

"You could pay her online."

"But she could claim she did not receive the check on time. After all, they mail the checks out. Also, it's less convenient for her to have to go to the post office to get the check if she is not at home when delivery is attempted."

"Your call! Now let's go down and be with the children for a while before we go to dinner."

"You go down first, and I'll be down in just a few minutes. I want to wash my face and put on some fresh makeup."

When Mark left the room, Donna sat for a while just thinking about what had transpired. She knew she would have to give in to Becky's demands, but she was happy to feel that Mark was really in her corner. Maybe things would be better around the house if she did not fight Becky, and she could even use this to get whatever she wanted from Mark. He would have to be grateful, and she would definitely use that when the time was right.

"Life is a series of compromises," she said out loud as she prepared to join the others in the den.

CHAPTER 20

DONNA WAS ENJOYING HER ROLE as office manager in Mark's new practice. They did not drive to work together as Donna wanted to have her own car there so she could leave if there were errands to do or for whatever reason. She tried to get along with the staff, but she did detect an undercurrent of displeasure when she told them do something that was different than what they were accustomed to doing. It was really the staff that he brought with him from the old practice that was giving her the most trouble. The people whom she hired as new additions were much more willing to accept her as their boss. Whenever she complained about this to Mark, he would tell her to let it go. He wanted the staff from the old office to be front and center so that patients who followed him would feel comfortable. He also trusted them to tell patients that his father or brother was not in at the moment if someone came to the new office thinking everyone had moved, not just Mark. Donna did see the merit in his thinking but vowed to herself that she would get rid of the old staff just as soon as the practice was established and on solid ground.

The one thing that Donna did insist on was that there would be no pension plan for the staff. She could not understand the stupidity of paying for a pension plan for everyone. She wanted a separate corporation set up to take care of pensions for her and Mark. This, she saw, as a major cost savings, and while the old employees complained, there was nothing they could do about it. It was one victory for her, and Mark seemed grateful for it.

The next situation addressed was health insurance. She and Mark and the family had health insurance through the other corporation, so she arranged for the cheapest insurance for the employees of the practice. She arranged it that they had to pay a portion of the premium so the cost to the practice was kept at a minimum. The second corporation, which she claimed provided administrative duties for the practice, was a secret. The corporation was in her name, and she collected a hefty fee for the administrative tasks she supposedly performed. Mark was content with the concept since it was saving him big bucks at the practice, and he was even putting household expenses on the corporate books. He repeatedly expressed how grateful he was to have her set these things up and to help handle the staff. Little did he know that most of the administrative fees she collected went directly into her personal account as a nest egg should she ever need it. Donna knew one thing for certain: she was never going to be poor again, and she was never going to be dependent on anyone.

When Mark complained that not enough patients followed him, Donna went into action to help drum up patients for the practice. She called all the doctors who used to work at the center and who were not part of the new facility and told them she would pay them for each referral made to Mark. This payment would also come out of her corporation so there was no link to the practice as she knew it was totally illegal to do such a thing. Legal or not, it worked. Mark's surgical calendar was filling up, and he stopped complaining to her about her spending money. It was a very good thing as she wanted to redo the house to make it hers and that cost money, lots of money. Debbie needed new clothes too. Both she and Donald were growing in leaps and bounds, and Donna made sure they had only the best clothes available. Her children were not going to be dressed in Kohl's specials like she had been when she was growing up. Donna felt that if they dressed well, they would be treated with respect. Respect was most important to her as she remembered what it felt like back in her Freeport days when she had received no respect and everyone took advantage of her. That was not going to be repeated, especially for Debbie. Donald was more able to take care of himself, and he seemed to have a good support system at school. He had friends, and they often did things together and for all intents and purposes, it seemed as though drugs were not a part of their lives. But Debbie was more insecure, and Donna feared that she would try using sex to get friends just as she had done back in the day. Donna never told Debbie about her life, but she did discuss the pitfalls of having sex with different guys and how that did not lead to true friendships but instead led to a girl having a bad reputation and being used and abused.

Debbie would listen to her mother, but Donna sensed that whatever she said went in one ear and out the other. She kept seeing herself as a teenager in her daughter and feared that Debbie would repeat her mistakes. Donna decided that the best way to help prevent Debbie from promiscuous behavior was to keep her very busy after school. It was easy for Donna to arrange her schedule so that she was home when school was finished, and she filled Debbie's day with singing and dancing lessons. There was little time to even do homework let alone get together with outside friends. If Debbie insisted on being with her school friends, she had to do so at Donna's house when either she or the nanny would be present.

Mark often commented that she kept Debbie on too short a leash and that the kid might revolt and start doing the very things Donna wanted to prevent.

"You don't understand. I know what it is like to be a girl and to want to be accepted."

"I do understand, and believe me, I worry about Becky and Marcie just as you worry about Debbie. I just feel that the kids that are kept too strictly are the ones that get in trouble as soon as they have any freedom. You cannot always be there to supervise her. The time will come when she will have to be on her own and make her own decisions."

"I know you are right, but now is not that time, and I will continue to monitor her especially until she goes off to college."

"Then she will really break free if you do not give her some freedom now. When I was in college it was always those kids who came from strict homes that got into the worse trouble."

"Believe me, I get it. I just don't need a teenage pregnancy."

"You sound like someone who has been there, done that.'

"I know how hard it is for a pretty girl to survive high school and remain a virgin."

"Not too many virgins graduate these days."

"Don't be flippant with me. You know what I mean, and if you are honest with yourself, you feel the same for your daughters."

"I don't hover over mine as you do."

"To each to his own!"

Donna was happy that the conversation ended without them having an argument. It seems like lately all she and Mark did was disagree, whether it be about the children, the practice or household expenses. He seemed to have a really short fuse, and she was getting increasingly tired about fighting for what she wanted. There were times she really just wanted to walk away, get her own place for her and her children, and to start over once again. Unfortunately, her nest egg was not large enough yet, and she still had not gotten him to void the prenup. She was working on having the deed for the house put in both of their names. That would offer her some security as the house was worth a hefty figure, and if they were to break up, it would have to be sold and she would be entitled to half of the value. Mark was having a hard time with the concept, but she was sure she would get him to agree one way or another.

CHAPTER 21

DONNA'S BEHAVIOR WITH DEBBIE made Mark wonder what she had done as a teenager. Whenever he asked her about her youth, all she would say was, "What happened before you, remains there. I do not care what you did before me, and you should not care about what I did. That is old history and has no bearing on today."

This really did not satisfy Mark. He knew from experience that parents most often try to prevent their children from repeating history. He knew that Donna had been a single mom prior to getting her break with Craig, but he did not know the circumstances of how she became pregnant and what had happened to Donald's father, who was not a part of his life and never discussed.

He had asked Craig to fill in the gaps, but that too went nowhere as Craig felt he could not discuss Donna without her being present. Curiosity was really getting to him, and the more Donna restricted Debbie, the more he was sure there was darkness in her past and the more he wanted it revealed to him. He knew of no friends that had known Donna during her teen years, and June and Jim would not indulge in any conversations about her youth. Mark felt that if he could gather information, it might be helpful should he need it to pressure her in the future. With this in mind, Mark contacted a private investigator who was a patient of his. He asked him to find out whatever he could about Donna's past.

It did not take long for the investigator to get back to Mark and to fill him in on Donna's teenage activities. It turned out that there were many people in Freeport who still remember the pretty but wild girl who sought acceptance through sex. He found out that she had been nicknamed the "Whore of Freeport." The investigator even found Rob who claimed he thought he was Donald's father but could not be sure as there were others who were intimate with Donna at the time she became pregnant, so it could have been any of a number of guys who fathered the kid. Rob had no interest in becoming a part of Donald's life and preferred to keep his existence anonymous.

The investigator did not find any proof of any sexual involvement between Donna and Craig. As hard it was to believe, theirs was a business relationship and a friendship but nothing more. This gave Mark some comfort because he could not accept knowing those two had a physical relationship as Craig was still a factor in their lives.

The other fact that was revealed by the investigator was Donna's ruthlessness. He reported in detail how she had ruined Steve's life and his future professional opportunities. It was clear that she had tried to destroy Steve because of his infidelity, and her payback was extreme. His advice to Mark was not to cross the bitch as he was sure she would return the favor in excess. This made Mark feel extremely uneasy as Donna was too involved in his practice and could hold that over him if they were to ever break up. He could imagine her going after his future earnings as well as a sizable settlement. One thing he learned was that Donna was no Sara and would never give in as easily as she had. This became a major concern for him as they continued to argue about just about everything and she continued to ask to be on the deed of his house. He knew there was no way he would ever put her on his deed and he also knew he would make sure there were accounts that she would never know about so he could protect his financial position going forward. He vowed to himself that he was and never would be another Steve.

Mark felt that the money he spent on the investigator was well worth it. He put the written report in the bank vault that he'd rented without Donna's knowledge. He decided that the vault would also be a place he would hide cash for an emergency fund. He knew he would never reveal the facts about the investigation unless he was forced to do so. He also had the private eye investigate Donna's actions at the center and her culpability in the Medicare and Medicaid improprieties that had been charged to the center and blamed on Steve. Mark was sure that Steve was not smart enough to initiate the activities and that it was probably Donna and Craig who had set up the fraudulent policies with Donna being the lead and Craig being in the background. Mark's suspicions proved to be right on the mark, and it was made clear to him that Donna and Craig had thrown Steve under the bus to save themselves. Mark knew for sure that he had to prevent her from doing the same things at his office site now that she was making it a multidisciplinary facility and could easily have patients shifted from one specialist to another even though there was no medical need to do so.

All of this put a strain on their marriage. Mark was having a hard time not confronting Donna with the information he had acquired even though he knew he had to keep it to himself, and she was having a hard time with him not accepting her recommendations for the office. The central issue that was forever present was the deed on the house and Mark's continued refusal to put her on it. Donna called him an ingrate and accused him of taking advantage of her. She even threatened to leave him at one point, but all he could say was, "Where do you think you can go? This is your home and the home of your children. Remember, we do have a prenup, and if you leave, you will get nothing. So stop making idle threats and just calm down."

Donna hated him for saying that but also realized the truth in his words. If she left at this point, she would get nothing despite having helped him to establish his practice. Theirs was not a long-term relationship, and any court would view her as a gold-digging woman who wanted to take advantage of him. Donna began to feel trapped, and that was not a feeling she liked. She wondered why Mark had all of a sudden taken such a hard line with her. Something had changed, and she really wanted to know what. In the past, all she'd had to do was stroke his manhood and he would give her anything she wanted. She was determined to find out why and how his attitude had changed. Unfortunately, there was no talking about it. As soon as she brought up the subject, he would just turn his back on her and walk away as though he was afraid he would say something he did not want to say. Donna decided that the best defense was to let things subside and not continually make an issue. She was going to be little miss perfect wife and the perfect mother to his bratty kids.

Donna did not really mind having her role in the office management diminished. She really hated working with Mark and listening to him reprimanding the staff and the patients. He was like a man with no patience, and it showed by the number of patients who cancelled their surgeries and never returned to the office. The staff also reflected his impatience because of the constant turnover of personnel. Instead of taking his constant abuse, Donna directed her energies to staffing the other offices in the building and managing the other practices. She resented Mark's interference with the other practices and his almost violent refusal to allow her to cycle the patients though the building. However, she was making enough money from the fees she charged the other doctors to manage their practices, so she was content that way. Some of the doctors felt her fees were too high, but she would just tell them to "Pay up or leave!" There were no other options as she knew she could fill their spots should they decide to leave, and leaving would be a tremendous burden on them. After all, she had all the billing numbers tied to the present office, and if someone were to leave, that person would have to apply all over again to become part of the various networks, many of which were closed to new applicants. She often laughed to herself that it was amazing how easy it was once someone made a pact with the devil. The doctors also could not open another office in the immediate vicinity as they had to sign a non-competition agreement before joining. If they were to leave, they could not open an office within a ten mile radius of not only the office but the hospitals as well. Plus the leases

Craig wrote were not able to be broken, so here again, she had them. If they were to leave, they would still have to pay the lease rate and all the expenses tied to the lease, including the management fees.

Donna made sure all the money she earned was hers and hers alone. Mark was not a partner, nor was Craig, who was just paid for his legal consultations. It was the old story of what was hers was hers and what was Mark's was hers too. She expected and, in reality, demanded that Mark pay all the household expenses since the house was solely in his name. He even paid the entire credit card bill each month while she put her earnings into the bank under her name alone and did not even reveal where the bank was. This was her payback, and she was really enjoying it while her nest egg was growing. There was no feeling as good to Donna as having money that she could call her own. It gave her confidence as well as pleasure. She knew that someday her net worth would be large enough that if Mark did not give her what she wanted, she would tell him to fuck himself.

CHAPTER 22

JAN HAD, AT FIRST, thought her world had come to an end. Everywhere she turned, Mark was challenging her very being. Not only had he abruptly left the practice, but he had taken several staff members with him. He tried to put the boat in receivership because he claimed he owned it after having put up a small amount of money toward its purchase. He actually took them to court over the boat, and it was Jan who made the judge realize that it was an act of vengeance. Looking back on her court appearance, Jan was astonished that she was able to keep herself together while Mark sat so pompously at the table with Craig at his side and Donna playing footsie with Craig. When they left the court, Fred could only tell her how proud he was of her and how happy he was to have her on his side.

"I only told the truth in there."

"I know you did, but I know how hard it was for you."

"It is hard to believe that he is our son, a son we raised and gave everything possible to."

"You have to stop thinking of him as our son. I think of him and that horrible woman as vermin who are not worth anything or any time. He is dead to me, and you need to think of him in the same way."

"If he were dead, I would have closure, but this way I know I will still see him at times and hear about him, and that is hurtful."

"Believe me, I get it, but we have more important things to dwell on than that bastard. We have a practice that we need to make sure survives and another son who deserves our allegiance."

"Howard and you will always have my allegiance, and I will do anything within my power to help you both whether it be professionally or privately."

"Having you at my side has always been my greatest asset, and I know Howard feels the same way."

"You make it easy, and I have always tried to be a good wife and mother despite what Mark thinks or says."

"He no longer counts, and whatever he says or thinks is of the same value as the garbage. I really think that everyone will be seeing it that way in short order."

"Right now I really do not care what everyone thinks."

"Good for you! Now we should get back to the office and start re-staffing it."

"I guess this means that retirement will be put off for both of us."

"What would we do if we did not work? I love what I do, and now that Howard is doing the surgery and the hospital work, it is really easier for me than it ever was."

"Yes, I get it. I actually am enjoying being in the office more than I have in years. The tension is just not there. Howard is much easier to work with than Mark ever was, and I find people are actually smiling while they are working. Of course the staff that remains is so loyal that they are a pleasure to have around. They even make the patients feel welcomed."

"You will see that everything will work out, both professionally and personally. I am already seeing referrals from doctors who had stopped referring to us because they lost confidence in Mark and did not want their patients to be treated by him. That is a very good sign for the future."

Fred and Jan walked into the office hand-in-hand. They both knew their love for each other would survive and that together they could face whatever came their way now and in the future. They also knew that they would forever have Howard in their circle of love and that their strength would always give him the strength to face whatever challenges came his way. His strength would also bolster them as he was and always would be the caring and considerate person he always was. It would never cease to amaze them how different their children were. It was as if they were raised in different households by different parents. Both Jan and Fred had to wonder if they had given Mark too much and made life too easy for him. He had been such a sickly child with a rare allergy to strep organisms, and they always had been afraid he would stop breathing, so they constantly hovered over him. He had wanted to go to an Ivy League college; they paid for it. No matter what he wanted, they had given it to him with no strings attached. They even had given him the down payment for his first house.

Howard, on the other hand, had gone to college on a full scholarship and constantly refused any financial help from his parents. He even had given in when Mark refused to pay him the same salary Mark was given for the first year in practice.

For Jan, the only pain was caused by her knowing she would not see the grandchildren. She knew she would never want to put them in the middle of a family dispute, and she made it clear to Sara that she would rather step away than cause them any pain. After all, a bad father was better than no father, and Mark had made it perfectly clear that he would not tolerate them having a relationship with her, Fred, or Howard. He knew this would hurt her, and if there was nothing else he could do to cause her the same pain, this was his best bet. It just completely reinforced Jan's feeling about him and made her resolve even stronger to not let him destroy her, Howard, or Fred. Secretly, she was amazed at the strength she found within herself.

CHAPTER 23

Mark found himself feeling challenged by his knowledge of Donna's past. He felt he could not trust her and began to wonder about her relationships with the other doctors in the building, mostly with Craig. Despite everything the investigator had said, he still viewed Craig as a romantic figure in Donna's life. He could not believe that they had never been intimate, especially since Craig had done so much to help her through the years. There was no point in discussing this with either of them as he knew he would never get the truth, and since he needed Craig for his legal advice, he decided to keep his mouth shut. It was obvious that no matter what their relationship had been in the past, they were not engaging in a sexual relationship now. To Mark it almost seemed as though Craig was taking a step back from Donna and having less and less to do with her. Mark really wanted to talk to Craig about this change in attitude but knew he could not do so and still have a professional relationship with him. Right at this point in time, Mark needed Craig for potential legal advice more than he needed confirmation about Donna's past or present actions. He also was afraid to push Donna too far as he knew she could just leave him, and that could present a financial burden that he was not prepared to face at this point in time. While he had a prenup, he also knew that it was only as good as the paper it was written on and that she was smart enough to be able to get around it and make him pay big time for ending their marriage. After all, she had helped him establish his practice, and there was a record of her involvement that could be used against him. His only course of action was to stay in the marriage and build his practice and his financial portfolio and to let her do whatever she wanted to do as long as she did not mistreat the children.

This resolve did not exclude loud arguments between him and Donna. There were times she would just drive him so crazy that he could not control his anger. It never mattered if other people were around or not when these arguments erupted. The children would just run down to the basement to escape, but when they erupted in the office, the staff never knew what to do. Everyone was talking about them yelling at each other, and even the patients were not spared hearing them go at each other. Soon it was all over the community. It did not take long for word to reach Jan that there was constant discord at Mark's office. Jan would only say that it was not her concern and that she did not want to even discuss him or his office. But if she was really honest with herself, she would admit that it gave her satisfaction that all was not perfect in his life. It did not take long for members of the staff that had followed him to start leaving. Jan heard that he refused to offer them any of the benefits they had when they'd worked with her and Fred. That and the constant arguing made life too stressful for many of them, especially when Mark carried the arguments over to them and yelled at them for whatever infractions he imagined they had committed. It was always someone else who was responsible; it was never he or anything he did that caused a negative reaction or perception. Jan could only feel grateful that she no longer had to deal with his mood swings or accusations.

Donna, on the other hand, did not give a crap about the fighting. She just continued to do whatever she wanted and completely ignored Mark. The crazier he got, the more she ignored him, and that resulted in his getting even crazier. If he yelled at her, she would just turn her back on him and walk away or just leave the building. Later, he would come to her all apologetic, and he would tell her how much he loved her and how important she was to him. He even suggested that they renew their vows to cement their love. The final result of all of this was for Donna to receive an expensive gift, which she often would sell and keep the money in the Donna account, as she called her hidden nest egg. It was fun watching her account grow and knowing that someday it would be large enough for her to search for greener pastures.

There was something important missing from Donna's life, and that was satisfying sex. Since their marriage, Mark had become a selfish lover. He no longer seemed to want to take the time to satisfy Donna; he just wanted to satisfy himself. While Donna tried to tell him about her feelings, he just continued to ignore her needs, and her resentment grew with each so-called love making event. Donna tried to masturbate, but that never left her feeling satisfied or, more importantly, loved. She thought about going elsewhere for sex but then decided that was not a good idea because if Mark were to suspect anything like that, it would mean the end of their relationship, something she could not afford at this juncture what with having two children living at home and receiving no child support for either of them. Steve could not give her any money for Debbie since he lost his practice and was now working as a salesman trying to sell chiropractic equipment. His commissions were small, and he was barely able to support himself, let alone give her child support. In some ways, she felt fortunate that she did not have to pay him any maintenance.

Donna did try to interest Craig in having a relationship with her. It would be easy to hide that from Mark as she and he spent a great deal of time together just as they always had in the past. Donna was still helping him manage his real estate properties. Unfortunately, Craig did not want anything but a professional relationship with her. He claimed he was being faithful to his wife, with whom he had established a better and loving relationship now that their children were older and less demanding. Donna did not believe a word of that, and in her heart of hearts, she knew that he was turned off by something she had done, though she had no idea of what that was. Craig refused to discuss his feelings, and for that matter, he refused to discuss anything personal with her. Their only discussions were about the properties and any legal problems that continued to result from the activities at the center. Donna hated being frozen out of his life but kept her feelings to herself since she liked the money she was earning.

For Donna, her life with Mark reminded her of the days when she was whoring. She did what she had to do to satisfy him, but it was without feelings or desire. She did what she had to do for the financial gain and for nothing else. The emptiness she felt was discouraging and festering within her. She could not even discuss her feelings with June, who would only tell her how lucky she was to have all the material things Mark provided. After all, she had the big house and seemed to have all the money she needed. Whenever Donna would start to complain, June would simply tell her how fortunate she was and how she should be grateful to Mark for the lifestyle he provided to her. Donna could only think that June's attitude was part of the generation gap, but there was no arguing with her, nor was there any point to doing so.

Donna did find happiness in buying things. She showered Debbie and Donald with gifts and the finest clothing. Of course, she never thought to buy anything for Becky or Marcie. This only created more jealousy between the children and more friction in the household. Even Mark could not help but notice how his children were excluded from receiving the expensive gifts that were lavished upon Donald and Debbie. Donna's only answer to him was that if he wanted to buy things for his kids, he could do so. She was not his personal shopper and never would be. When Mark would complain about her putting the things on his credit card, she would only say that it was the cost of having her in his life. If he complained that she was spending too much and that his earnings were down since the separation from the original practice, again she would just ignore him and walk away. There was no doubt in her mind that if she was going to live like a whore, she was going to be an expensive one. Now all she really wanted was to get her name on the deed to the house, and if with-holding sex was the necessary component to get what she wanted, so be it. She knew she would get what she wanted and, if necessary, as a last resort, she would threaten Mark with whatever was necessary to achieve her goal. It worked when Mark came to her and asked her to loan him some money as he needed it to make payroll at the office. In essence, Donna told him to pay up or shut up knowing that if he came to her it meant he had exhausted all other avenues for the needed revenue.

"What do you want from me?"

"It is quite simple. I will give you the money, and not as a loan, if you put my name on the deed to this house. It is only fair that I receive something for my money, and you will not have to pay it back. Obviously you are over your head in loans and you are having problems repaying the money or you would not be here asking me for any."

"You know how I feel about this house."

"Yes, I do. But I also need some security, especially if you are taking my money and there is little chance I will ever see it again. The house has real value for both of us, and if we are both on the deed neither of us can do anything without the other's approval. In reality, it protects you and me."

"You are not really giving me a choice."

"Take it or leave it. That is my offer."

With that, Donna left the room knowing she had finally achieved what she had so long sought. He would put her name on the deed because he had no other avenue to travel, and she would have the security she so wanted for herself and her children. Since it was obvious that Mark was and probably would continue to have financial issues, being on the deed at least guaranteed that if things went really south with his practice, she would come out of this mess with something.

CHAPTER 24

LIFE HAS A HABIT of taking strange turns just when you do not expect them. That was exactly what happened to Donna when she was called to come and meet with the guidance counselor at Donald's high school. Donald had always told her things were going great at school and that he was really doing well even though he rarely did homework at home. His claim was that he had enough time during his study period to do the homework and the necessary studying. Donna felt that there was no reason to challenge him. She always felt that she lavished her children with all the things they needed or even just wanted. In return, all she asked was that they do their part at school. So when she received the call from Mrs. Gaston, she was alarmed, especially since the guidance counselor stressed that time was of the essence and asked that they meet that very afternoon. Mrs. Gaston refused to discuss any issues with Donna over the phone, which further alarmed her.

Donna agreed to a three o'clock meeting, but when she hung up the phone, her concern rapidly grew. Donna could not help but remember what she had been like in high school and, even worse, what Rob had been like. The last thing she wanted was for her children to make the same mistakes she had made. It was even worse today as it was almost impossible for a person to get a decent job without a high school diploma. Her dream was for Donald to go to college and earn a degree in something he was interested in doing. Then his future would be ensured. It was only while she was sitting, looking at the phone that she realized that she had never really discussed his future with him, and she had no idea as to what his interests were. It was really strange because she had always considered herself to be an involved mother, but maybe she was too involved in her own life and not enough in Donald's. Mark had repeatedly questioned her about the boy, his goals and interests. But looking back at it all, she knew she had done little to get involved, and she wondered if that was why the counselor was calling.

"Oh well, I'll know soon enough," she said out loud as she typed in Donald's cell number. He answered immediately.

"Hi mom, what's up?"

"I just got a call from your guidance counselor, and she wants to see me this afternoon. What is going on?"

"That crazy bitch. All she does all day is make trouble. She'll probably tell you a bunch of lies just as she has with many of my friends."

"What kind of lies can I expect?"

"She told James' mom that he keeps cutting classes and will probably fail out of high school. But you cannot fail out of high school since you have to attend. The woman's just a nut case."

"What do you expect she will tell me?"

"I have no clue. I come to school and do my work, so I don't know what her beef is."

"Why aren't you in class now? I think it is odd that you can answer your phone and keep talking to me."

"I have a study period, so I just walked out of the room to talk to you when I saw it was you calling. After all, you hardly ever call me during school hours, and I figured it had to be important."

"Go back to your study hall. Please remember that I will want to see you after I meet with Mrs. Gaston. I am sure she will have some serious complaints, and you and I will have to deal with them."

"I'll be home for dinner. Will you be there?"

"See you then."

As she disconnected the call, she could not help but think how strange it was that he was asking her if she would be home for dinner. Had it been so long since she'd had dinner with her kids? For a moment, she could not remember the last time they had actually sat down to eat together. Whoa, what was happening to her family? All of a sudden, Donna felt as though a knife was in her chest. She was really all caught up with everything but her kids. Of course, she did run around taking Debbie to singing lessons and acting lessons as well as cheerleading and other after school activities. But Donald was another story. He no longer needed Donna to take him places. He had friends with cars, and they drove him wherever he wanted to go. He would just leave her a note telling her where he was. It was then that she realized she never really checked on him. He could tell her he was at a friend's house, but he could be anywhere and she would not know the difference. Thinking about this made her dread the meeting with Mrs. Gaston even more. She remembered telling June that she would be at a particular friend's when she was really having sex with one of the boys. Today it was probably even easier to find a house without a parent being home; most parents worked and had set schedules, which gave the kids more freedom than ever before.

Donna's nerves were on high alert by the time of the meeting. She walked into the guidance office expecting the worst, and her expectations were heightened when she saw the principal was also in the office. He rose as she entered and extended his hand to shake hers.

"Thank you for coming. We know how busy you are, and if it weren't important, let me assure you, we would not be here."

"I get it. All I want to know is what is going on and if Donald is in some serious trouble."

"Donald is a nice boy, and he should be passing his classes. But he is failing, and worse than that, he is using drugs and hanging out with a bad crowd."

"Do you have proof to support that accusation? After all, you are saying something very serious, and I need to know your proof and why I was not informed before this. If he is failing, why haven't his teachers contacted me?"

"They have tried. They called your home but never received a call back. They even sent letters home, but by the look on your face, I am assuming you never received the letters. He is cutting classes and we have no idea as to where he goes or what he is doing except that when he does come back, his eyes are all glossy and he definitely smells of marijuana. I know this for a fact because I stopped him just yesterday as he was reentering the building."

"Have any of you confronted him?"

"Not directly. We wanted to have you involved before the school takes any steps. You know we are obligated to get the police involved where we think drugs are an issue."

"I appreciate you calling me before doing that. I definitely will speak with Donald tonight. How bad are his grades?"

"As of now, he is failing in all classes. There is still time for him to recoup, but it will take a great deal of effort on his part and on yours. He has the IQ to pass, but he has to go to class and do his homework and study for his tests. He is doing none of that. He will need tutors to catch up with the work already done, and I am sure you can afford to get him the help he needs. But it is up to him to accept that help."

"History does have a way of repeating itself. I was not a good student when I was in high school."

"So you have first-hand experience with what we are talking about. I am sure you understand how hard it is today for a young person to get a decent job without a high school diploma, at a minimum. Today it is as though every job wants a college degree. It is funny, but when I was in college one of my professors said a baby should be given coupons at birth: one for high school and another for college. Our society has almost come to that level. It worries me that a kid like Donald cannot complete high school, and he will be left with no options except criminal ones. They all see drug money as easy money. Unfortunately, they are right about that, but we do not want to see him go down that path."

"Thank you, Mr. Hilton and Mrs. Gaston. I truly appreciate you taking the time to meet with me. I will definitely discuss this with my husband and together we will come up with a plan to help Donald. Please let me know immediately if he cuts classes or if you suspect that he has been using any drugs at all. You can call me on my cell. I want you to know I care and I thank you for caring."

"We appreciate your attitude. We were half expecting you to defend him and deny that there could be any credibility in what we were saying."

"I already told you, I was a problem in high school, and in reality, I probably did a lot worse things when I was his age. That does not make it right; but it does make it believable. I was lucky to have a guardian angel who changed my life. Since there is no angel for Donald, I will have to step up and do whatever is necessary. Please keep me in the loop and give me a chance to work with you."

"You got that from us and from all of his teachers."

With that, Donna got up and left the office, making a concerted attempt to keep her head high and not look like a defeated person. Once in the car, she first called Mark and filled him on the meeting. His only response was, "I told you so." Donna immediately knew she could not expect him to become involved. She also knew it was her fault that he was not involved in Donald's life. She had always said that she would handle her kids and he had to handle his. Her next call was to Steve, the only father Donald ever knew. Steven listened but had little to say as he too felt excluded from parenting Donald.

"Donna, you have to talk to him and get him to understand the seriousness of the situation. He has not been coming to my house at all. So I am out of the loop and probably out of his life."

"Why haven't you told me that he does not come to your house for visitation?"

"I thought you knew. Even Debbie never questioned that he was not here."

"You are saying she was aware that he was just not coming."

"We never really talk about it. We just accepted what is."

"I wonder where he goes when I think he is at your house."

"He goes wherever he goes when he is supposed to be in school. You have to remember how easy it was for you to find places to go."

"That's part of the problem. I remember all too clearly. I really did not want my kids to make the same mistakes I made. I never saw this coming my way."

"Let me know if there is anything I can do. The boy does not think of me as his father any more, so I have little-to-no authority with him, but if I can help, I am here for him."

"Thank you, Steve. I really appreciate you taking the time to discuss this and you offering to help. That is more than I can expect from Mark."

"Mark is also your problem. I think you have to begin to see that he is a selfish person who does not extend himself for anyone."

"You are talking about my husband."

"Been there, done that!"

With that, Donna disconnected the call. There was no point is any further discussion as she knew Steve had a point and she was not prepared to accept his evaluation, nor was she prepared to defend Mark. Her next call was to Donald. Once again, he answered quickly.

"Hi, Mom. Did that bitch fill your head with lies about me?"

"You are to meet me at the house immediately. We have much to discuss, and I want to see you alone. I will be home in ten minutes, and you had better be there when I walk in."

"That does not give me much time."

"You have had too much time already. Be there!"

Donna just sat still for a few minutes trying to compose herself. She knew there would be little to gain if Donald perceived her as hysterical. She had to be in control of the situation and of herself. Her next call was to Craig.

"I need advice as to how to handle Donald," she said and then proceeded to tell him about the meeting at the school.

"I need time to think about this. The first thing I would do is to have a sit down with him and lay your cards out on the table. I think he has to be grounded. Homework has to be checked, if not by you then by a tutor. His allowance has to be cut so he will not have money for drugs. That's a start, and after I think about it some more, I will talk to you in greater detail. My immediate thought is that a military school might be an answer, but let me think before you speak."

Donna felt empowered as she put the car in gear and headed home. She knew she would implement the immediate things Craig suggested and go from there. There was no way she was going to back down no matter what Donald said or did, and she also knew she would be at home every day after school to monitor his activities. No more relying on the nanny who Donald could walk all over and get his way. Maybe it was actually a good thing that she did not have to be at the office all the time.

When she walked into the house, the sweet smell of weed greeted her. Donald was in the shower, but his clothes were on the floor in the laundry room, and they reeked. Donna took them with her and stood outside the bathroom door waiting for the shower to stop. When Donald walked out of the bathroom he was shocked to see his mother standing with his clothes.

"What are you doing?"

"Holding your stinking clothes, and just in case you think I do not know the smell of weed, think again."

"My friends were smoking, not me."

"Don't bother to lie to me. I get it, and now you are going to get it too."

"What are you going to do? Spank me?"

"Grow up and show some respect. Maybe I haven't been the best mother, but I care, and now things are going to change around here. Get dressed and meet me in the kitchen."

"Aye, aye, captain!"

Once the two of them were sitting at the table, Donna basically told Donald the things Craig recommended and told him he was not to see any of his friends and that he was completely grounded. She went on to tell him that his grades had to improve and that she would be checking his homework daily.

"You have to be kidding me. I am not a baby."

"Then don't act like one. I am not kidding you. From this point forward, you will take lunch to school, and there will be no allowance since you have been using money for the wrong things. You will turn around your grades, or you will be in a military school before you know what hit you. Until your grades are passing, there will be no social life for you, and I do not care how you stomp your feet or yell. I am setting the rules for this house, and you will obey them."

"What if I don't?"

"There are schools that are more like prisons, and you will find yourself in one of them. That is a promise, not a threat."

"It takes one to know one."

"Yes, it does. I am not denying that I was a problem student when I was in high school. Believe me, I know all the tricks. Times have changed, and today it is impossible to get a job and make a living without an education. I will not see you ruin your life for a little pleasure now. Get it into your head that you will live by my rules or life will become impossible for you."

"What does Mark say about your new rules and regulations?"

"You are my problem, not his. You never really wanted him as a part of your life. So what does it matter what he thinks or says now? In reality, he would be in favor of my rules as he basically makes Robert adhere to them."

"I'm not Robert. He's a dork."

"Maybe you need to be more of a dork."

"Oh, come on. There is no way I can be a computer geek, and you know it."

"What do you think you can be?"

"I like things like cars and stuff like that."

"Okay, I see nothing wrong with being a car mechanic."

"Why do I need school for that?'

"You need school to learn to think and to expand your horizons. Who knows, you might someday want to be an engineer or to design cars. You can't limit yourself now, and besides, every job these days wants the person to have a high school diploma at least. You need to pass your classes and get your diploma. Once you have that, we can discuss the path you want to take from there. You are anything but stupid. You can and will do this. Am I making myself clear?"

"Clear as mud."

"It may be mud to you, but it is clear to me."

"You can't be serious about me not being able to see my friends."

"I am totally serious. Once you start doing better at school, we will readdress that issue. Until then, consider yourself totally grounded. Am I correct to assume that you have no idea as to what you have to do for homework?"

"I did not go to class today."

"I will call the school and get your assignments so you can start right now."

"I left the books in my locker."

"Get your jacket. We will go to the school together and get whatever you need."

"You embarrass me."

"Too fucking bad. You should've thought about that before you screwed everything up."

Donna walked boldly into the school with Donald trailing behind her. She could feel his embarrassment, and it did bring back painful memories of her own high school days. If only her mother had been more forceful and more demanding, maybe she would not have made the mistakes she made. But that aside, Donald was going to graduate, of that she was certain. She was convinced that she would monitor his homework daily and physically take him to school each morning. She knew she would even check up on him throughout the day to make sure he did not cut out. If he behaved like a baby, he was going to be treated like one.

She could sense Donald become more and more nervous as they approached his locker.

"I can handle this," he said with affected conviction.

"What's in that locker that you do not want me to see?"

"Nothing, I just know where everything is, and there are things I do not have to take home. There is no point in dragging things back and forth."

"We are going to empty the entire locker."

"You sound like you do not believe me."

"Take it as it is. You are giving off vibes that make me feel that there is something in that locker you do not want me to see. Once a liar, always a liar. You lied about going to school, so why would I believe you now?"

"You can't treat me like this in front of everyone who is in the school. I will be the object of all the jokes because of you."

"The longer you put this off, the more visible we are. Let's get that locker open, and let's get it done."

With that, Donald hung his head down and opened the locker. The mess inside was horrible. Obviously, he just used it to stuff things into it, and he was not taking out his books.

"You had better get the garbage can over here. We need to throw some of this shit out."

With that, Donna started pulling stuff out of the locker until she came upon a bag of weed and another bag of unmarked pills. She felt her knees buckle as she held the bags in her hands. It was all too obvious to her that Donald was not only using the drugs, but also he was selling them as there was far too much in the locker for personal use.

"Don't say a word to me. I know what you have been doing, and nothing you can say can make this any better. You have been playing me for a fool, and the only good thing here is that I am the one who opened this locker and not the school officials, because your ass would be fried if any of them found this crap."

With that, Donna stuffed the drugs into her bag and continued to empty the locker of all its contents. The books were handed to Donald, who had turned an ashen white while standing beside his mother.

"I am sorry. I never meant for you to find that stuff."

"That is not the problem, young man. The problem is that you have that stuff, and you have been selling it to your so-called friends. You are lucky that you are not going to jail."

"Your rules will make my life worse than being in jail."

"Nothing I could do could make your life worse than jail. You really screwed up this time, and we will work together to turn things around or you will find your ass in military school before you can catch your breath. Am I making myself clear?"

"I don't know if I can do what you want. I am very far behind in class, and I have no clue as to what is really going on in school. None of my friends are doing any better than I am, so there is no one to help me. I also am not sure I can cold turkey it. I am used to using weed."

"You will cold turkey it. As far as your studies are concerned, you will be home schooled for now. I am thinking that the best path is for me to hire tutors to come to the house to work with you. That way you will not be tempted to follow your so-called friends."

"You are saying that I am going to be a prisoner in my own home."

"Like it or not, that is the way it is going to be. You do not deserve my trust anymore."

"Like mother, like son."

"I have not denied that I made mistakes as a teenager. I just do not want to see you destroy your life. Times have changed, and things are much different now. You have done things I never did, and you have done things that are illegal. I do not want to have to visit my son in jail. Get that through your thick head."

"How long do you propose to hold me prisoner?"

"As long as it takes to get your diploma and to get you on the straight and narrow. There will be no drugs, no booze, no friends, and no sex. You will not lie to me ever again, and you will be respectful to me and Mark. Am I making myself completely clear?"

"Mark does not give a shit about me. He's all for his own kids, and you know it. And if you think Steve is some kind of knight, think again. He's the one who started me on the drugs, and he is a good source for them. Don't think for one minute that Debbie is completely clean."

"What the hell are you saying?"

"I am saying that Steve is one bad dude. I would not be surprised if he was dipping into the golden hole with his own daughter. I have seen him touching her in ways that guys touch girls before going all the way."

With that, Donna had all she could do to control the car she was driving. Her hands were shaking, and she was feeling faint. How could she have possibly believed that Steve could be a decent father, and if what Donald was saying was true, Debbie was being abused, and that was too horrible to comprehend. She wondered how she would be able to get to the truth. Victims of child abuse were always told to keep everything secret, and if Debbie would not come clean, she would not be able to deny Steve his visitation as no court would take Donald's word for anything without proof. This day was going from bad to horrible quicker than Donna could believe. As she pulled into the driveway, she turned to Donald and asked "Are you telling me the truth, or are you making something up to divert my attention away from you?"

"What would be the point of my lying to you? There is no way you are going to change your mind about me being a house prisoner. I know you. But just maybe, you can do something to help Debbie. After all, she is my little sister, and whether you believe me or not, I love the kid."

"If you love her so much, why haven't you said something before this?"

"Drugs are good. I did not want to cut off my supply."

"Great—just sacrifice your sister."

"We all do whatever we have to do to get what we want. You are an example of that, and you know it. You married Mark for his money. You are his whore, and you know it."

"That is not true. You are just lashing out, and before this conversation deteriorates any further, you had better go to your room and sleep off whatever you have taken. I have some calls to make so that I can set up your tutoring sessions, and then I will talk to your sister when she gets home. You are room-bound, and don't even think about sneaking out of the house."

Once Donald was safely in his room, Donna thought about calling Mark to discuss the new events of the day but decided against that. He was in the office and probably seeing patients, so her call would be an interruption, and there was really little he could do or say to change things. She did call Craig to get his legal opinion regarding Donald's accusations about Steve.

Craig suggested, just as she knew he would, that she talk to Debbie in a calm and nonthreatening manner to see if Debbie would confirm what Donald had said. If there were any mention of any undesirable behavior, they would have a suit against Steve that would stand up in any court.

"Don't be shocked if Debbie denies everything Donald said. If there is anything going on, she may be too embarrassed to confirm it. She is very young and may just think that is the way fathers treat daughters. I am sure you never had that type of conversation with her."

"You're right. Why would I ever bring up anything like that?! I have no predisposed images of Steve, but I never imagined that he could abuse his own daughter."

"We can't jump to conclusions. If Donald is into drugs as much as you think, he could be making this all up as a diversion."

"Believe me, I thought of that. I even said it to him, but he held firm, which is why I kinda believe him. He said that Steve was supplying the drugs, and that is why he never said anything or did anything to protect Debbie."

"What a mess! Does Mark know anything about all of this?"

"No, he's at the office, but I will tell him tonight. My guess is that he will be furious and will try to throw Donald out of the house. That's something that will not fly with me. You know I am a tiger when it comes to my kids, and I will do anything I have to do to fight for them."

"I get it, but I also understand that Mark may not like Donald having an influence on the other kids. You cannot watch him twenty-four-seven. He is too old to have a sitter or nanny, and what are you going to do when you go to work or even go shopping or out for dinner with Mark?"

"I'll work it all out in time. Donald is not really a bad kid. He just made a bad turn under the guidance of a bad person, if what he has said about Steve is true. No car, no money, and no freedom can help him find the straight and narrow. Right now I am more worried about Debbie."

"I get it, and if I can do anything to help, just call. If Debbie gives any information that confirms that Steve has behaved inappropriately in any way, we can get his visitations limited to having someone there with him and Debbie. The courts are very strict about that. Keep me posted."

Hanging up the phone, Donna immediately became aware that tears were running down her face. She felt like her life had suddenly come to a total stop and everything was is chaos. Part of her wanted to call June for comfort, but she did not have the energy to do anything at the moment except sit in the kitchen and cry.

CHAPTER 25

MARK ACTUALLY EXHALED as he turned onto his block. It had been a miserable day at the hospital. First, two cases cancelled at the last minute leaving a gap in his schedule that could not be filled and thereby leaving a gap in his income. One of the OR supervisors thought she knew better than he when it came to treating patients, and that had resulted in a huge argument. He was further infuriated that he was the one called to the CEO's office and reprimanded for yelling at the supervisor. She should have been the one called to the office. He all but told the CEO that he could take his hospital and shove it; there were other hospitals where Mark would be more than welcome to bring his cases. After all, money talks and bullshit walks, and he planned to make them beg to have his cases. The patients he then saw in the office were no better. All he had were complaints about his surgeries and threats of suits. All in all, it had been a terrible day, and he was exhausted. Now all he wanted was a strong drink and some quiet time.

As soon as he walked into the kitchen and saw Donna's face, he knew his plans for a quiet evening were shattered. It did not take her long to unload the entire day's events. After hearing all of it, all Mark could think and say was, "I told you so. You always give your kids too much freedom, and discipline is not part of your vocabulary. Maybe if you had set stricter rules, you would not be here now."

"That is a real help. You telling me that all of this is my fault is absurd and not at all helpful. I need your support and help now."

"What the hell do you want me to do? You never have allowed me to get involved with your kids or to discipline them in any way. Now that there is trouble, you want me to get in the middle of things and solve everything for you. Really, Donna, that is asking too much, and I really doubt that anything I would say would have an impact on Donald—or Debbie, for that matter. They view me as your fuck and your bankroll and nothing more. I would not doubt it if I were to discover that Donald has been helping himself to my money and things to help pay for his drugs, and if that is the case, hell will break out around here."

"Are you threatening me?"

"I am not threatening you, I am telling you something. If that kid has been stealing from this house, I promise you I will press charges."

"I don't need your threats. I need your help."

"Call Craig. He is the one you always go to for help."

"He is not my husband, you are. I always wanted us to be a family, and I have always treated your kids as though they were mine. Why can't you do the same for Donald and Debbie?"

"That last statement is an interesting one. You have never treated my kids like your own. Your brats get everything new, and my kids get the hand-me-downs. You do everything for your kids, but you will not drive mine to any events or give them any quality time. You think I don't know this. Well, think again. You put on the big show when there are other people around, but in reality, you make the kids feel unwanted. It has been an ongoing battle to get the kids to remain quiet about you and not to complain to Sara, who, I might add, is just waiting for the complaints to take me back to court. I am beginning to think that marrying you was one of my biggest mistakes and that you have ruined my life in so many ways, not the least being starting my own practice and relying on you to manage it. You are never there except to pick up your check, and I have to do everything else. All the bullshit you said about us being a team and working together was pure fabrication."

"I am sorry you feel that way. I am doing my best, and if you don't like it, there is the door."

"That is where you have it wrong. This is my house, and if you don't like it, you can leave. The sooner the better as far as I am concerned. I have had a really bad day too. It seems my office manager is not confirming cases, and we are having cancellations at the last minute. Worse even than that, patients are complaining about their surgeries and even threatening to sue. Does that sound like a good day to you? Look, I need a drink and some quiet time; so you attend to your son and just leave me alone. Your problems are your problems, not mine. I have enough of my own to deal with."

With that, Mark walked out of the kitchen and into the den. Donna could hear him opening the bottle of liquor and then hear him storming up the stairs to their bedroom. After hearing the door slam, she knew he would hole up there for the rest of the evening and there would be no talking to him or reasoning with him.

First, she tried to call Debbie, but her phone went right to voicemail, something that was going to be forbidden going forward. Donna left her a message to call home immediately and then went up to check on Donald. He was lying in bed and complaining of a severe headache.

"It's all your fault that I feel this way," he yelled at her as she opened the door.

"That is something you got totally wrong. It is all your own fault. Not getting your drugs when your body wants them can lead to severe headaches; so get used to the feeling. Do you want anything to eat, and do you have water? You need to drink lots of water to dilute the drugs in your system."

"I am not hungry, but I guess I could use some water. Would you mind getting me a bottle?"

"I'll be right back with it."

"Hey, Mom, what were you and Mark arguing about? I could hear you up here even with the door closed."

"He had a bad day, not that I had a good one."

"I hope I am not the cause of it. I really don't want to destroy your marriage along with everything else I've done."

"I just hope you have not been helping yourself to anything that is his, and if you have taken any money or anything, please let me know before he finds out."

"I swear that I have never stolen anything of his. I have taken money out of your purse when I needed money, and that is the truth."

"Do you have any idea as to where your sister is?

"No clue. Maybe you should call her father; she might be there."

With that, Donna turned and walked out of the room to get the water for him and to call Steve. If Debbie was indeed there, there would be hell to pay. Steve denied seeing Debbie, and when he questioned Donna, all she would tell him was that Debbie was not answering her phone and that she was concerned as to where she was. Donna asked Steve to call her immediately if he heard from Debbie. She then proceeded to call Debbie's friends, and by the time she located the kid, her anger had grown out of proportion.

"You know you are never to put your calls to voicemail when you are not at home."

"I am sorry. We were working on a school project, and we just did not want to be interrupted."

"I want you home immediately. I am leaving the house now, and I will be at Diane's in just a few minutes."

"But we are not finished with the project."

"Consider yourself finished for today. I am just a few minutes away, and I want you to come home with me."

"You have to stop treating me like a baby."

With that, Donna arrived at Diane's house and rang the doorbell. She could hear the loud music coming from inside the house. Obviously the project was a party, and she was sure that there were boys there as well. Debbie actually opened the door and looked at her mother with the widest eyes Donna had ever seen.

"What the hell is going on here? Where is Diane's mother, and does she know you are having a party here? God, I can smell the pot from the doorway. What else is going on?"

Donna then pushed her way into the house, and everyone froze immediately upon seeing her. There were boys without shirts and girls in underwear, and the smoke was everywhere. Donna demanded to know where the parents were and learned that they were out of town, which explained how the party could be so open. Donna then demanded that everyone get dressed and go home.

"This party is over but don't think for one minute that Diane's parents are not going to know about it. I want all the weed left with me, and I demand that everyone get the hell out of this house or I will call the police. Diane, I am sure your folks are going to be furious with you just as I am with Debbie. You both have violated their confidence and mine."

"Is there any way that you will not tell my folks?" Diane asked in a very little voice.

"No way in hell. This behavior has to stop before you and Debbie get yourselves into unbelievable trouble. Have the two of you been smoking pot too?"

"No, Mom, I really did not smoke it. I swear."

"What about you, Diane?"

"I did try it, but I don't like it. I just want to be popular and have friends."

"These are not the friends you should have. These are users who are using you to do things they know are wrong. Believe me, if push comes to shove, they will push you under the truck. You know there are laws against having a pot party in your house. All that needed to have happened was for one of the neighbors to call the cops and you would be in serious trouble right up to your pretty neck, and your so-called friends would be nowhere in sight. Don't be naïve!

"Now, Debbie you get your things. You are coming home with me. Diane, if you want, you can come too as I don't think you should be here alone. When are your folks coming back?"

"They said they would be home on Sunday. They just went to Puerto Rico for a few days."

"Call them and ask them to come home tomorrow, and until then you can stay with us."

"What should I tell them is the reason I need them to come home?"

"Try the truth. Look, I have had a really bad day, and you both have made it even worse. I am done here, and so are you. Let's go."

Once in the car, Debbie tried to apologize, but Donna would have none of it. All she would say was that Debbie was grounded for an indefinitely long time. She would be allowed to go to school but had to come directly home afterwards, and there would be no visits from friends. What she really wanted to discuss was Donald's allegations about Steve's improper behavior, but that would have to wait until she had Debbie alone. It was hard to believe that her life was unraveling all in one day, but regardless of her own disappointments, she knew she had to try to save her children, and that was her primary objective. She knew that she was going to put her kids before her marriage and before everything else in her life, and if Mark did not want to help, so be it. She would do it alone. At least Debbie's grades were still good, so she could still go to school, unlike Donald, but Donna knew she was facing a hard road ahead with both of them.

Once home, Donna sent Debbie and Diane directly to Debbie's room, telling them they were to wash up and then come to the kitchen for dinner. There was to be no telephone and no television. After dinner, they were to get their homework done, and in the morning she would take them both to school. Donna made it clear that she was going to call Diane's parents, as Diane had failed to reach them, and fill them in on what was going on. It was her sincere hope that they would return by the end of the next school day, and then they could deal with their daughter while she could do the same with Debbie. Of course, that was exactly what Diane's parents said once they were reached. They, too, were upset and understood the importance of the situation. They could only thank Donna for taking care of things and not getting the police involved.

"We are indebted to you for what you did to protect our daughter," Jim, Diane's father, said. "Today things are much more complicated than they were when we were kids. We could drink at a friend's house and the parents would not get in trouble. Today, the parents are responsible even if they are not home and have no knowledge that a party is going on in their house. I am shocked that Diane would expose us to that potential danger. She knows how serious it is for the parents and how much trouble can come from things like this."

"She is still a kid, and kids do stupid things to earn acceptance. I really believe that both of the kids only wanted to feel that they are popular. They both swear that they were not the ones smoking the pot, not that they should be excused because of that. I have grounded Debbie for an indefinite period of time, and once we are alone, I expect to have a real heart-to-heart with her. I know you will do the same with Diane, and hopefully we will not be in this situation again."

"We totally agree with you, and thanks again for caring about our daughter."

"No problem. I will take them to school in the morning, and I will pick Debbie up right after school. Do you think you will be back in town by then?"

"Absolutely! We will probably see you at the school in the afternoon."

With that, Donna hung up. Now all that was left was to tell Mark about the rest of the day's happenings. This was not going to be an easy conversation, but it was one that had to take place. Donna was sure that there would be some very nasty comments made about her children. She also knew she would have to hold her tongue and not bring his kids into the conversation as that would only escalate the whole thing to another level, one she was not prepared to go to at all.

After checking on the girls and Donald, Donna decided to pour a glass of wine for herself to help her relax while she waited for Mark to open the bedroom door. She even thought of calling Craig to get his prospectus on the situation but decided against that. This was one time she had to stand on her own and face the music. Hopefully Mark would be of some help, but she doubted that as well.

Mark eventually walked into the kitchen like a raging bull. He was still shouting about what a terrible day he'd had and how the office was totally lacking in management.

"You know you are supposed to be the office manager. Where were you today when I needed you? You didn't even answer your phone. I don't understand. It is not like you don't cash your check right on time."

"Sometimes there are things that happen that are more important than your precious office. I really don't appreciate you coming at me like this again. I told you about what happened with Donald when you first came home, or are you too drunk to remember that conversation? You don't have to be such a nasty bastard."

"Now we are down to name calling! How lady-like of you."

"Look, I have had a really bad day, and the last thing I need or want is to have an argument with you. I actually need your help and advice, but if you are in such a 'you' mood, I will just leave you to your misery."

"Maybe it is a good idea to leave me alone. Maybe it is even a better idea for you and your brats to leave this house permanently. I can manage without your constant problems, and if you leave, I can actually hire a real manager to help me with the office."

With that, Donna just looked at him and realized she was dealing with an unstable person. There was no reasoning with him and no point in trying to tell him about the children or anything else that was bothering her. She almost felt sorry for him because his self-induced stress was driving him absolutely crazy, and there was no reasoning with a crazy and drunk person. Donna just got up and left the room. She quietly went into the guest room and locked the door behind her. Like everything else that had happened on this awful day, this too would have to be dealt with in the morning. What she would do was something that required some thought and planning and even some legal advice. One thing was for sure: she would make Mark pay for the way he was treating her.

Donna was really surprised when she opened the bedroom door and smelled coffee. She was even more surprised when she saw it was Mark in the kitchen actually preparing breakfast for her.

"Listen I am really sorry about last night. I know I was really rude, and I was taking my frustration out on you. I hope you will accept my apology."

"We both had a bad day, and we were both on edge."

"What happened that made you so on edge?"

At that, Donna unloaded a recap of her day and all the problems. While she truly expected Mark to blame her for the actions of her children, she really did not care. She needed to unload, and since he was willing to listen, she just laid it all out like a flood of words.

"Whoa, your day was certainly more stressful than mine. Now I am doubly sorry for the way I acted. What can I do to help?"

"At this moment, there is little anyone can do. Donald will be home-schooled for now, and hopefully we can get him through high school. Debbie knows she is grounded, and as soon as I have her alone, I will address Donald's accusations about Steve. God help him if what Donald said is true. That is probably the most upsetting development because I never expected Steve to behave in any way that could be harmful to his daughter."

"We both know he is one solid dirtbag. Nothing he could do would really surprise me."

"But she is his daughter!"

"She is still one very pretty girl, and she is developing sexually. One never knows what a guy like Steve could be thinking."

"Now, what is going on at the office, and how can I help you?"

"We are not getting the number of cases that I expected to get when I opened the office. I know that Fred and Jan are badmouthing me to everyone at the hospital, and Howard is doing his best to follow in their example. Can you believe that there are those who actually think Howard is a better surgeon than I am?"

"We both knew that it was going to be a hard go when you broke away. In reality, we can do with less for the time being, and I am sure the practice will start to grow. After all, our ads say we have moved. So many of the patients who would go to the other office will come to us, and once you get them there, they will stay."

"It is hard when they ask where Fred or Howard is."

"Just tell them they are out of the office but you can take care of them. I would avoid telling them that Fred and Howard are not part of the practice. I also think having the other doctors in the building will eventually be very helpful. The cardiologist and dermatologist will increase the traffic to the office, and that alone will increase patients for your practice. I have arranged to manage their practices, and we will get income from that as well. I can also make sure that all surgery is referred directly to you."

"We need quality people, not like the ones you had at the center."

"The two I have are real quality.

"Are you sure there is enough physical space to make it work?"

"Absolutely. We can alternate the days each works so that each has more than enough space. And don't forget, you are getting rent money from each of them, so that too will help relieve some of the pressure on you."

"Thank you so much. You are my rock, and I promise to treat you in a way you deserve. You can also count on me to help with the kids. I truly believe that Debbie is a good kid who just wants to be accepted by her peers. Donald, on the other hand, seems to be having major problems in school. Maybe doing homeschool will make a difference, but you do realize you cannot keep him here like a prisoner. He goes with a tough crowd, and the more you insist that he not see his friends, the more he will want to do just that."

"I will not write off the kid. If he can get his high school diploma, at least he could get a decent job. It is my first priority where he is concerned."

"Who is going to tutor him?"

"The school is recommending someone who can tutor him in the various subjects. They also think he will benefit from a one-on-one situation."

"Go for it; we have nothing to lose. I just worry about how he will react when he sees his friends.'

"One problem at a time, please."

"You do not have that luxury. What are you going to do with Debbie?"

"I am going to try my best to prevent her from getting pregnant and ruining her life."

"Get her a prescription for birth control pills. You cannot stop what you cannot stop, but you can prevent what you fear."

"I don't want my daughter to be considered an easy girl, and I really think that if I level with her, I can get her to see the pitfalls."

"Good luck! Look, I really have to get to the office. Call me if you need me, and once again, I am sorry about last night."

"Let it go! We were both edgy, and things just got out of control. Love you!"

With that, Donna took her coffee and went up to see what the girls were doing. She knew Donald would still be asleep, and there would be no point to waking him. The girls were up and dressed.

"We heard you and Mark talking, so we did not want to come down and interrupt you."

"Both of you have to come down and have some breakfast before I take you to school."

"We are ready, but you really don't have to take us to school. We can still get the bus."

"Remember you are grounded and you are not to be with any of your friends until we sort this whole thing out. I will take you to school, and I will be there to pick you up too. Diane's parents will meet her at the school as well."

Both girls knew there was no arguing with Donna, so they just grabbed their backpacks and went to the kitchen.

That afternoon, Donna was parked outside the school waiting for Debbie. It had already been a long day trying to get Donald set with home tutors. She had finally arranged for two different tutors, both of whom were certified teachers, and between them they could get him the necessary credits he needed to graduate with a regular diploma. While he bitched and moaned about the entire situation, she felt good about things and knew that one day he would appreciate the effort she had made. The world had definitely changed, and in the current atmosphere, a high school diploma was the minimum requirement for getting a job.

Once Debbie was in the car, she immediately tried to explain what had happened the day before.

"I really do not do drugs, and I really wanted to just leave Diane's house, but I was afraid to leave her alone."

"I get it, and I really want to believe you. The next time, if there is a next time, call me immediately, and I will come to wherever you are. That situation was potentially dangerous, and who knows what those boys could do once they were really high. I get it that all girls want to be popular, but remember, it is not worth it in the long run. You know that I became pregnant when I was just a little older than you are now, and if you think it was easy, think again. I was lucky to have met Craig, who helped me make a life for myself and for Donald. I really do not want to see you in that same situation."

"Do you ever hear from Donald's father?"

"No, he wanted nothing to do with the baby or me, and his parents behaved in the same way. They claimed they could not be sure that the kid was his, and they did not want him to ruin his life by having a kid to support and all. I have learned through the grapevine that he is a real dirtbag today, and I am really happy to have him completely out of my life. It was all a difficult lesson to learn, and I do not want you to fall into that trap. Do you understand me?"

"I get it, and I want you to know that I appreciate you being so honest with me. Most moms never want their kids to know their mistakes."

"Now that we are talking about being honest with each other, I need to ask you a question, and I need a really honest answer." With that Donna pulled over to the side of the road so she could look at Debbie and see what her eyes were saying even if her mouth was saying something different.

"This sounds serious. What do you want to know?"

"Donald tells me that while you both were with your father, your father made inappropriate remarks and even touched you inappropriately. I need to know if that is true."

"Dad was just fooling around. He did say that I am getting to be very sexy, and Donald really lost his cool. I was sitting on his lap at the time, and he was rubbing my back but nothing more than that."

"You are too old to be sitting on his lap. I do not want you to do that in the future. Men get really excited when a pretty girl sits on their lap, and that can lead to trouble. I want to know if your father initiates that sort of behavior again. Also you are not to go there and be alone with him. Donald has to go with you as you really are in no position to protect yourself."

"But he is my father!"

"He is still a man, and a man whose moral integrity is questionable. Believe me, I know, and I do not trust him for one minute."

"What do I say if he wants to do something just with me?"

"Just tell him you and Donald are a package deal. He can take it or leave it."

"If he leaves it, I will not get to see him at all."

"Fear not, he will take the deal, and if for some reason, he balks, it will only confirm that his intent is not honorable. I will be happy to let him know the rules, if that helps you."

"Let me try first, and if I have a problem, I will let you know and then you can step in to solve it. I would like to try first; you and my dad really are like fire and ice when it comes to getting along. I am sure you had your reasons to be angry with him, but it really makes it hard for me as I am always afraid to mention the other person to either of you."

"Sorry about that. You do not have to worry about talking about your father to me. I need to know what goes on when you are with him. I have my reasons not to trust him."

"Can you tell me why?"

"Let's just leave it that he was unfaithful and dishonest when we were married. Once a person lies to me, I can never trust the person again. He hurt me not only as his wife but also as his superior at work, where he caused everyone a great deal of trouble."

"Just for the record, he denies ever doing anything wrong at the center, and he denies ever having cheated on you."

"You can believe whatever you wish. You know me well enough to know that there is no reason for me to lie about your father. I have always tried not to involve you in my relationship with him, and we would not be having this discussion now if Donald had not voiced his concerns. Your brother loves you and wants to protect you. I think that is admirable."

"Do you think it is possible that Donald is making more of the situation to try to deflect your attention away from him?"

"Whoa, you sound more grown up with every passing moment. No, I believe what Donald saw and what you confirmed that he saw, and I really feel that is potentially troublesome. Make no mistake, if your father ever does anything inappropriate, I will skin him alive."

"I get it, Mom. Believe me, there is no way I want to be on your bad side. I promise I will always make Donald come with me, and I will always tell you if there is anything to worry about. You have enough on your plate, and you do not have to worry about me and my father. Now, can we talk about my being grounded? It is absurd that I have to be taken to school and picked up every day. I promise to come directly home after school, and I will not see my friends after school unless you give me permission to do so."

"That sounds like a possibility. I also need you to promise to always call me if there is any sort of problem, whether it be during school or after school."

"I promise, but I will need my phone back to be able to do that."

"I get it, but I do not want you involved in group chats or posting on Facebook. Am I making myself clear?"

"Clear as can be."

"Also, no going on any of those so-called social sites. I do not want you chatting with some pervert."

"I am not that stupid."

"You know that I love you and just want the best for you. You are a really smart girl, and you have the chance to get a good scholarship to a good college. Just don't screw it all up."

"I love you too, and thanks for caring about me."

With that, they hugged, and Donna put the car into gear and proceeded home knowing she had done all she could. Hopefully, Debbie would actually listen and not ruin her life. It would be nice if she could actually marry someone she really loved and who really loved her and not marry for financial stability or social position.

Once home, Debbie went directly to her room, claiming she had a lot of homework to do. Donna went directly to the bar and poured herself a large glass of wine. As she drank the wine, she felt herself come back down emotionally, and she felt that she was actually thinking with her mind and not her heart. It was then that she decided to call Steve.

"Look, you bastard, if you ever touch Debbie again in any manner that could possibly be construed as inappropriate, I will see to it that you are never alone with her and that you face charges as a sexual pervert."

"Hold on! Where is this coming from, and why are you accusing me? I am her father, and there is no way you could possibly prove that I have ever done anything wrong."

"You may not believe me, but I do not have to prove anything. All that has to happen is for Debbie to tell the authorities what she has already told me about how you touch her and have her sit on your lap and you would be skinned alive."

"She told you that? Well, she is one hell of a liar!"

"I doubt that, especially since Donald has also told me the same thing. From now on, you will only be able to see Debbie if Donald is there."

"That's not fair. I have my rights as her father to see her according to our divorce agreement, and you have no right to change that agreement or impose any restrictions on me."

"If that is the way you want it, expect a court order for supervised visitation. No judge in his or her right mind would take the chance that you could do something inappropriate. My solution is a simple one and does not involve legal intervention. Take it or leave it; it's up to you. And one more thing; if you ever give Donald or Debbie drugs or supply Donald with drugs to sell, I will make sure the police are notified. You can bet your bottom dollar I will be there to testify against you."

With that, Donna disconnected the call. She felt relatively certain that Steve would accept her terms because being labeled a sexual predator or drug dealer was the last thing he needed. If that were to happen, he would not be able to be with children, and his reputation would be further damaged in a way he could not survive. She had to wonder what she had ever seen in him, but it was obvious to her that her choices of men were all flawed. Even Mark left much to be desired. He was such a hothead and so selfish that as soon as things did not go his way, he flew off the handle and made everyone's life unpleasant, to say the least. She was beginning to wonder how much longer she could take his mood changes and the way he was monitoring every dollar she spent. No expense was too much when it came to things he wanted or if it were for his kids, but anything she bought, whether it be for the house, her children, or herself was subject to scrutiny. It was obvious to her that if she wanted to stay married to him, she had to get a job independent of him so she would have her own money and not have to answer to him. As she finished her second glass of wine, she decided to call Craig and ask him for help in finding a position.

Donna was well into her third glass of wine when Mark came home. While his mood was initially better than it had been the previous evening, he soon became agitated when he realized that Donna was over the edge, if not downright drunk.

"Now I have to come home to a drunk! Is that fair play considering I worked a full day and you were a no-show at the office, as usual?"

"I am not drunk, just a little tipsy, and I am feeling really good. So there; and if you don't like it, too bad. I am not one of your children, and I am not doing anything socially inappropriate. I am entitled to have a few drinks to relax, so there!"

"I think this is disgusting, especially in front of your children. Yesterday you were all bent out of shape because of Donald using weed, and today you are drinking yourself into oblivion. You are a really good example for the children."

"Go fuck yourself."

With that, Donna went up to the guest room and locked the door, leaving Mark to fend for himself.

CHAPTER 26

IT DID NOT TAKE LONG for Donna to secure a six-figure job at a multidisciplinary medical facility. The chief doctor was a client of Craig's, and he wanted to mimic the center but not violate Medicare or Medicaid rules. He saw Donna as a perfect fit since she knew the rules and regulations better than anyone else. For Donna, the job represented liberation. Now she was freed of Mark's restrictions, and she felt like a whole person instead of being a kept woman. It proved easier than she thought to make the necessary arrangements for Donald's homeschooling, and she really did not have to be there while the tutors were with him. She even arranged her hours so that she could be home shortly after the tutors left so she could continue to keep an eye on him.

Initially, Mark was furious with her decision. He felt that she was abandoning him and his needs at his office. Donna convinced him that if he needed her, she could be there in the afternoon but that it was more important that she felt whole again and that this move would actually help their marriage survive.

"We will be able to talk to each other about our day and not feel that we are constantly in your office," Donna stressed. "Also, the added income will help with the household expenses so you will not have to carry the entire burden."

"That part is good, but I worry about you being out there and maybe meeting someone else. I really do not want to be the odd man out."

"Don't worry about that. There is no way I would even think about having a relationship with someone at my new office. They are geeks, and besides that, I know how bad it is to be involved with men with whom you work. Believe it or not, I have learned my lesson in that department. Look, this is a golden opportunity for me and for us, and I really want to take it."

"I guess that leaves me with no choice."

"I guess so, but if it doesn't work out, I can always quit. After all, I will not be under contract, and even if I were, it would only hold me for thirty days."

"Okay, then; give it a try."

"Glad that's settled.

"Now, let's have a drink to celebrate the opening of a new chapter in our lives."

"Don't you think you have to go easy on that stuff?"

"I said a drink, not a bottle, and yes, I will go easy from this point forward, but one drink is not being abusive. We need to celebrate."

CHAPTER 27

ONCE DONNA STARTED HER NEW JOB, it was as if she started a whole new life. She was her own person for the first time in years, and she knew she had self-worth. She also enjoyed the fact that she no longer felt that she had to answer to Mark when she wanted to buy something for herself or her children. Before she felt that she was on an allowance and she could not go over the limit without encountering Mark's distain. She did take it upon herself to buy the necessary groceries, and that seemed to please Mark as he felt she was contributing to the running of the household. But that was the only part of her having a job that seemed to please him. He resented the time she was giving to the job, and he resented her independence even more. His mood swings were becoming more and more apparent, and when the swing took him to the dark side, as Donna called it, there was no reasoning with him. During those times, Donna made it clear that she wanted nothing to do with him. If it were late at night, she would lock herself in the guest room. If it were happening during the day, she would just leave the house and even take the kids with her. Sometimes it worked and he would just calm down, but sometimes it would infuriate him even more. At other times, he remained the sweet Mark she had fallen in love with, and they did have good times together. That was what was keeping her in the relationship—that with the lifestyle she was really enjoying by being his wife. One thing that was for sure: she was going to continue to build a nest egg for herself so she could protect her future should her marriage fall apart.

It was also interesting the way her children treated her once she had a real job. There seemed to be renewed respect on their parts, and even Donald was willing to accept the house rules and complete his studies. Remarkably with the homeschooling, he was actually on a path to receive his diploma. Now he was talking about going to mechanic school so he could learn how to repair cars and motorcycles. Both he and Donna considered this a viable choice for his future as he always loved motors and there were good paying jobs out there for well-trained mechanics.

Debbie was another story altogether. She was definitely college-bound, and this was another subject of confrontation with Mark. He saw no reason to let her go away for college as there were several good colleges right on Long Island. To him it was a waste of money to allow her to go away while Donna felt it was an opportunity to give her independence and a chance to be on her own. Debbie really wanted to go to the Boston area for college as it was close enough for her to come home and yet far enough away to give her independence. Donna told her that if she could get a decent scholarship to help defray the costs, she would make it happen even with Mark's disapproval.

As for Mark's children, that was a totally different story. They continued to be combative, and when they were at the house, Donna felt she could easily go out of her mind. They refused to listen to her even if the request was for something really simple. The only way Donna felt she could coexist with them was to ignore them completely. This was rapidly becoming another source of conflict between her and Mark, who wanted his children to be treated in the same manner as hers were. Donna's only reply to Mark was to let their mother mother them. "I will never be their mother nor do I want to be."

CHAPTER 28

WORK WAS HER OASIS. It rapidly became her escape from the pressures at home, especially when Mark was home from the office. She truly enjoyed the success she was having and the recognition she was receiving. Her bosses continually told her how happy they were to have her as a part of their team, and they in turn continued to raise her salary as a way to show their appreciation. As for the staff under her supervision; that was another story. Many of them resented her and did their best to sabotage her efforts. It rapidly became apparent that she would have to discharge some of them and recruit her own staff. When she discussed this with her bosses, they simply told her to do whatever was best for the office. They did not feel any loyalty to the present staff and often felt as though they were being taken advantage of by them. And so it started: Donna recruited and replaced staff members, and the entire tone of the office improved immediately. The remaining old staff quickly fell into place as they feared losing their jobs, and Donna's control was complete. Soon she actually started to use some of her work time to do personal errands as she was not needed in the office to get the work done and to have things run the way she wanted it to be done. The free time also afforded her the opportunity to meet the various reps from the different venders, and those meetings often included luncheon dates. Donna loved the socializing especially with the men, with whom she flirted without reservation. And if by chance the luncheon date became an afternoon delight, all the better. Sex with Mark had become boring and predictable. The men she met offered some newfound excitement with no strings attached. She made it a rule not to see the same man more than once and not to enjoy an afternoon delight too often so as not to draw any attention to her activities. Of course, she kept her phone on at all times.

She sometimes wondered what would happen if she actually became attracted to someone with whom she could have a relationship. That person would have to have a substantial bank account and a socially acceptable way of life for her to leave Mark. No matter what Mark's faults were, Donna did enjoy the socially acceptable position she had as his wife. There was no question she had come a long way from the cashier at the supermarket, and she was not ready to give it all up for anyone who had less to offer in the way of security and position. The only man who could be a real possibility would be Craig. In her heart of hearts, she knew she loved him and would do anything for him, but he never showed any romantic interest in her and he would never leave that bitch to whom he was married. Donna had always thought it was just because of financial considerations, but now she was not really sure that was the real reason. She actually wondered if he really loved her and that all his complaining was just talk for talk's sake. She also knew that Craig's attitude towards her had changed ever since that day in her house when he as much as told her she was a selfish bitch, though he did continue to help her, even getting her the job she now had. That was something she did not quite understand. Why would he help her and yet ignore her? She concluded, "That was men! It was best to love them and leave them and not expect anything from them."

Donna also could not help but wonder if some of the outrageous behavior Mark was exhibiting was due to his jealousy of how well his parents and Howard were doing. He really thought that once he left the practice, the patients would follow him and their practice would fail. Now it seemed that, even if he lied to patients and claimed his was the practice where the father was or told the patients that Howard or Fred were not in on the day the patient came requesting one of them, he could not retain the patient. In fact, Donna knew it for a fact. Many patients left his practice extremely angry that they had been lied to, and they felt scammed. Every time this happened, Mark would be extremely angry and come home in a foul mood. He would then proceed to take his anger out on Donna and the children, even though they had nothing to do with initiating the problem. If Donna questioned him, he would blame her for forcing him to break away from the original practice, something she claimed she neither did nor wanted. Though if she were to be really truthful, she had wanted to take over Jan's role, but that was something that Fred would not entertain for a moment. Fred never really trusted her, and he saw right through her ambitions and knew she would really hurt Howard if she were ever to be a part of the practice. That really amazed Donna as she always thought that Fred was an extra nice person and that she and he had a good relationship. He had seemed to accept her into the family more readily than Jan ever had. Jan, for whatever reason, had remained loyal to Sara and seemed to blame Donna for causing the marriage to break up. Jan also saw between the lines, that Donna would never treat the children properly and greatly resented her for that reason. Thinking about that actually brought a smile to Donna's face. In the end, she had the ultimate victory by convincing Mark not to allow the children to see Jan, Fred or Howard. She could only imagine how hurtful that was to them as they were always particularly close to the children.

Then there was Mark, who always relied on Jan. Donna knew he missed having her to bounce ideas off of and to give him advice. Though Donna tried to fill that role, she knew she never could as Mark made it clear that he did not trust her advice. That mistrust intensified after Donna took her new job. Mark made it clear that he felt she no longer cared about him or his practice, and he seemed to withdraw from her and refused to discuss the office or any other problems with her. Donna accepted this without question and continued to feel that the gap in their relationship was getting greater and greater and that justified her afternoon delights because no one was there to know what

Mark was doing in his office. It would not surprise her if he was using the office to meet other women. She never questioned his late nights nor the fact that he often failed to answer his phone when she tried to call him.

This was all the more reason for her to continue to build her own nest egg. The more money she was able to squirrel away, the more secure she felt, though she very much doubted that he would divorce her, especially since the house was now in both of their names. No way would he want to have to give her half of its value, nor could he afford to pay her any settlement or buy her out of the house, especially while he still had maintenance and child support to pay Sara. All in all, she had what she wanted from him: some form of financial security, social position, and freedom to do whatever she wanted to do. It was actually fun having her luncheon dates and knowing she was cheating on Mark. In reality, no matter what she did for him or how she treated him, it did not make him any happier or any more fun to be with, and sexually he was a non-entity.

CHAPTER 29

Donna started noticing a pain in her jaw. It did not seem to come with exercise, but it was definitely becoming more and more noticeable. She finally went to Mark and asked his opinion regarding the pain.

"I think you should see a cardiologist. Women can develop heart symptoms that are very different from men, and pain in the jaw is one symptom. You can see the guy who is renting space in my office. He can run whatever tests are necessary, and then we can go from there."

"I would think that if the pain is from my heart it would get worse after exercise, and it doesn't."

"I don't think we can just ignore this. You should get it checked out, and if it proves to be nothing, all the better."

"It is important to me that my office does not get word about any of this."

"No one in my office even knows where you are working; so that is not an issue."

"Can he see me tomorrow evening so that I do not have to take time off?"

"He'll do whatever I want him to do. I'll set up an appointment for you."

"Thanks, I really appreciate your help."

The next day, Donna had her appointment and her stress test. To her utter amusement, she was told that her heart showed some minor irregularities and that she had to take medications to help regulate her heart. This was an emotional blow to Donna, who viewed it as a sign of getting older, something she feared and did not want to admit. Mark took the news as a "so what?" He kept telling her it was no big deal and just to do what she was being told to do and get over it.

The doctor tried one heart medication after another, but the pain in Donna's jaw just kept getting worse. She finally decided to consult her dentist to see if there was a tooth causing the pain. The dentist told her that she had a cyst on the root of the last tooth, and he thought that could be a causative factor in her pain. He recommended that the tooth be extracted.

"This tooth is not doing anything in your mouth. There is no tooth above it, so you will not miss it at all."

"Are you sure that is what is causing my jaw pain?"

"Look, Donna, I can only say what I see on the x-ray. That tooth should be gone, and if it helps the jaw pain, all the better. It is a potential source of infection, and that can only make matters worse."

"Will you remove it?"

"I want you to see an oral surgeon for this. The tooth is a root canal tooth, and most likely it will break into pieces when they try to extract it."

"Let me think about this. I really do not see any rush in having the extraction, and you can watch the cyst to monitor it. If it gets bigger, then I will do something about it immediately."

With that, Donna left the dental office and just rode around in her car. She did not like how she was feeling on heart medications and especially did not like the weight gain and the swollen hands and feet. All of that was interfering with her luncheon dates, so it was impacting her quality of life. She felt she really had to know if indeed she had a heart condition. After looking up her symptom on WebMD, she knew the only way to be sure was for her to have an angiogram. If there really was a blockage, the doctor could put in a stent right then and there and she could go on with her life, most likely, without the medications. Right then and there, as she sat in the parking lot at field six at Jones Beach and looked out on the surf, she decided she would make an appointment for the angiogram, and Mark would just have to take her. If he refused, she knew she would ask Craig for help, and she was sure he would take her.

Once she made up her mind, it did not take her long to get her records together. Using Mark's name as the referring doctor, she sent her records to the chief of the department at St. Francis Hospital for his review and for him to schedule the angiogram. Mark kept fuming about her decision, but she stuck to her guns. Knowing for sure, one way or the other, was going to be better than what she now had. If it showed she indeed had a heart condition and the stents did not help or were not the treatment of choice, she would be more willing to stay on the medications. If the angiogram revealed no heart involvement, then she knew she would seek out the cause of her pain. Mark did agree to take her to the hospital if for no other reason than it would look bad it he refused. He made her wait for an appointment on his day off so he would not have to miss office hours or OR time.

The day of the test finally came, and she and Mark went to the hospital together as the instructions told her they would not release her unless someone was there to drive her home. While Donna had no idea, the test was over basically as soon as it began. There was no blockage and no heart involvement. When the doctor told this to Donna, all she could think was, "Why is there still pain in my jaw?"

Mark suggested that the pain was in her head and not in her jaw, something Donna did not find humorous.

"You made me see that quack in your building. Obviously he knows nothing, and in reality, he could have harmed me. All he did was give me meds I did not need, and when I complained to him that I was actually feeling worse on his meds, he just told me it would take time for my body to adjust. Adjustbullshit. Now I want to know why I have pain in my jaw and down my arm. Your telling me it is in my head, is not helpful."

"Do what you want. Just don't ask me for anything. You obviously do not have any respect for my opinions."

"Thanks for your sincere concern."

"Hell, no matter what I say, you will take it the wrong way. I am sorry you have pain, but I have no clue as to why. What more can I say?"

"Nothing!"

Donna knew there was no point in continuing the conversation. She was on her own, and she would go further if the pain intensified. Where she would go or who she would see was another matter that she would investigate and hopefully find the right solution. Mark was a dead end, just like he was on all matters affecting her. He was the ultimate I/me personality and was only concerned with himself. All she could think of was how she had been so easily fooled by him, and she now wondered what she ever saw in him. She could only wonder, as she watched him drive them home, if he always had been so selfish and self-centered. She did not remember that being the case while they were dating or even when they were first married. Things really had changed once he broke away from the family practice, and it was as if he was blaming her for the breakup. There was no doubt that the jealousy he had toward Howard was consuming him and eating at his very core. Worst of all, there was no talking to him about the situation. Any mention of the family would be followed by an eruption of anger and days of no communication whatsoever. With that thought in mind, Donna simply closed her eyes and pretended to be asleep for the rest of the ride home.

Once home, Donna was surprised with the reaction she received from Donald and Debbie. They were both so happy to hear the results.

"Does this mean no more pills?" was all that Debbie could say.

"I always knew you were too tough to have a heart condition," was Donald's comment.

"Yes, it means no more pills and no heart condition. I guess I'll be around for a while longer to bother you."

"We'll take that!" both Donald and Debbie said in unison.

Donna smiled at her children as she made her way upstairs to her bedroom. Right now all she needed was some rest. She was never good after receiving anesthesia, and this was no exception.

"Everyone for themselves as far as dinner is concerned. I need to get some rest."

CHAPTER 30

DONNA AND MARK DEVELOPED A LIVING ARRANGEMENT that most closely resembled that of roommates, not that of a married couple or lovers. They each went their own way whenever it pleased them. Every so often, Mark would demand sex, and Donna would submit with an attitude to get it over with as quickly as possible. Mark was even more of a selfish lover who was only interested in getting his own satisfaction. He did nothing to enhance the experience for Donna. Sometimes Donna felt like a whore performing sex for financial benefits, but she did not care. She was still having her lunch dates, and the men knew, in no uncertain terms, that if she was not satisfied, there would definitely be no repeat performance. When the lunch went particularly well, the practice also benefitted with better pricing, so Donna looked like a hero.

Then one day Donna noticed that the bridge on her lower left side of her mouth was loose. She immediately made an appointment with her dentist who advised her that the bridge had to be replaced. He recommended that she have implants placed so that the new bridge would be permanent. He also again recommended that she have the last tooth on that side extracted since he saw a cyst on the root and felt that could be a factor in her persistent pain. Donna made an appointment with the oral surgeon to have the implants but declined to have the extraction as she wanted that tooth to be used to hold the temporary bridge. The oral surgeon agreed and planned to extract the loose teeth that were holding the bridge and to place the implants at the same time; a rather customary procedure.

The day of the extraction came, and Donna went to the office by herself since, of course, Mark was busy at his office. The plan was to use local anesthesia, so her driving home was not an issue. The extractions went fine, but when the dentist started drilling for the implants, the pain was excruciating. Donna could only think it would be a blessing if she were to pass out, and the poor oral surgeon was sweating as he attempted to finish the procedures.

"We are never going to do this again. In the future, you will have to have general anesthesia before I will try to do any type of procedure on you."

"There is no argument on my part. I just hope you got the implants into the bone far enough so that they will hold and the bridge can be attached."

"It looks like they are in and in good position, but I can tell you I have never seen anyone have as much pain as you had despite the fact that I kept injecting more and more local anesthesia."

"I don't get it either. I have never had a problem with local anesthesia. This whole thing is too weird, but I have to go home now and put my head down. I still am in pain."

"Are you able to drive?"

"Yep, I'll make it home, but you have to give me something for this pain. I promise I will only take it when I get home if I cannot stand the pain."

"I have the prescription right here for you. Unfortunately, we cannot call it in as it is a narcotic and the pharmacy requires a hard copy of the RX."

"Just give it to me, and let me get out of here."

Driving home was a frightening experience, and Donna kept hoping that she would make it home without hurting anyone else. Once home, she knew she could send Donald to CVS to have the prescription filled, and hopefully it would knock her out.

As time passed, Donna realized the pain in her jaw was getting worse. Obviously, the teeth that had been extracted were not the causative factor. So once the permanent bridge was in place, she decided to have the tooth with the cyst removed hoping that would finally resolve the pain. She again returned to the oral surgeon who decided to extract the tooth under local anesthesia since the extractions were not the problem last time and there was not going to be any implant this time.

The extraction was rather routine even though the tooth did fracture.

"It was a root canaled tooth, and they usually fracture when they are extracted. I really do not see you having any problems with this procedure, and I doubt you will need anything stronger than Tylenol for pain."

"That's good to know. I just hope it helps the pain in my jaw."

"I expect it will as the cyst was in the bone, and that causes pain. I did get the whole cyst out, so you should be okay."

With that, Donna left the office feeling that maybe she had finally found the reason for her pain and hopeful that the pain would be gone for good. She decided to be good to herself and go home instead of going back to the office. It would be nice to be able to get some rest before Mark came home and started complaining about how hard his day had been and how ungrateful she was for everything he did for her and her brats. Donna knew she was not in the mood for his nonsense, so she decided she would just lock herself in the guest room and pretend she was in too much pain to come out. As for dinner. He could just fend for himself. He was probably getting used to fixing his own dinner or bringing something in to eat as Donna was cooking less and less, claiming the pain was sapping her energy.

CHAPTER 31

THE PAIN JUST NEVER REALLY LEFT. In fact, at night Donna now had such horrible earaches in addition to the pain in her jaw, that she would just lie in bed crying. When she complained to the oral surgeon, she was told that she was no longer as young as she once was and that healing just took longer. Mark remained totally unsupportive and even remarked that she was a horrible failure when it came to her wifely duties.

"I never thought you would turn into such a hypochondriac. Do you really think you will get more attention if you continuously complain? Maybe you should stop having those lunches with the salesmen. I hear you are quite the number."

"What the hell are you talking about?"

"I'm talking about a conversation I had with the guy from Moore Surgical. It seems you left quite an impression on him, and he just had to share it with me."

"I don't even know who you are talking about. We do not do any business with Moore Surgical, and I would have no reason to have any type of lunch with their salesperson, whoever he is."

"Donna, remember this is a small world and what comes around goes around. I will not stand to be made to look like a fool whose wife is fooling around. You will find yourself out on your ass, and I will fight you for every penny should you seek a settlement."

"Don't threaten me. I have done nothing wrong, and I resent your accusations. While we are on that topic, remember I own half of this fucking house; just if you've forgotten that little fact."

With that, Donna turned away from him and just laid there seething. One thing was for sure, she had to be more careful if she were to continue with her luncheon dates, but she very much doubted she would do so. The pain in her head was making it harder and harder to even concentrate on sex, so the whole thing was not worth the energy. One thing she knew for sure, she would never allow that bastard from Moore to even set foot in her office. It was always the agreement that what went on during lunch stayed at lunch, and neither party would ever discuss it with anyone. Now it was only a question of if she wanted to confront him or just let it go and just hurt him in his pocketbook. Her inner voice said to let it go, because if she were to confront him and make it an even bigger issue, he could, most likely, just go back to Mark with more questions and damaging information.

In the morning, Donna again called the oral surgeon and complained that the pain was becoming intolerable. They made an appointment for her to see Dr. Russ, who was an expert on nerve pain. She went to see him that afternoon, and he took panoramic x-rays and told her that the dentist who took the tooth out probably damaged the nerve with the injection for the anesthesia. He recommended that she take Neurontin, a drug to quiet the nerve, and he thought all would quiet down in a few weeks, especially since the extracting doctor told him it was a normal extraction with only the minor complication of the tooth breaking, something that was a routine occurrence.

"What you are experiencing is very similar to TMJ, and while it is very painful, it usually responds to Neurontin."

"I hope so as this pain is starting to really impact my life."

"I understand, and I really want to help you. Please let me know how you are in two weeks as that is about how long it might take for the drug to do its thing."

Two weeks passed without any resolution. In fact, the pain was intensifying and going up the entire side of her head. Someone at the office suggested that she try acupuncture, which she did try, but that too offered no relief. Donna found herself desperate to escape from the suicidal pain in her head. It was at that point that Craig appeared at her office.

"Just stopped by to say hello since I haven't heard from you in ages."

That was all Donna needed to allow the floodgates to open and the tears to roll down her face.

"What the hell is going on here? I have never seen you like this, and I have known you a long time and have been through too much stuff with you."

Between her cries, Donna told him all about the pain and how it was getting worse each day. She told him she did not know where to turn or what more to do, but the pain had to stop.

"Mark is of zero help. He thinks this is all in my imagination. He just keeps telling me I am a hypochondriac and that I am as much fun as a dirty, wet dishrag. Craig, this pain is real, and it is driving me crazy."

"You need to see a neurologist. Your face is not symmetrical, and it is obvious that something is going on."

"I feel like my lip is tight and being pulled into my head, and I do see that my bottom lip is much smaller on the left side than it is on the right side. I also find that I cannot wear my contact in my left eye, and I really do not feel the eye when I do wear it and try to take it out."

"Let me call this doctor from my club. I know he is a neurologist and has an office here on Long Island. Hopefully, he will be able to see you and make a proper diagnosis. So far you are just seeing quacks who do not know anything."

With that, Craig pulled out his phone and started making calls. Within a few minutes, he had an appointment for Donna that very afternoon, and he even suggested that he go with her, an offer she readily accepted. Once again, it was Craig to her rescue.

Dr. Horowitz did all the usual things a neurologist does. He tested her ability to raise her arms and feet, watched her walk, and used a light to test her eye movement, something that really bothered Donna. It was when he took out a textbook and started showing her pictures of the facial nerves that Donna became really scared.

"Usually TMJ affects these three nerves but does not extend to the forehead or affect the eye in anyway. I want you to have an MRI so we can see what is going on inside that head of yours. I want you to have it really soon."

"Is there a special facility that you would recommend?"

"We have it right here in the office, and I will make sure you can be seen tomorrow, if that is all right with you."

"I appreciate your help. This pain is making me crazy, and there is no escape from it."

"You can get dressed, and I will be back in just a few."

With that, Dr. Horowitz and Craig exited the room, and Donna just knew they were talking brain tumor. Her only thought was that it should not be a glioblastoma. A friend of hers had just recently died from that, and he had gone faster than anyone could believe. In June he was a vibrant man, and in September he was gone. During that interval, he had gone from looking like a man in his early sixties to a man in his nineties. Sitting in the exam room, Donna vowed to herself that if that were to be her diagnosis, she would make sure she just ended her life on her terms not on the disease's terms.

"Be here tomorrow at ten, and we will have the results before the day ends. Don't leave here thinking this is some life-threatening thing. I really think we are dealing with a benign entity, and you are going to be fine."

"That makes me feel better. Thank you for your help, and I will be here tomorrow. Should I stop taking the Neurontin?"

"You can stop since it is not helping you. There are other meds we can try, but let's first see what is going on here."

Donna was grateful that Craig was with her. He had a way of keeping her calm and rational. All Donna could think was she did not want this to end up in the oncologist's court. There was definitely something scary when that cancer word accompanied any diagnosis. She could remember how she felt when they told her years ago that she had breast cancer. The surgery, the radiation therapy, and the Tamoxifen all took a toll on her, but she'd known she had no choice as the children were so young and she needed to be there for them. There was no way she wanted to do that dance again.

The next morning, she planned to go for the MRI alone as Mark was too busy to go with her and she really did not even want him to be there. When she told him about Dr. Horowitz, he just sneered at her.

"He is just another quack who is going to find that there is nothing wrong with you. "

"There is no point talking to you. You are one uncaring bastard."

"When all else fails, we resort to name-calling, which is very ladylike, I might add."

"I am beginning to hate you. You are so selfish it is unbelievable."

With that, Donna stormed out of the room and went directly to the guest room and locked the door behind her. There was no point talking to Mark about anything. All he cared about was himself. It was good that Donald was away at Lincoln Tech in Mahwah, New Jersey where he was studying to be an auto mechanic, something he always had been interested in doing and something he was proving himself to be really good at. Debbie was in her freshman year at Boston College and was loving every minute of it. She'd received a full academic scholarship, so neither she nor Donna had to be beholden to Mark for any help with the tuition. Donna found it comforting that her children were on their way to becoming successful adults and that they would be fine if something were to happen to her or if she just decided to throw in the towel and get away from Mark, a thought she'd had long before the pain started but was becoming more and more frequent.

Mark was having his morning coffee when Donna came into the kitchen the next morning. She really thought he had left the house or she would not have come downstairs as there was no way that she wanted to engage him at this early hour. It was a bad day when it began with evil words and more evil thoughts.

"And good morning to you too," Mark said with that silly smile on his face that made him look like a child who stole a candy bar.

"Good morning, I thought you had left for the office."

"Actually, I was waiting for you. I am really sorry about last night. I was off, and I took it out on you."

"It is beginning to seem like you are off more than you are on these days."

"And you are sick more than you are well. We both have our problems."

"You give me the impression that you think this is all in my head and that there is nothing really wrong. That hurts because while the pain is in my head, it is real and getting worse each day."

"I guess it is just that I cannot deal with anything happening to you. I need you in my life and it is beginning to feel like you do not want to be there anymore."

"If you want to be there, you need to revise the way you treat me. I will not be bullied like you bullied Sara. I am my own person, and sick or well I can take care of myself."

"I see how well you take care of yourself. When in trouble, you go right to Craig as though he is your knight in shining armor."

"Leave Craig out of this. He is a great friend and has always been there for me, long before you were ever in the picture."

"I cannot help but feel you want him to be more than just a friend."

"Don't be ridiculous. If we were to be romantically involved, it would have happened a long time ago. You would never have become part of my life."

"I have to admit I am jealous of him."

"He is more a man than you will ever be. Maybe you should see how he treats people and try to copy him. Lately you have been treating everyone like they are beneath you and you are some type of entitled person. Personally, I am getting quite tired of it all."

"Whoa, you know how to hit a man below the belt; don't you! While we are at it, how do you think you have been treating me? You are so wrapped up in how bad you are feeling, you don't take any interest in me or what is happening in my life."

"That is like the pot calling the kettle black. You have not been there for me at all. I see you as being the ultimate selfish person who is totally wrapped up in himself. That is probably why you could not get along with your family and why your kids really do not like coming here to spend time with you."

"Your short term memory must be affected by your pain. It seems to me you were instrumental in encouraging me to make the break from the family practice. I still hear you saying that I deserved more money than anyone else and that they were taking advantage of me. To be frank, I got tired of hearing about it from you, and that was a main reason I did what I did. As for my children, you treat them like second-class citizens, and that is why they dislike being here."

"Interesting. Now it is all my fault."

"Well, isn't it right that you wanted me to break away from the family practice and you wanted to play a bigger role in my professional life?"

"That is correct. Your father and mother refused to allow me to work with you in their practice. I now see that they were right. When I was in your office, life was hell, and you know it."

"Oh, that was all my fault too. When you were in my office, you treated it like it was your playground. You came and went at your own will and left the work to everyone else. I am sure you don't do that now. You really took advantage of the fact that you were the doctor's wife, and the rest of the staff resented you."

"What did you expect? Did you think for one minute I would be like your mother and devote all my time and thoughts to your office? Well, if you did, you now know you were wrong. I have to say your parents were right about us working together; it did not work out for either of us. I am much happier working for strangers who appreciate me and the work I do. My bosses have respect for me, and they will do anything they can to help me through this time. They only want me to promise to remain with them. That is more than my husband has ever said."

"Donna, I did not stay here to fight with you. I want you to know that I support you and am here to help you in any way that I can. I am sorry you are in pain and sincerely hope we can find the cause and get it better."

"I thank you for that, and hopefully once this stupid pain is better, we can get our marriage better too. Right now all I can say is the pain is terrible. I know you do not believe me, nor do you think the pain is real. Look at the time. I have to get to the MRI office. Will you be home for dinner?"

"Why don't we go out tonight? Hopefully we will have good news and can celebrate and, most importantly, try to recapture what we used to have. I want this marriage to work."

"I'll call you when I am leaving my office. I have a lot of work to accomplish today, so I do not know what time I will be out of there."

"Let me know how the MRI goes. I will be at my office all day as there are no cases at the hospital today, so you can reach me any time."

With that, Donna grabbed her pocketbook and her coffee and raced out the door. Once in her car, she allowed herself to replay the morning's conversation in her mind. Obviously, Mark wanted something, and whatever that something was, it had to be to his benefit. It suddenly occurred to her that the house was probably at the core of his new interest in her health. If she left him, he would have to sell the house or buy her out of it as her name was now on the deed as half owner. That might prove to be her biggest coup yet. That house was always his paramount possession, and right now he was in no position to buy her out as its value had increased and he did not have the cash available. No way was his practice performing at the level of his expectations. With that thought, Donna had to smile as she knew she had him just where she wanted him to be, and it was her deck of cards to deal, not his.

CHAPTER 32

THE MRI WAS PAINLESS AND QUICK. Donna left her cell phone number with the receptionist and requested a call as soon as the results were ready. That call came in the late afternoon just as she was finishing up at the office.

"Donna, the MRI shows a mass near the trigeminal nerve. It is a trigeminal schwannoma."

"What the hell is a schwannoma?"

"It is similar to a neuroma, but it should be removed as it is in the brain and it is the cause of your pain."

"Is it cancer?"

"No, it is a benign lesion, but it is one that requires a specialist to remove it. That is why I want you to see Dr. Stein at Weill Cornell. I want you to call his office as soon as possible and make an appointment with him."

"Thank you, Dr. Horowitz. I will do that right now."

"Keep me informed, and if there is anything I can do, just call."

"Thanks again."

With that, Donna's next call was to her oncologist at Monter Cancer Center. What she wanted more than anything was assurance that this schwannoma was not cancer.

"Have no worries. A schwannoma is a slow-growing tumor that is benign, but because of your pain level and the fact that the trigeminal nerve is involved, it should come out. I know of Dr. Stein, and he is a good surgeon who really knows his craft, and you will be in good hands with him. Let me know what he says, and if he wants to speak with me, I will be happy to do so."

Donna made an appointment with Dr. Stein for his earliest available time, which was on a surgery day for Mark, so she knew he would not be able to come with her. Once again, she asked Craig to go with her as there was no one else upon whom she could rely. She knew Mark would not be happy that Craig was going with her, but she also knew he would not rearrange his schedule to be there, so what was the point?

The appointment was strange to say the least. Dr. Stein simply said he did not want to operate on her as the lesion was too close to the brain stem, and he felt it would be too dangerous to do the surgery. He suggested that she see the doctor who was the head of their radiation department as the best path would be for her to have radiation therapy to decrease or resolve the lesion. In quick succession, Donna saw two other doctors before she landed in the office of Dr. Forman who agreed that radiation was the way to proceed.

"We need to schedule a new MRI, and it would be best to have it done here. Once we get that done, my team will meet and decide on a course of treatment for you. If you like, you can schedule the MRI now, and then we will get everything going as soon as possible. I understand the level of your pain; it is suicidal pain."

"Thank you for that. I feel better already knowing someone is taking my pain seriously. Up until now, everyone has made me feel that I am being ridiculous and exaggerating the pain. Let's get the necessary appointments scheduled, and let's get this thing under control."

"I am with you on that. I will have Maria come in and get the MRI scheduled ASAP. Unfortunately, I doubt we can do it today, so you may have to make another trip in; but we will see what can be done."

"I am prepared to do whatever is necessary, and the sooner the better."

With that, the doctor turned and left the room, leaving Donna to her own thoughts and fears. It was scary to think of getting radiation in her head and even scarier to think of it affecting her brain. Thoughts of Donald and Debbie flooded her brain, and she wondered what would happen to them if something went wrong and she was no longer there to help them. Mark would definitely be a nonentity when it was her children involved. He was always telling her they were her problem and not his, but he did expect her to take care of his kids even though they treated her like dirt.

Before she could let herself get all worked up about the children, Maria came into the room with a big smile on her face. "I am able to get the MRI done right now, and that will save you another trip into the city and allow us to start getting your treatment plan worked out."

"That is great, and I really appreciate you getting it scheduled. Just tell me where I have to go, and I am there."

With instructions in hand, Donna went down to the MRI lab, and in no time, she was done. Craig was right outside the MRI suite, and Donna was just so happy to see him. He was her rock and was always there for her. It was still strange to her that he showed how much he cared and yet never wanted to take their relationship to another level. Donna always knew that she would do anything he wanted as she owed him more than she could ever repay. They were both quiet on the trip home. Each was totally involved in their own thoughts and fears.

Donna really attempted to go about her daily life as though nothing had changed. She went to work, did the food shopping, and whatever chores were necessary. The only thing she avoided was any contact with Mark. She really did not want any type of showdown with him, and she knew that any conversation could likely lead to an argument. Mark made it clear that he did not believe that there was anything seriously wrong with her. It was hard for Donna to comprehend that a doctor could be so callous and uncaring and so utterly selfish. He was proving he was a total disappointment to her as a husband, a friend, a supporter, and someone who could influence important people and advance her social position. She came to realize these were the real reasons she had married him and that he never really loved her, nor did she really love him. Leaving him was beginning to look like a real solution, but that would have to wait until her health was restored and she could be sure that she could support herself and her children. Of course, she would get half of the worth of the house if she were to divorce him, and that was probably the only reason he was not threatening to divorce her. His finances were not in a good position what with his payments to Sara, the upcoming college expenses for his kids, and the fact that his practice was not doing anything close to what he expected. The latter was making him increasingly crazy and jealous of Howard, who he saw as having it all. Of course, he believed it was totally her fault he had left the family practice. He repeatedly made it clear that he resented her for not continuing to work with him in his practice as that had been the original plan. Donna could only laugh to herself at the thought of it. Their working together was a disaster, and she could not stand to see the way he behaved in the office, not only to the staff but to the patients as well. He was constantly telling people how great he was and how they had to do whatever he wanted. If he did not get what he wanted or desired, he would become a screaming manic, calling everyone names regardless of if that person was an employee, a patient, or a member of the hospital staff. Donna did not imagine this as she repeatedly heard about Mark's outbursts from the venders who came to her office. Now he was treating her the same way as he treated others, and all she could think was that he was becoming increasingly unhinged and her physical challenges were adding to the stress for both of them. Once the tumor was gone and she could have her life back, she would face the necessary decisions, and that was for sure.

The next day, Donna received a call while she was driving to work; it was a call no one could ever be prepared to receive. It was Dr. Lee, the head resident in Dr. Forman's group.

"We cannot start radiation until you have additional testing. Your MRI shows advanced metastatic bone cancer, which was most likely caused by the breast cancer."

"What are you saying?" Donna screamed into her cell phone as she pulled over to the side of the road.

"I am saying we need to determine if the cancer is the same as the breast cancer was and how extensive it is. Your skull has multiple lesions."

"Can't you just zap all of the lesions?"

"There are too many, and we need to be sure before we formulate a treatment plan."

"What do you want me to do?"

"You need to schedule a bone scan and a PET scan ASAP. You can do that here or at the cancer center on Long Island. After that, a bone biopsy will be necessary to determine the exact type of cancer with which we are dealing, and then a treatment plan can be formulated and started."

"Whoa, I never expected this. What about the schwanomma? Is there a brain tumor?"

"There is no schwanomma. What we are seeing is a large bone tumor pressing on the brain, but we need the PET scan to be sure that the brain has not been penetrated by the tumor."

"This all sounds horrible. I am not sure I can grasp all you are telling me right now. Are you giving me a death sentence?"

"Let's not go ahead of ourselves at this point in time. We need the necessary tests, and once we know more, we can make intelligent decisions."

With that, Donna disconnected the call and sat in her car crying like a baby. There was that horrible cancer word again, and all she could think was that this time it could spell the end of her life. Even in the best scenario, she was sure her life would never be the same. All she could think to do was to call Dr. V, her oncologist, and ask him what to do. She could feel herself shaking as she placed the call, and she knew she would be hysterical if he did not take it or if he was out of town. Luckily, neither happened, and his calming voice started telling her how they would go about getting the tests done as soon as possible, and they would be able to find a way to make things right.

"Don't look at this as a death sentence. We have many women living full and rich lives after having this diagnosis, and you are a tough cookie, so if anyone can do it, you can.

"I don't feel so tough right now. To be blatantly honest, I am scared shitless, and I am not even sure I can drive."

"That is one of the problems of having cell phones. You can be reached anywhere. Get yourself together and call me in an hour. I will get the bone scan and PET scan set up and we can start things going."

Donna again disconnected the call, and still crying, she called Craig and told him the news.

"Whoa, I never expected this. Have you called Mark?"

"No, and I think I am too upset to call him and have to deal with him. I am fairly close to my office, so I will just drive there. I will let you know what Dr. V sets up for me once I call him back."

"You know I am here for you and will take you wherever you need to go."

"You have always been there for me ever since that day in the supermarket in Freeport. I can never tell you how much you have meant to me and how grateful I am for all you have done. I love you and always have."

"I love you too. You are the sister I never had, and while I know you would have wanted a different relationship, that is the best I can offer. I am just sorry you have to face all of this, and I realize that without me, you have no one to lean on now that the kids are away."

"You are so right about that. Mark will probably bail on me once he knows the diagnosis. There is no way he will want to take care of me if things get really tough. He is too selfish and too self-centered."

"You should have known that at the beginning of your relationship. I never could understand you getting involved with him in the first place.

"There is no point in looking back on it. At the time, I thought he loved me and would do anything for me. I even looked at this breaking with the family as a sign of his devotion, but it really was just his selfishness and greed that drove him, and I was stupid enough to encourage him."

"Stupid is as stupid does. There is no point to this conversation, as we can do nothing with the past. You will need to tell him about this diagnosis and soon. Then we can all formulate a plan to help you get through all of this, and get through it you will."

"Thanks for the support. I will let you know what Dr. V says as soon as I speak with him. For now I guess I had better get to the office."

"Do you want me to stay on the line as you drive?"

"Not necessary. I think I have it more together right now. Thanks."

CHAPTER 33

As she was driving, **Donna** knew Craig was right. She had to tell Mark, but she knew she was going to wait until she knew the dates of the upcoming tests and could talk to him in person. That would make it easier for her to gauge his reaction.

Once at the office, she ran right into the ladies' room as she was sure her makeup had been destroyed by her tears. There was no reason to share her news with the office personnel until she really knew what was ahead of her and how much time she would lose from work. One good thing was that she was not dependent on her job for her health insurance as she was covered under Mark's plan, so if it proved that she could not work, she still would have the insurance even if he were to leave her, something that was a distinct possibility. "For better or worse, just as long as it would benefit Mark," she thought as a sinister smile crossed her face. Down deep, she had to admit to herself that she really was not sure how she would react if he were the one with the cancer. She really could not see herself in the role of nursemaid.

"Selfish is as selfish does," she said out load as she left the bathroom.

By the time Donna got home that evening, she had her appointments set for the bone scan and PET scan. She knew she could go for the tests by herself as they were going to be done in Lake Success, so it was not necessary to inconvenience anyone, and if she really wanted company, her mother could go with her.

She was glad she had gotten home before Mark, so she had some extra time to prepare herself for the upcoming conversation. As she expected, it did not go well. All she heard from Mark was how he was going to manage the household and do everything if she could no longer take care of things.

"You know this is not about you. I am the one with cancer, and I really do not give a shit about how you are going to manage. You are one selfish bastard, not that I expected anything different from you," Donna yelled at him as she ran out of the room and ran to the guest room, locking the door behind her. She threw herself onto the bed and smothered her tears with her pillow, not really knowing why she was crying. She had known what his reaction was going to be, so it did not surprise her. What she had not expected was the feeling of being all alone and the knowing that no man would ever want her once her condition was known. She was indeed damaged goods and would be so for the rest of her life. She could only wonder if Mark wanted her life to be a short one, and she knew, at that moment, she would do everything possible not to let him have what he wanted. She was going to make his life as miserable as possible, and if he left her, she would take him for all that he was worth and then some. No judge would go easy on a guy leaving his sick wife. There was justice in life.

When Dr. V called following the scans, Donna felt as though her life had completely fallen apart. The cancer involved almost all the bones in her body, with large lesions in both hips, which was where they wanted to take the bone biopsy. She knew there was no point in telling Mark as he had no sympathy, so she called Craig and just cried into the phone.

"You can beat this. I have been doing some research into the whole condition, and there are new drugs on the market that can keep it in check. Let's face it, if you were never to get any worse than you are and they can do something with the lesion pressing on your brain, you could live a relatively normal life. Just don't give up, because then the cancer will win."

"It's hard to fight without any support from my so-called husband."

"Forget about him. He is not worth your thoughts. You have to fight for Donald and Debbie and for me, because I care about you."

"Thank you as always."

"I will take you for the biopsy, so don't fret it. It really is no problem for me especially since it can be done out here."

"Thanks again. I'll let you know when they schedule it."

Donna's next call was to her mother, who immediately told her to come home where she could have some help, but Donna refused. Donna knew that if she left the house, she could lose her rights to it, and there was no way she would take any chances to give Mark any advantage over her. Her last calls were to her children, who both wanted to come home to be with her. She assured them they could do nothing by coming home and that they needed to stay in school.

"I just want to let you know that I love you more than words can express, and the greatest gift you can give me is to succeed at school so you can make something of your life," Donna told each of the children.

The next weeks passed as a blur with Donna in robot mode. The biopsy confirmed the cancer was the same as the previous breast cancer. A plan was established for the radiation to address the painful lesion, and Donna arranged car service to take her to the city for the treatments so no one needed to be inconvenienced. After the five treatments were completed, Donna started Ibrance and Faslodex, the two medications specific for her type of cancer, and before she knew it, life fell into a routine. She had to go for regular blood tests but was able to resume her full duties at the office despite feeling very fatigued at the end of the day. The only permanent change was that she no longer shared a room with Mark, and he no longer seemed to care. Donna was sure he had something going on, but she no longer cared what he did or with whom he did it. She truly hated him for his selfishness and lack of caring, but she refused to let him have the satisfaction of her leaving him; she knew she had to wait it out for him to leave her so she could get what she felt she deserved.

She knew that he was aware of her plan, and she was sure he had his own plan to try to force her out or to see her die, neither of which was going to happen.

CHAPTER 34

IT WAS STRANGE LIVING IN THE SAME HOUSE with a man who was merely a roommate and with whom she rarely crossed paths. For Donna it was definitely better this way as she was able to get the necessary rest she needed so desperately. As for sex, that was no longer important to her. She had no interest in accepting any invitations from the men who came to her office. The medicines made her feel dry in places she would rather not discuss, and sex was no longer enjoyable but rather painful. As for Mark, he had absolutely no interest in her; sexually, socially or even humanly. He showed his true colors, and Donna knew there would never be any going back to any type of a relationship with him. He repeatedly told her she was damaged goods and no man in his right mind would want to have anything to do with her. One day, when she could not control herself, she simply told him to leave and get out of her life for good.

"You can leave, bitch. The door is open, and once you step through, it will hit you in the ass and lock behind you," Mark replied with a sinister smile on his face.

"Since this house is half mine, I am not going any place until you buy me out. Have you forgotten that I am on your precious deed?"

"I sincerely doubt any court would honor that ridiculous statement. After all, you did not put up any money to buy this house, and in fact I owned it before our marriage. It is not considered marital property."

"Your memory has to be failing you. When you needed money to try and save your precious practice, you signed an affidavit stating that since I was giving you, as a loan, the money from the sale of my house, I became an owner and my name was added to the deed. You have never repaid that loan. That makes this marital property, and you are free to check with your lawyer about that fact."

"I will sue your boyfriend, Craig, for malpractice for tricking me to sign such a ridiculous statement."

"Actually, Craig had nothing to do with it. It was your lawyer who created the paperwork. Craig was out of town at the time, and you needed the money immediately to meet your payroll. Your friend Arthur handled the whole thing. And if your short memory is that bad, let me remind you again that you desperately needed money. I would only turn the money over to you if you signed on the dotted line. Have I refreshed your memory?"

"You are one solid bitch."

"You are one selfish bastard. I really do not care if you are fucking someone else, nor do I care about your financial situation. I only want to protect myself and my kids. Understand this, I hate you and everything you stand for. It is not my fault that I have cancer, and while I may be damaged goods, as you say, my mind is working just fine, and I know what a horrible person you truly are. You think you can bully everyone, but know this, you cannot bully me. You bullied Sara into a bad deal. You tried to bully your parents and your brother, but they stood up to you and are doing better now than they ever did with you in their practice. If you want out, pay up and you can be out. I would be happy to never have to see your puss again."

With that, Donna turned her back on him and went directly to the guest bedroom, locking the door behind her. She could hear him throwing things in the kitchen but decided to ignore him and to avoid any further contact with him. She was sure he was capable of inflicting physical harm on her, and that she definitely did not need. She knew that if she were to fall or receive a direct hit, she could easily fracture one of the many bones afflicted by the cancer and that healing would be a challenge. She decided that from here on out, she would further minimize her contact with Mark and she would continue to maximize her credit card purchases for which he was responsible until he cut her off from them. She was sure that, too, would happen. After all, he was a shrewd person, and he knew all the tricks of the situation as well as she did. Luckily, her job made her financially independent, and once she got the money from the house, she felt she would be on easy street. Even her health insurance could be through her job now that the insurance companies could not deny insurance due to pre-existing conditions, so she did not need Mark for that. She just wanted to make his life as miserable as she could because, for her, there was definite joy in watching him suffer, even if it were from a distance.

CHAPTER 35

FOR DONNA, treating her cancer and living her life as it now was became the new normal. She actually cultivated a nice group of friends from the office. They would often enjoy going out for dinner after work. She always made sure she went back to the house to sleep so she could never be accused of deserting the place. When Debbie and Donald came, they all spent time in the house and they all avoided Mark while they were all cordial toward his kids, who rarely came to the house. Mark had actually become a rare sight at the house, and Donna was sure he was really living elsewhere, and that was fine with her. As she expected, he did cancel their joint credit cards, but that had little bearing on her lifestyle.

Donna had the house appraised by a certified appraiser and knew that the house was valued at $1.2 million, less than she expected but enough so that half would buy a decent place. She went so far as to have Craig send Mark a certified letter with the appraisal and a suggestion that an agreement be effected so that they could both move on with their own lives. No answer was forthcoming, but Donna was sure one would eventually come forth as it was costing him too much each month to support the house, and he probably had expenses where he was currently living as he liked to appear as the wealthy man.

It did not take long before Donna received a notification that he was putting the house on the market and wanted to accept the highest bid. Craig responded for Donna, stating that no bid lower than $1.2 million would be accepted unless Mark was willing to make up any difference in the selling price so that Donna received her $600,000. While Mark was not happy with that ultimatum, he eventually accepted the agreement, and the house was put on the market at a price even higher than the appraised amount. Donna cooperated with the showing of the house and made it completely clear to the agents that she had to have a written offer before any sale would be possible. She did not trust Mark and could just imagine him selling the house for a greater amount and just giving her the six hundred thousand minimum. Houses in the area were at a premium because inventory was down and waterfront property was very much in demand.

The house sold quickly after a bidding war with the final price being $1,500,000. The furniture was divided up through arbitration, and Donna quickly found a modest home with just enough room for herself and her children in Freeport, something that she found somewhat ironic since she was once again back where it all started. She thought she'd had it all when she married Mark, but now she knew she really had it all. She had her self-respect, her independence, and the knowledge she could make it on her own. Things that had been important were no longer important, and life had taught her to enjoy every day and make something of each day.

CHAPTER 36

MONTHS PASSED, and Donna heard nothing about Mark, his practice, or his lifestyle. Even the vendors who came to her office seemed reluctant to talk about him. This struck Donna as rather unusual, and previously they seemed to enjoy gossiping, especially if they had something negative to say. Donna, for her part, tried to separate herself completely from Mark. She even had her name changed back to her maiden name so that people she met did not make the connection to Mark.

Her work gave her great satisfaction. The people in her office really appreciated her, and everyone knew she was doing an exceptional job managing the office and managing her cancer care. They often commented on her strength.

Even her relationships with Debbie and Donald seemed to improve now that Mark was out of their lives as well as hers. There were daily calls from them, and they all enjoyed sharing stories about their day and their activities. Donald was particularly excited to be completing his course. He had excelled and was offered a very good position with a car dealership near his school. While Donna regretted that he was not coming home, she respected his decision and encouraged him. There was something to be said about having to pay your bills and keep a roof over your head, and she sincerely hoped that would prevent Donald from making the same mistakes he had made while he was in high school.

As for Debbie, she still had a long road to follow in college and was determined to go directly into a graduate program. She had secured a financial package for graduate school so as not to put the burden on Donna and had actually started working at the college so her classes could be taken care of financially. The money from her package was slated for living expenses. Donna was so proud of her and just knew for sure she would make something of her life without being dependent on any man.

Life was good. And so Donna was totally unprepared for the shock of seeing Mark being led to a police car with his hands cuffed behind his back. Channel 12 was covering the story as breaking news, and it was reporting that Mark had been charged with domestic violence after he had mercilessly beaten his new girlfriend, who was now in the hospital fighting for her life.

As soon as Donna saw the story, she called Craig.

"It is just luck that you were not his victim."

"I know, but I never for a moment would think he was capable of something like this. Yes, he was always capable of slapping someone or completely losing his temper and just cursing out the person. But to beat someone to the point of that person being near death is not something I would ever have thought he could do. He has to have gone over to the dark side of life and has to have completely lost his mind and his self-control."

"He could lose more than just his mind. The medical board does not favor doctors with any type of criminal record, especially something like this. If he is proven to be mentally incompetent, he will lose his hospital privileges and most likely his license to practice."

"As a surgeon, if he loses his hospital privileges, he could not work anyway. Of course, this type of negative publicity cannot help his practice in the first place. Who would want to have surgery with a mentally unstable person?"

"Just be happy you are out of that relationship."

"Me too! I knew that before our divorce was final. He was losing it more and more. People in his office would call me and complain about his outbursts, but there was nothing anyone could do.

"I cannot help but wonder what Jan and Fred must be thinking. This has to be a shock for them as well."

"My guess is that nothing he could ever do would shock them. I am just surprised that you would even think about their reaction. "

"I actually think about them a lot. They proved to be so right about him. Had I listened, I would never have encouraged him to leave the practice so that I could work with him and be the big shot. Jan warned me that that path had many obstacles, but I just would not listen. What with the financial difficulties from the office and his feeling he was alone, I am sure that all did not help his mental condition."

"I am sure you are right. Hindsight is always 20/20. Unfortunately, we can never undo the past."

"I, for one, have learned from the past and know where I was wrong. That's something to be said."

"Let's hope."

"Craig, you have always been there for me whether I was right or wrong. I am finally grown up and able to stand on my own two feet. Life, for me, is good, and I am in a good place both mentally and physically. Now I really have it."

9 781480 986244